DEAD SEXY

DEAD SEXY

A Novel

KATHY LETTE

ATRIA BOOKS
New York London Toronto Sydney

ATRIA BOOKS
1230 Avenue of the Americas
New York, NY 10020

ISBN: 0-7434-5688-2

First Atria Books hardcover edition June 2004

10 9 8 7 6 5 4 3 2 1

ATRIA BOOKS is a trademark of Simon & Schuster, Inc.

Manufactured in the United States of America

For information regarding special discounts for bulk purchases, please contact Simon & Schuster Special Sales at 1-800-456-6798 or business@simonandschuster.com

For John Mortimer, the literary love god,
in celebration of his eightieth birthday.

No woman is an island

* * *

How can we win the sex war when we keep
fraternizing with the enemy?

Contents

Contents

The Differences Between the Sexes: Origin

Women are from Venus.

Men are from, well . . . Home Depot, mostly.

1 The Charm Offensive

God, apparently as a prank, devised two sexes and called them "opposite." For 5,000 years the sex war has raged, with still no truce in sight. While birds, beasts of the field, invertebrates even, all pair off happily, breeding away without the aid of French ticklers, nipple-window bras, videos entitled *Moist* or *Thrust*, Viagra, She-agra, clitoris-orientation classes or Internet dating sites listing GSOHs—the male and female of the human species are constantly at war. We're supposed to be the higher animal life form, but you don't see octopi going on dating-quiz television programs to get laid, now do you?

This is what Shelly Green thought to herself as she waited at the altar of a church on Euston Road, on a dark, damp February day, a sweat stain the shape of Ireland beneath each armpit of the posh frock she'd been tricked into wearing on the pretext that she was going to play classical guitar at a Valentine's Day wedding.

She just didn't know it was going to be her own.

The TV presenter, sporting a tangled, unruly hairstyle that

few men outside a heavy metal band would dare to contemplate, was relaying events via a handheld microphone to his viewers across England.

"And we can now reveal that the winners of our computerized matchmaking competition here at Channel Six are . . . Shelly Green and Kit Kinkade!" he announced with lunatic fervor. "Their prize? Each other! Plus one hundred thousand pounds. Each!! A white wedding in Gretna Green, a reception in the faaaab-ulous Balmoral Hotel, a honeymoon on the sensaaaa-tional, unspoilt Réunion Island, a two-bedroom flat in the Docklands and—" he verbally drum-rolled "—a Honda hatchback! All of which the little love birds get to keep *if*, and I underline *if*, they can stay hitched for one whole year! What do you think, viewers? Has the computer played Cupid? Have two soul mates been united? Or will we watch as Kit and Shelly break up in a frenzy of mutual recrimination and toxic incompatibility? . . ."

The maps beneath Shelly's armpits now grew to encompass all of the British Isles. She glowered at the gaggle of sixth-form pupils in their prime position in the front pews. They were the ones who'd tricked her into this debacle. An acned, teenage crew, they'd taken up music to get out of Home Ec and Woodwork, but had lucked upon the only teacher who didn't make them feel like pond-scum. These students liked their beloved music teacher enough to realize that she, a late and only child, was still grieving for her mother who'd succumbed to ovarian tumors three years earlier. To kick-start Shelly's life again they'd secretly entered her name into this reality television marriage competition, a crime for which, Shelly silently swore, they could expect detention involving a lot of trigonometry for the rest of their natural bloody lives.

"So, isn't this every little girl's dream, Shelly—to be married on Valentine's Day?" The coiffured presenter thrust the mike into her startled face.

"I don't like the idea of getting married on any day," Shelly replied, stunned. "I don't even like the idea of men all that much!"

Shelly's music students, overhearing this blurted confession, looked stricken. There was bound to be some legal penalty for forging their teacher's signature on the entry form. The announcer looked equally alarmed. He abruptly reclaimed his microphone and launched nervously into an upbeat spiel, for the benefit of any new viewers, on the program's premise. Basically, having been matchmade by computer from thousands of entries, after this "gorgeous" photo opportunity, bride and groom would be chauffeured by limousine to Gretna Green. This village just over the Scottish border, he explained, was a traditional elopement destination which didn't require the usual month's notification of the intention to marry. During the five-hour trip, the nation would hold its breath—and the station would sell loads and loads of advertising—while the "winners" decided whether or not to accept the computerized marriage proposal.

But just as Shelly was summoning up the courage to stop the presenter mid-flow and call off the whole idiotic stunt before the PR people could bundle her into the courtesy limo that was purring curb-side, the flustered frontman announced the arrival of her "intended."

"From the three final male contestants, a systems analyst from Ipswich and" —the presenter consulted his clipboard— "a solicitor from Milton Keynes, how could you not fall for a man who answered Cupid's request on his attitude to love with, 'About my height, only fatter'? And folks! Do you know what? The computer agreed!"

As the presenter went on to describe Kit Kinkade to the viewers, including his response to a question about his attitude to sex (apparently, as far as Mr. Kinkade was concerned, sex was nobody's business, except for the horse, dog, wife and two hookers involved), a top-hatted-and-tailed streak of chic moved debonairly, Fred Astairely down the aisle towards Shelly. "*Height* six foot one. *Complexion* olive. *Hair* fair. *Age* thirty-five years. *Profession* doctor" reached the altar, spun towards Shelly on a Cuban heel and cocked his top hat rakishly over one eye. With his tanned face, butter-blond shoulder-length hair, fleshy mouth, green eyes and chiselled physique (despite his diamond ear stud, this was a Real Man, the kind of guy who could take a cold capsule and still operate heavy machinery), it was clear that Mr. Kinkade was a GP who had a five-mile line to get into his waiting room and a five-year waiting list to make it into his Palm Pilot.

When Shelly first saw her intended groom, she smiled so hard she pulled a muscle.

Kit's eyes slid up and down Shelly's body and she felt her face burn.

"*Height* five foot four. *Complexion* fair. *Hair* brunette. *Age* thirty-one years. *Profession* musician" tensed, squared her shoulders and sucked in her abs so violently it felt as though she had a vacuum cleaner strapped to her vertebrae. Shelly had been so engrossed in her intended's appearance that she hadn't given much thought to what his first impressions would be of *her*.

The high-school music teacher suddenly felt gawky in the soufflé of white chiffon one size too small she'd dug out of the back of her wardrobe for the non-existent gig at the nonexistent wedding. She also knew she'd become rather bland over the last few years since she'd cut her hair, stopped wearing makeup, lost her mojo and given up on life. Human Muzak, that's what she was, just fading into the background. If Shelly could see herself as others could see her, she was pretty sure she wouldn't take a second look.

"You lied" were the first words her computer-chosen hubby-to-be ever said to her. "On your form." Shelly was so amazed to note that her groom was chewing bubblegum at the altar that she didn't register right away that the honeyed twang was American. "Five four, blue eyes, natural charm . . ."

Oh God, she cringed. What else had those bloody kids said about her? She ran her fingers through her ragged locks. Shelly's hair, cut on the cheap by a pupil's mum, was not exactly a designer style. It was more as if she'd been knocked down in the street by a runaway lawn mower which had then done three-point-turns all over her cranium. Or perhaps—she started to panic beneath his cool scrutiny—she should have given a bit more thought to cuticle buildup? Didn't everybody know that "natural charm" simply decodes as being too lazy to bleach her moustache every four weeks?

"Well," she stammered, "nobody is ever going to admit that they're ordinary looking, are they?"

"Naw," Kit clarified. "You lied about your eyes. They ain't blue—they're aqua." And then he gave a slow smile, a rich glint of wickedness lighting up his own lovely orbs. "Not to mention your hot bod. You shouldn't wear such tight dresses so poor unsuspecting guys can see how sexy you are. The only part of you that's safe to have on display is your big toe . . . or maybe an elbow."

Well, Shelly mentally amended, perhaps she could just go for the limo ride. I mean, what harm could one limo ride do, hmmm? That would give her time to work out how the hell she was going to get out of this preposterous situation without landing her pupils in deep disciplinary doo-doo for forgery and conspiracy to commit public mischief.

* * *

"Look," Shelly confessed the moment the smoky-windowed limo lurched into the London traffic heading north and Kit had detonated the Dom Perignon with an optimistic pop. "Actually I'm a misogamist."

"Really?" Kit Kinkade's laser-like eyes burned into her. Shelly had to check that she didn't have any more holes in her body than were strictly speaking necessary. "You hate women? I thought all chicks were lesbians—emotionally. It's just that when it comes to comin', you need us guys." He grinned saucily.

"No! Not a misogynist. Misogynist is just Greek for 'man.' " (It was something her mother used to say.) "I'm a misogamist. I'm allergic to marriage." This disclosure was evidently of profound concern to the man beside her. One long leg jerked as though it had been struck by an invisible neurologist's hammer. Shelly quickly preoccupied herself with guzzling bubbles from the crystal lip of her frothing flute, while he composed himself.

"Yeah, me too," he faked, breezily. "Allergic to normal marriage, that is. But this ain't normal, is it? How many failed 'normal' relationships have you had? Squillions, right?" He paused to toss in a fresh piece of bubblegum. "Well, me too. Which is why arranged marriages are the way to go. Once marriages were arranged by tribal elders and family . . . but, well, my folks are dead."

"I'm so sorry," Shelly said, with compassion. "You must miss them dreadfully," she added, pained by a sudden stab of the grief that had coagulated around her own heart.

Kit shrugged. "Nope. Mum only ever broke off talkin' about her complex gynecological problems to tell me again what a waste of labor pains I was. Got a picture of her someplace"—he started rooting around in his wallet—"topless, in the Readers' Wives section of some shitty magazine. Not that she was a 'wife' for long, mind you. I only saw my dad once. For Thanksgivin'."

"How was it?" was all Shelly could think to say. Talking to Kit Kinkade was not so much a conversation, more a rush of verbal vertigo.

"Novelistic. *A Streetcar Named Desire*. Act One, Scene Four."

"Actually, that's a play, not a n——" Shelly began, but Kit plunged on.

"He had a house that was mobile but ten cars that weren't, ya know? Oh, I guess his phone was mobile too, come to think of it. With a speed dial to the UFO report hotline."

If only Shelly could stop thinking about how the champagne and bubblegum would taste mixed together on his luscious lips, she'd be able to say something sensible along the lines of "It's been lovely meeting you, but clearly our differences in education are going to mitigate against a happy union." Instead of which she could only manage a faint query. "If aliens really exist, why do they never abduct sensible Brits—only weird people from Texas?"

"Arkansas, actually," he corrected, with a wry, lopsided smile.

"And your father?" Shelly tried not to watch him moistening that succulent mouth with his tongue. "Where is he now?"

"Dead. Cirrhosis of the liver. Mind you, he hid his transvestite tendencies from his family to the very end, so that was somethin'."

"Oh," Shelly said. She seemed to be saying "oh" rather a lot. "I'm sorry," she added diplomatically. "About your father dying, I mean."

"Don't be. I only went to the funeral so that I could drive a wooden stake through the coffin lid, screamin', 'Take that! Oh creature of the night!'"

"Oh." (There was that "oh" again.) "So we're both orphans then." She waited for him to inquire about her story, to show mutual concern. But Kit Kinkade just blew a diaphanous bubble that obscured half his handsome face. They were well into the second bottle of Dom Perignon and his tenth hilarious family anecdote and he still hadn't asked.

And it was just as well really as there wasn't much to tell, she admitted to herself, hovering over a grotty loo in a Midlands motorway service station. Her beloved mother had been abandoned by Shelly's dad—a drug-addled, promiscuous Celtic rock guitarist with a band called I Spit In Your Gravy. Next she was ostracized by her Bible-thumping Welsh family for having a child out of wedlock. Shelly's mum, although intellectual, had eventually become, out of necessity, addicted to Reader's Digest DIY manuals, with special editions devoted to Adjustable-track Shelving Systems. She watched videos entitled "Adding a Spur Socket to a Ring Circuit." They didn't need a cleaner in their flat but a mechanic. Unable to afford even package holidays, she'd subscribed to *Practical Caravanning* magazine. Yes, Shelly thought, it was a safe bet that her small family unit was never going to be made into a TV situation comedy.

"Anyway, where was I?" As they passed by Birmingham, Kit shrugged off his satin-lined black jacket. Shelly couldn't help noticing how the man's tight silk shirt worshipped every inch of his musculature.

"Oh yeah. Arranged marriages. Once upon a time, couples were matched by tribal elders, right? Well, this millennium they're matched by computers. Now I know you're a Brit, so you're naturally pessimistic—your blood type is B minus, am I right?" He grinned. "But just think about it. A house! A car! Not to mention the big buckaroos! Twenty-five thousand pounds each today, another twenty-five thou at the end of the week if we can stay hitched, plus another fifty if we make it to the end of the year!"

"Money isn't everything, Kit."

"I know—there's also MasterCard and travellers checks!" he

joshed. "Plus, an amazin' vacation. This beach resort at Réunion is so exclusive not even the tide can get in."

Shelly smiled. He was quirky, yes, but also quick-witted. She liked that in a Love God. "Look, Kit, it's not that I'm averse to going somewhere hot with a lot of vowels and a turquoise sea—and all for free—but . . ."

"But what? Hey, Shelly, at our age, tempus is fugitin' like there's no tomorrow."

Shelly perked up. "In vino veritas," she toasted back. But he looked at her blankly.

"Latin? You speak it?" she asked, rather pointlessly. Her mother had drilled it into her, along with the rudiments of music.

"Don't try that educated shit on me, kiddo. I left Arkansas Maximum Security High at fifteen." He popped his gum again. "I'm an autodidact."

Shelly had to admit that she was linguistically stumped. "What does that mean?"

"Self-taught . . . It's a word I taught myself." He smiled cockily. "And you?"

"I did my formative sulking and angsting in a Cardiff Comprehensive, and then on to the Academy of Music."

"Hey, I'll show you my attempted-suicide scars if you show me yours." Kit drained his glass in one long gulp, exposing a café latte–colored throat. "Nah. Actually, it weren't that bad. The most dangerous thing was avoidin' the pedophilic gym teacher. Not easy in a Catholic boys school whose motto was, 'We pull together! We aim higher!' "

A guffaw, as urgent as a sneeze, exploded out of Shelly, surprising her with its vehemence. Kit laughed in response, a smoke-frayed, sexy, late-night laugh, which kicked Shelly's pulse up into double time.

"What have you gotta lose, Shelly Green? Say yes and I promise to say real nice things about you, you know, on national television when we get back to London after the honeymoon. And of course you'll say I'm better hung than a Pakistani pachyderm." He winked. "And that you've now discovered, contrary to what women's mags reckon, that size really does matter."

"Size of ego you mean, of course," she ribbed, caustically. "And in that case I'd say you're extremely well endowed. I'm sorry, but I'm never getting married, Kit. Wedding dresses are white because all kitchen goods are white," she stated, passionately. "That's what 'wife' stands for, isn't it? W.I.F.E.——Washing, Ironing, Fucking, Etc.?" (Her mother again.)

Kit took her chin in his hand, turned her pale face towards him, tilted back her head and trickled champagne down her throat from his own mouth. "So, what are ya sayin', Shelly?" His mischievous lips pouted with petulant charm. "You don't believe in love at first sight?"

Shelly swallowed, then brushed his hand aside. "I don't believe in love at *second* sight, let alone first." But despite her practical approach to romance—that love was a powerful self-delusion, genetically designed to bond people for breeding; that romantic love did not exist until Hollywood arrived to promote it—she found that she was already fantasizing about the cute little joint message they'd leave on their answering machine.

The eyes the American now turned on her were clear and assessing. "How can ya not believe in love?" Kit nonchalantly extracted a Marlboro packet from the waistband of his Calvin Klein underpants and lit up. "Don'tcha wanna be besotted? Entranced? Enraptured? Iridescent with lust and longin'? Intoxicated by orgasmic bliss?" Shelly glanced pointedly at the non-smoking sign beside his head. "Have you ever been married before?" He eyed her critically, between smoke rings, before teasingly amending his query to, "Or on a *date* even?"

"God. I've been on so many blind dates I should be given a free dog!"

Kit threw back his head and laughed with that insouciant abandon that Shelly found simultaneously sexy and unsettling. "Have you ever even been in love?"

"Only once. With an oboe player. I absolutely adored him. Despite the fact that he was a lactose-intolerant, anally retentive vegan."

"So what went wrong? Lemme guess. He said he couldn't go down on you because he was vegetarian."

Shelly snorted. Champagne spurted attractively out of both nostrils. But it didn't stop her from feeling an electric heat pulse through her thighs. She shifted in her seat and attempted sobriety. "When it comes to the Sex War, let's just say I have now declared myself a Conscientious Objector." (Hence, she thought pathetically, her dates of late in an Internet chat room, typing one-handed and, on one occasion, with her *nose*.) "Anyway, that's why these . . . friends of mine kind of concluded that it would be safer for a computer to pick a partner for me and entered me in the bloody competition. Under false pretenses. I'm afraid I knew nothing about it."

Kit's eyes clouded with disappointment for a moment before he verbally rallied.

"But your pals are right, Shelly!" He popped open another bottle. "Love's arrow is about as accurate as a Bush bomb on Baghdad. I've always attracted the worst women. Life's rejects." He stubbed out his cigarette with his heel, then tossed it out of the limo window where it landed on the nose of some ancient statue in some town square where they'd detoured for fish and chips.

(Obviously not a classicist type.) "Show me a psychopath and I'll show you a girlfriend."

Shelly gulped down a lungful of tepid, centrally heated oxygen. "Um, Mr. Kinkade, perhaps you should take me through *your* dating history, excluding pets and relatives." She'd meant it to come out as light banter, but couldn't keep the trepidation out of her voice.

"Sure. Well, I've only been in love a couple of times. The first time I fell for the gal because she loved animals so much—until I found out she was on parole for it."

"A case of puppy love?" Shelly was trying to sound suave but urgently refilled her glass for fortification.

"Yeah, and she had the porno movies to prove it. When I complained about her choice of co-stars, she told me I was oversensitive and shot me."

Once more, "Oh" was the only reaction Shelly could manage at short notice.

"Only in the leg." He hiked up his trousers to reveal a muscled calf, marred by one puckered bullet hole. Kit gave an insolent smile, which split his lively, cordial face; a cordiality belied by the odd scar, Shelly also noted. Okay, the man was dissolute but fascinatingly so. His broken nose gave him the look of a streetwise Greek god; the way Hercules would have looked if he'd played in a rock 'n' roll band.

"And what about the second time?"

Kit's expression hardened. He bit his lip and looked away. "Let's just say, to find my princess I've had to kiss a lot of frogs. Nothin' amphibious about *you*, though." He placed his hand on Shelly's chiffoned knee and her fanny did a fast fandango. His touch gave a wake-up call to her senses, a hormonal reveille. The sad truth was that she'd been celibate since her mother died. If she was ever called upon at school to give the sex talk, she'd be lecturing from *notes*. Her clitoris had taken to sending the odd sexual SOS along the lines of *"Remember me?"* If it weren't for Mrs. Palm and her five daughters (although the two elder daughters usually sufficed, with the other three fighting over the VCR), she would have dried up completely. Yes, there was a lot to be said for celibacy, and most of it began with *"Why me?"*

"Only trouble is—men and women," Shelly persevered, brushing away Kit's hand like a bothersome fly. "We're not just from different planets—we're from different galaxies. It's never going to work, is it?"

"Well, it ain't our fault. I mean, men's needs are simple. Football, food, music and"— his warm hand stole back onto her leg, a little higher this time—"sex. It's you gals who want so goddamn much!"

With the third bottle of champagne warming Shelly's blood and fizzing to her brain, she found herself melting towards this loquacious Lothario beside her. "I don't want much! Just a man who agrees that everything is his fault and always puts himself second," Shelly teased flippantly. "And is smart enough to realize that women are superior."

Kit threw back his head once more to laugh. There was an animal vigor about him, a sense of dangerous heat. And not just because of the limo's now overexuberant central heating, for which she felt most grateful when it caused Kit to unbutton his shirt and reveal his trampoline-taut abs and pectoral pillows. "Of course women are superior." Kit met her gaze defiantly. "I mean, you must be smart, 'cause look who you chose to marry? Us guys!" He winked. "That's what makes it so goddamn annoyin'" when you whine about it bein' a man's world."

"Oh come on! It's much, much easier being a bloke."

"Howja figure that?"

"Okay . . . Wrinkles and gray hair add character. You can eat a banana without every man in the vicinity imagining you naked. You don't have to commit suicide if someone turns up at a party wearing an identical outfit to yours." Shelly began tipsily counting off points on her fingertips. "You never have to shave below your epiglottis. You don't care if nobody notices your new haircut. Nor did the hairdresser charge you double for it! Your phone conversations take thirty seconds, tops. You're always in the mood. You're————"

"Hey," Kit Kinkade interrupted, "with the right man *you'd* always be in the mood too." His elongated vowels left a verbal vapor trail. "You need proof that it's a woman's world? Well then I have two words for you, kiddo." He leant back on the leather seat, arms spread along the back of the upholstery, smugly pleased with himself. "They are 'multiple' and 'orgasm'. Another reason the sex war is your fault. We men are so givin'. While you chicks are so selfish and demandin'! You're always callin' out, 'Don't stop! Don't stop!' for hour after exhaustin' hour. To delay orgasm we're s'posed to think of somethin' awful. Well, I once thought of Andrea Dworkin, Anne Widdecombe and Barbara Bush naked, and delayed my orgasm by three goddamn months!" Kit opened his mouth wide and guffawed again, that cynical, rude, jazz-joint American laugh which had slightly irritated Shelly at first but which she was now starting to find unaccountably enchanting.

"At least all your orgasms are real!" she fenced.

"As I said, with the right guy . . ." His voice was silken, with hands to match—hands that were now straying beneath the hideous soufflé. And she wasn't stopping them. It wasn't as if Shelly had ever actually faked an orgasm. No. Her trouble was that she'd only been with men who'd faked foreplay.

But not this one. The air in the limo was suddenly crackling with sexual heat, like a fuse burning towards a bomb. "Ah, I see you're already contracepted."

Shelly, breathing hard, managed to cant a brow.

"Panty hose," he clarified with cheerful rascality.

"Hey, if suspenders were so great you guys would be wearing them. And anyway"—she snapped out of her sensuous trance—"what the hell do you think you're doing?"

A little light caressing was one thing, but this cocksure Yank had adroitly started to peel down the waistband of her tights. "Hey, your ladyship. I'm so sooorry. I didn't see your bustle and bonnet. How nice of you to pop in from Victorian England." His fingers began brushing back and forth across her lower belly until, despite herself, she was soon arching like a pussycat.

But as his hand strayed lower, she seized it in a vice-like grip. "Holy hell. Where do you think I am from? Strumpets R Us?"

"You think too much. If done right, the woman shouldn't be thinkin' about anythin' 'cause she'll be in a coma of sexual stupefaction. She'll be a coma-sexual." Kit's fingers stole back under her panty hose waistband. She gave an involuntary sigh of pleasure. This man could find libidinous places where women didn't even have places. He was a carnal cartographer, mapping out her erogenous zones—and then double-parking in all of them.

"Men are . . . luckier . . . because you can . . . extricate emotion . . . and not feel guilty later. I mean"—Shelly swallowed hard as a sexual surge set her nipples on fire—"you can just make love to a perfect stranger, right?"

"Christ no!"

Shelly felt disappointment course through her.

"I don't want her to be perfect," Kit explained cheekily, "I want her to be really dirty and bad." Then he kissed her—hot and startling. She tasted the warm, salty interior of his mouth and felt a dark throb of desire worthy of a scene in a bodice-ripper.

"You'll be emotionally scarred forever, but hey"—he laughed cavalierly—"it'll be an experience you'll never forget."

A part of Shelly knew this was true. She knew it was dangerous to make love to Kit Kinkade—he was so exotic, so, well, "out there." Like encountering a Tasmanian Tiger, or a poltergeist. But her body had started without her. She registered a feeble hope that her panty hose would protect her from her baser instincts, but he used both hands now to tear the crotch of her tights right in two and she felt her traitorous legs yield enthusiastically for him without consulting Mission Control. His fingers lingered over the equatorial flesh of her inner thighs and then on to the, oh God, she remembered too late, very tropical jungle between her legs. Houston, we have a problem.

"I don't bikini wax in winter," she blurted, cutting short the kiss and attempting to cross her legs. If he thought panty hose were unsexy, what would he make of her secret undergrowth, she fretted, trying to ignore the pleasure building up in her blood.

The stranger's supple fingers parted her thighs once more.

"You might discover the legendary lost temple of the Xingothuan tribespeople down there, you know," Shelly panted into his mouth, her voice embarrassed, but still thick with lust. "Or maybe a couple of *Big Brother* contestants who don't yet know the series is over."

He planted a warm kiss in the curve of her neck. He was all concentrated heat. The smell of him was spicy and wild. Shelly didn't need to rub his groin to know that he was as keen as a pot of Dijon—but she did anyway.

And then he bent her back and nipped a line of kisses down

her throat and breasts. The nerves in her body jumped wildly as his head disappeared beneath her synthetic soufflé.

"I s'pose now would be a good time to tell ya *I ain't vegetarian.*"

As the limo sped past Manchester to her right, then Blackpool on her left, if the soundproofed window had not been smoked, the driver would have seen his passengers fling themselves at each other with primitive abandon. Glimpses of Cumbria and Carlisle kaleidoscoped past Shelly as Kit playfully wrestled with her on the carpeted floor of the limousine. To Shelly's astonishment, she discovered in herself a passion so fiery that not even that daredevil oil well capper Red Adair could have quenched it. The world and its reason was obliterated by sensation. When Shelly, clawing at Kit's hair, cried out, she wasn't sure whether it was an orgasm or demonic possession. Would Kit thrust his tongue inside her again or call an exorcist? But whatever it was, she wanted more.

"Wow!" Her face whipped up from the limo floor to gaze down at him in admiration. Kit Kinkade smiled, smugly. If he'd had a snooker cue, he would have blown suavely on the tip. And then he crawled up her body, found her mouth and kissed her lubriciously, deliciously, letting her taste her own juice as they breathed in the essence of each other, the "ussence" as Kit called it, that intoxicating pheremonal ambrosia that Mother Nature gave men and women so that we would occasionally stop fighting each other.

When Shelly found herself grabbing urgently between Kit's legs, he gently pushed her back onto the leather seat. And then he said the words every woman fantasizes about one day hearing (along with "Scientists have discovered that celery was fattening all along"): "Pleasin' you is what gives me pleasure."

Now, the handful of men with whom Shelly had been intimate had possessed an insectine sexual attention span. They had been abrupt and arrogant, making the sex joyless and functionary. It seemed to her that most men only performed their bit of perfunctory cunnilingus for the penis payback, the erotic IOU that it implied. Which is why Shelly pinched herself now to check that she wasn't wet-dreaming. But no, seconds later, she was more than just a thought on the tip of his tongue. She heard a languorous, low moan and was startled to realize that it had come from her as she writhed once more beneath his mouth. The pleasure was simultaneously exquisite and excruciating—as though she were swimming through warm then icy spots in a deep, delicious pool.

When Shelly climaxed for the final time that trip, the sensation was so long and strong and bone-marrow-meltingly spectacular that she could only describe it as an out-of-body orgasm. She was a coma-sexual! She touched his face, amazed. When she eventually managed to draw in a quavery breath, it was to confess that she'd just experienced an orgasm longer than Wagner's Ring Cycle.

"Ring Cycle?" asked Kit, licking her salty juice from his lips. "What the hell's that? Zsa Zsa Gabor's theme song?"

"Zsa Zsa Gabor?" quizzed Shelly, stroking the slivers of amber in his hair.

"Wagner?" queried Kit.

But it didn't matter. High on endorphins, they wore smiles so huge they were off the Richter scale. They just grinned their euphoric complicity into each other's besotted eyes. It was nothing short of a magic moment. Hell, it was so magical, she wouldn't have been surprised to learn that Gandalf was behind it.

"So, Shelly Green"—Kit kissed her forehead—"now do you believe in love at first sight? . . . or should I walk by again?"

The Differences Between the Sexes: Intelligence

Why do men like smart women?

Because opposites attract.

2 Détente

"Now do you believe in love at first sight? Or should I walk by again?" was what Kit had asked her and Shelly had tried to answer. But having been set free, her heart was now taking up all the room in her mouth. Her lower body arched enthusiastically into his in reply.

"Hope I still respect you in the morning," she finally managed to say. But, to her surprise, Kit pulled away.

"Only thing is, sugar, I'm savin' myself for my weddin' day." He looked at her, his face all dreamy and dishevelled. "Will this be my weddin' day, Shelly?"

Shelly Green saying "yes" to a marriage proposal was as likely as spotting Bin Laden on a pub crawl. But the misogamist faltered. What was going through Shelly's mind was a mixture of: 1) Phwoarrrr. 2) A house, a car and enough cash to buy that Fleta guitar she'd coveted since graduation. 3) Carpe diem or, in Kit talk, why the hell not, babe? 4) I'm thinker than I drunk I am. Weeks later, she would confess that it wasn't the alcohol she'd found intoxicating, but his complete absorption in *her*. If she married this man she might get to touch him on a semi-regular basis . . . Now that's what she'd call an indecent proposal!

"Shelly . . ." The way he murmured her name in that velvety voice sent a sizzling current of lust humming against her lower spine. "What've you got to lose, baby?"

Indeed. Not even her job; her students had whispered upon departure that they'd organized a sub to take over her teaching workload for the next two weeks. In a brutal rush of honesty, Shelly also admitted to herself how tired she was of waking up on New Year's Day with nothing to regret. For too long she'd felt that her life was talking to her, but looking over her shoulder for someone more interesting. Her mother would have thought she was tragically undermedicated, but, Shelly realized with a burst of mind-boggling optimism, she was bloody well going to say yes. Why? Because her life had hit a minor key. Because she was all overture and no opera. Because she felt overcome with nostalgia for something she'd never had. Yes, initially she'd been furious with her students for entering her in the *Desperate and Dateless* competition, but had realized over the past few hours that Kit Kinkade might just be the jolt she needed to hot-wire her life, to re-ignite her emotional engine. Adventure. It was the elixir of life. And she wanted to be invigorated by it. Her blood type was not B minus, goddamn it.

"Why don'tcha soar a little, huh?" Kit persisted, the green lozenges of his eyes sweetly upon her. "If you start killin' time, time will quickly start killin' you," he aphorismed. "The only place to live is the present—unless you're offered a château in the South of France, that is! Only one rule regardin' pussies too." He licked his lips with slow deliberation. "If you rest, you rust." He gave her a Casanova smile—a bad boy grin, all impishness and insolence. "So, what's it gonna be, baby?" he asked as they finally crossed the Scottish border.

Shelly had graduated from the Royal Academy of Music. She'd studied every composer from Monteverdi to Mahler. She could augment a fifth. She could augment a sixth in three languages, for Christ's sake! But she loved it when this cowboy called her "baby." Men subscribed to the Pleasure Principle and *they* ruled the world. Why couldn't females just give in to raw, uncomplicated desire? Why shouldn't women be guilty of Acute Lust in the First Degree?

"Hey, what other wedding list would include a flat and car?" Shelly said dryly. She guzzled down another glass of bubbly in celebration. "I now declare this season 'Bridegroom Open.'"

"Ain't that lucky 'cause whatta ya know? I'm a troth-plighter!" Kit enthused before flipping Shelly beneath him, parting her knees with his body and holding her wrists above her head with one hand. "We are goin' to that island but don't wax." He slid his free hand beneath the froth of her ruched-up chiffon and cupped her. "Your pussy's like a seventies soap actress—all attitude, shoulder pads and big bouffant. Your muff is Farrah Fawcett Major. When we do consummate this marriage, Shelly Green, I want you just the way you are."

They kissed for the next few miles until the limo pulled up outside the Blacksmith's Cottage in Gretna Green. According to Scottish folklore, the local village blacksmith, who married hot metal to hot metal over the anvil, could also forge a union between lovers. Shelly scrambled to sitting position, tugging what was left of her tights up from half-mast and glanced apprehensively at the scrum of waiting reporters.

Kit squeezed her hand. "Thank you, Shelly," he said with genuine feeling. Shelly detected a tousled tenderness beneath his bad boy bravado, a cryptic sadness which she couldn't quite decipher. "I know you've had some jackasses in your life, so I just wanna apologize in advance for any asshole-type behavior I might inadvertently inflict on you."

Shelly laughed as she groped for her shoes. "Jeepers, it's hard enough to get a man to apologize after, let alone before. You *must* be drunk."

"What you're doin' for me now—the chance to start over, well . . . this is the best day of my life," he confessed with heartfelt gratitude.

"Oh!" Shelly's misogamistic skepticism evaporated. "Mine too," she heard herself gasp, like some Doris Day clone.

"Really?"

"Uh-huh," she said, regaining her sarcastic equilibrium. "I saw Jennifer Aniston on TV this morning and she looked a little plump."

Kit tweaked her cheek. "Shall we?"

As they walked towards the Blacksmith's Cottage, all eyes were upon them.

"Well?" demanded the *Desperate and Dateless* presenter, who had flown up ahead. Would they or wouldn't they? Was it ditch or date? Tarry or marry? The crush of onlookers—media pundits, fate-fengshuists, radio rent-a-mouths, teams of oleaginous marketing men, puffed-up PR executives, romance astrologers, marriage counselors, "wee frees," and other Scottish Calvinists from the local Kirk and the computer technicians who'd decided that Kitson Kinkade would be Shelly Green's perfect life partner were signaling either "thumbs up" or "thumbs down."

"Ditch! Ditch! Ditch!"

"Marry! Marry! Marry!"

It could have been the Coliseum mob in Ancient Rome. The expectant silence of the TV executives was weighty upon her. But when Shelly took Kit's hand, the crowd exulted. A great outburst of applause shattered the air. Their synthetic excitement was diluted by the chants of the puritan protesters. Kit had to push past the dissenters, protecting Shelly inside his arms as they negotiated the cobbled courtyard. She could hear snatches of what their leaders were saying to the cameras about the sanctity of marriage.

"This competition has brought marriage to a new low. A disturbing illustration of a culture of instant gratification," pontificated one clergyman.

"'Winning' a partner for a lifelong commitment? When did marriage become relationship roulette?" demanded an elder.

"You have reduced a God-given institution to the level of a game show. What do you say to that?" another shouted in her direction.

The presenter shoved his mike into Shelly's face. "But I thought you didn't even like men? So tell us, have you agreed on a sexual cease-fire? An amorous amnesty?" The man was really on a roll now, Shelly thought. He could positively smell his Bafta Award on the media wind. "An emotional armistice? The bedroom—a demilitarized zone?"

"Well, maybe there could be a truce in the sex war," Shelly ventured tipsily. "I mean, underneath our differences men and women really both want the same thing, don't we? Love . . ."

Her voice was drowned out by caustic laughter from the waiting press. A truce? In the sex war? As if! Shelly's mother would have been horrified with her. "What must a woman do when a man is running around in circles? Reload and carry on shooting" was her catchphrase. Maternal warnings about the evils of men were practically tattooed on Shelly's brain.

27

"Well?" the announcer persisted.

Kit squeezed Shelly's hand. She felt euphoric. Like the elated first chord of Berlioz's *Symphonie Fantastique*. Shelly squeezed Kit's hand in return.

It was Them against the World.

When the blacksmith-cum-marriage celebrant asked if Shelly Green would take this man to be her lawful wedded husband she beamed at him. "Yes!"

When it was Kit's turn to pledge his troth, he eyed her more critically. She felt his gaze in the pit of her stomach. There was a pause. A Pinteresque pause. A longer pause than Shelly thought entirely seemly. A ripple of suppressed titters ran around the pews. The maps of Britain beneath her armpits expanded to encompass half of Europe. "Do you, Kitson Kinkade, take this woman, Shelly Green, to be your lawful wedded wife?" the marriage celebrant repeated.

"Um," he finally, laconically, replied, grinning cockily at Shelly. "Can I sleep on that?"

There was a detonation of tense laughter from the congregation. "GSOH! Good Sense of Humor. That's why the computer matchmade you two comedians," the TV presenter crooned in a professional simulation of politeness to his audience, while simultaneously gesticulating frantically for Kit to get the fuck on with it.

Kit blew a perfect bubble of gum in response.

"Will you, Kitson Kinkade, take this woman to be your lawful wedded wife?" the blacksmith persevered.

Shelly was starting to feel about as valued as a giveaway shampoo sachet in a fashion magazine. She gulped in a lungful of damp February air, which was sobering her up with a rush. She exhaled a thin stream of fevered breath. What had she been thinking? This man was way out of her league. He had prime pectoral real estate. Obviously her eyes had been bigger than her vagina. Forget GSOH. The entry form should have read NLP—No Losers Please. Then her students would never have entered her name.

Kit's gum bubble burst, making a noise like a small firearm going off. A sign, Shelly thought, that perhaps she should duck for cover in, say, *New Zealand*. Her "intended" licked the sticky residue back into his mouth with a lazy flick of that supple tongue. The DJ's eyebrows were now in his hair. "Hell, I will if she will," Kit finally, impertinently, announced.

There was the pronouncement of "man and wife," and a gold band was slipped on her finger in a snow blizzard of paparazzi flashbulbs and the blinding glare of TV news crews' camera lights. This was followed by the now familiar taste of those bubblegum lips which made Shelly's heart accelerate once more, blood grand-prixing through her veins. The throng of corporate sponsors and radio executives thrust out congratulatory hands and deluged the newlyweds with spectacularly insincere celebratory kisses.

The presenter made the obligatory sidesplitting jokes about giving the bride away—"What? Couldn't you get a good price for her?"—before shoving the microphone into Kit Kinkade's face. "Any marital advice for other desperate and dateless hopefuls out there?"

Kit Kinkade didn't miss a beat. "Well, boys, a lick in her entertainment center will get you everywhere," he winked. If the presenter's eyebrows hadn't been hovering two inches above his hairline by then, they definitely got airborne after Kit's postscript: "Yep! A little of Cupid's toothpaste goes a long way."

Shelly's smile was so tight, she thought it might cut off her circulation.

The Differences Between the Sexes: Commitment

Women want love and marriage and happy-ever-afters . . .

Men want a "meaningful" one-night stand—preferably with seven bisexual hookers.

3 Conscription

Wedding ceremonies should only be performed at Lourdes, because it obviously takes a *miracle* to make a marriage work, reflected Shelly throughout the media reception at the Balmoral Hotel, Edinburgh—a massive architectural mausoleum resembling a moored *Titanic* on Princes Street. After the press call, they were ushered into a side room to change into their complimentary "going-away" outfits.

Shelly, who was experiencing jaw-ache from constantly beaming for the official photographs, just kept on beaming when she was presented with a Versace gold lamé mini dress of the sort she would never, ever wear. By the time she'd beamed her thanks for her plane ticket to Réunion Island for the following day, complete with a suitcase of size-10 sun frocks and erotic underwear for her tropical holiday trousseau plus a key to the Balmoral honeymoon suite, her cheeks had cramps from smile-lag. As she'd sobered up over the last few hours she'd developed the charisma of a crash dummy. And Kit Kinkade, she suspected, was the oncoming speeding vehicle.

Shelly turned her back on her husband to coax the white chiffon down over her hips where it slopped around her like spilt milk—that thing you don't cry over, she thought, fighting despondency.

Kit refused his hotel room key, explaining that he was staying with friends. Handing over his hired tux, he next rejected the Armani designer suit offered to him by a PR flunky and wrenched some crushed clothing from a battered backpack—scruffy jeans with condom pack prominent in a torn pocket, frayed velvet shirt with shark fin lapels, switchblade . . . *Switchblade*?

"That's your going-away outfit?" Shelly asked, perplexed.

"Uh-huh."

"Where are you going to? An *orgy*? Why aren't you staying here at the hotel? With me?"

"Married five minutes and you're already tellin' me what to wear! And askin' where I'm goin'!" Kit wrenched the top hat from his head and pitched it towards the chandelier where it caught and dangled desolately. "Love may be blind, but marriage is a real friggin' eye opener," he stated bitterly.

"How . . . how do you know?" Shelly found her vocal cords again. "Your form stated that you've always been single."

"What?" Kit evaded her eyes. An expression flitted across his face like weather—a stormy thought.

Why did she have the feeling that she'd just pulled the pin on a conversational grenade? Reflexively she stepped towards him, then stopped herself. "If you feel that way about marriage, then why did you enter the competition?" she blurted, bewildered.

"I'm American," he improvised. "Compulsive behavior is compulsory." He laughed, but there was no smoke-frayed, late-night joy in it. Sadness flowed down his face.

Shelly got the feeling that this man flew by the seat of his pants so often he should have earned frequent-flier pant points. She forlornly recollected the runners-up she'd met at the wedding reception. That nice, sane systems analyst from Ipswich. Though fluent in Geek speak (an alien language of hot swappable expansion bays), he was also a newspaper and plastics recycler. And that solicitor from Milton Keynes. Shelly doubted that he would have confessed to the world that he liked to yodel up the Love Canyon.

"So why did *you*?" Kit tugged off his shirt, revealing those rippling pectorals and looked at her with naked curiosity. "Go in for the competition, I mean?" There was a newfound wariness in his voice.

"I told you. My students entered me in the bloody thing."

"Students?" Kit interrogated, gimlet-eyed. "You said *friends* had entered your name. You never said nuthin' about no students."

"My music students. I teach guitar at a London high school, rock guitar, if you can believe it."

"Your CV said 'classical musician.' "

"I didn't write it. The kids did. And I *am* a classical musician. Only nobody ever hears me play anymore." Shelly pressed her lips together, as if she'd just put on lipstick.

"Wait up. Don't you, like, perform?"

Oh, thought Shelly. Let's start with the easy questions first. When had she lost her nerve? Just after her mother's body had been ransacked by rogue cells. Shelly had frozen in the middle of the Bach Prelude from the fourth Lute Suite. Pain and humiliation she thought long blunted, erupted hot. And there, once more, was that tension twisting tighter inside her. The silence of Wigmore Hall had roared at her even louder than the klaxons of terror trumpeting through her blood. And since that cataclysmic moment, this award-winning musician with the virtuosic flair and supple fingertips had vandalized her talent; reduced to the peripatetic teaching of heavy metal guitar techniques to sweaty teenage members of school bands called Stomach Contents, Bowel Scum and Jerk to Inflate.

"Stage fright," she confessed quietly.

"So, really you're just a . . . high-school teacher?" Her husband launched a halo of smoke heavenwards.

"You could have found that out in the car if you'd stopped talking about yourself for two seconds."

"I thought you were an artist. You know what they say. Those who can, do. Those who can't, teach," he pronounced grimly, kicking off his trousers. "And those who can't teach, teach music."

If Kit's curiosity had been the only naked thing about him, Shelly might have been able to respond, but not while he was standing there in skimpy Calvin Klein's. This exquisite sight had turned her into a vegetative state. The only reaction he'd get out of her now would be photosynthesis. "Ummm."

She dragged her eyes, under police escort, away from the comely body of her lithe groom so that she could relocate her power of retort. "Oh well, Mr. Kinkade, at least you don't have to take off all your clothes to prove to people that you're a natural blond."

"Hey, dumb blonde jokes don't get my nuts in a knot 'cause just like Dolly Parton I ain't a) dumb or b) blonde."

With that he wrenched at his hair, which, to Shelly's astonishment, came off in his hands. He tossed the wig into the bin and fluffed out an electric mane of black curls.

She stared at him dumbfounded. Why the wig? Who the hell was this man? This man she'd just—Holy Mary Mother of God—*married*? Shelly began to reappraise the light in Kit Kinkade's eyes. It was looking a bit like the rich glint of lunacy. What had she been thinking? How could she have married a man she'd just met? Shelly had things in her *fridge* that had been around longer than he had! How could she have been intimate with a strange man? Who the hell was she all of sudden? *Blanche Du Bois*?

She felt herself developing a distinct facial tic. Kit Kinkade, now all Heathcliff hair and vagabond eyes, yanked his tattered jeans up over his peachy posterior, shrugged on the black velvet shark fin–lapeled shirt and tucked the switchblade down the side of his Cuban-heeled boot before slapping her playfully across the cheek with the first installment of their prize money—a wad of £25,000. "See you on the honeymoon, cupcake. Oh, and Happy Valentine's Day."

This didn't look much like a truce. This looked like a first-strike offensive. She had only one thought, something tearful along the lines of "I want my mummy."

As the door swung closed behind his sashaying ass, Shelly was left with a distinct feeling that marriage to Kit Kinkade would be a lot like having root canal surgery—only not as restful.

The Differences
Between the Sexes:
Religion

Many couples divorce for religious reasons. He thinks he's God, and she doesn't.

4 The Preemptive Strike

On Wednesday, February 15, the morning of the first day of her honeymoon, Shelly was riding higher than the polyester underpants beneath her new Versace skirt. She had decided to put Kit's erratic behavior at the reception down to nerves—or inebriation. She had married a drop-dead gorgeous, if somewhat zany, American Sex Pot whom she would soon be getting to know better in a duvet-ed environment. How could she not take up residence on cloud ten? Limo-ing it to the Edinburgh city airport from the hotel, Shelly was so high above cloud ten she couldn't even see it.

The libidinous truth was that Kit Kinkade had given Shelly Green her first ever orgasms. It had been miraculous. Biblical even—"I can see! I can see!" Neil Armstrong walking on the moon had not been more surprised than she was. One small step for man . . . one huge step for one woman! Their encounter in the limo had been so erotic she'd thought for a moment she was in a Swedish movie, only without the Ikea furnishings and ski knitwear.

Shelly knew she'd been wanton. She realized she'd been slatternly. She acknowledged this was not what Good Girls did. But she'd been a Good Girl all her life, and what good had it done her? Even her cat had forsaken her and taken up with the cardio-funk instructress in the apartment downstairs. As for her sex life, good God. The woman was practically *Amish*. Give her a white cap and a covered wagon and she'd be threshing wheat and churning butter any minute now.

No. There was a time to be bad. And this was it. Reckless. Impulsive. Wild. Caligulaesque. Those Roman Emperors would have nothing on her! Bring on the fatted calves! And not those things above your socks either. Woman cannot live by vibrator alone, she vowed.

Shelly was so hyped up she shot a roll of film before she even checked in—a whole roll of the fuselage from the Edinburgh airport car park. *There* was a slide night not to miss. Now, she thought, still patting her wayward hair into shape despite the hour she'd spent gelling it into submission in the hotel bathroom—where was her gorgeous groom?

She ransacked the departure lounge crowds with her eyes, but the only thing waiting for her at the terminal was a long line. She took her place behind a bearded man who was rummaging through his pockets looking for his passport or perhaps some anthrax.

"He's *left*? What do you mean he's *left*?"

"Last night. Flew to London and got an earlier plane to Mauritius. Changed planes at the Seewoosagur Ramgoolam International airport, try saying *that* when you're pissed, and is now at Réunion. The sneaky American bastard."

Imparting this wretched information was Gaby Conran, a small woman with the blunt features of something feral and forest-dwelling. She had a cultivated East End accent and wore fashionably ugly, oblong-framed specs, the type nerdy scientists used to wear in the 1960s. Even if she hadn't been vaguely introduced at the reception the night before it would be clear she was the director of the *Desperate and Dateless* reality television program by her amount of luggage. Scott went to the Antarctic with less.

Although the northern hemisphere was shivering beneath a thin blanket of damp, gray February fog, for the commissioning editors of Britain's television stations, who program three months in advance, spring was in the air. And when spring is in the air, a young woman's thoughts turn to love, especially if she's a commissioning editor. Unbeknown to Shelly, at Heathrow that very morning there were six different couples heading off on romantic holidays with film crews in tow. *Singled Out, Blind Date, Meet Market, Hormone Hell*—all dating game shows where the aim of the contestants is to get a shag, and the aim of the viewers is to see whether or not they get one.

"Why would he leave without me?" Marrying Kit Kinkade was obviously going to prove a tad more difficult than marrying a member of the actual human race. "Perhaps I should save myself the psychiatry bills and just divorce now?"

Gaby pushed her thick, black-rimmed specs up the bridge of her nose and blanched. "Look, all men are scum. It's beyond me how they don't drag their knuckles when they walk. But this Kinkade bloke is hot. Hot? He's gen-u-ine pool boy material! Most girls would be satisfied with a man who has his own hair and no visible body piercings. This guy's a cum-coaxing fuck pig. So stop whining. Besides, what about the flat? The car? The consumer goods? The spin-off advertising promotional work? The His and Her Hot Beverage Thermoses?" she added flippantly. "Listen, Mrs. K.

While men may not be the most romantic species on the bloody planet, they are great believers in technology, right? And you have been matchmade by a computer. Kinkade'll want to give it a shot. For the sake of science alone, let's persevere, shall we, love?"

Yes, for science—and that pert pair of Calvin Klein–clad buns, lusted Shelly on the flight from Edinburgh to London. Thoughts of how Kit Kinkade had taken his mouth to her on the floor of the mirror-ceilinged stretch limo had simmered in her subconscious all night. "Stairway To Heaven" had been playing over the speakers. But she hadn't just taken the stairway—she'd ridden the bloody *escalator*.

And so, once she hit Heathrow, Shelly didn't skulk back to her flat in Hammersmith. She did, however, slip into the ladies' room to take off her makeup, muss up her gelled hair and replace her sexy "going-away" outfit with duty-free jeans, T-shirt and running shoes before dashing, late, to the Air Mauritius ticket counter.

Although she sprinted all the way, Shelly was only marginally more terrified of missing the plane than catching it. It would be fair to say that Shelly Green was not a good traveler. She knew all the statistics—that flying is the safest form of travel; that she was more likely to be hit by lightning on her way home from buying the winning lottery ticket she shared with her best friend *Brad Pitt*, than die in a plane crash. But it didn't help. As she boarded the plane she was ushered right into Economy (with no press present, when it came to generosity it seemed the *Desperate and Dateless* TV producers stopped at nothing—literally). Her seat was in the row opposite the toilet block. Shelly reasoned that if a bomb didn't get her, the bacteria would. Sharing one toilet with twenty nationalities with varying and sometimes idiosyncratic approaches to personal hygiene was not her idea of fun.

Nor were the buttocks of the man who was now lowering his

bulk into the seat beside her. We're talking Elvis, the later years. The man's flesh remained suspended on either side of the armrest for a moment before oozing lava-like into the leather upholstery with a forlorn "phttt." Nothing like the warm cellulite of a stranger pressing into your thigh to make you feel truly relaxed and ready for a flight, Shelly reflected. A quick glance revealed a man who resembled an illustration in one of those 1960s sex manuals, all bearded and balding and primary-school-teachery. Shelly could see him making his own beer and doing improbable things to slightly hirsute women on jute rugs.

"So" —the gargantuan slapped Shelly's thigh—"what's it like to be married? In my book, if you want to fly it, float it or fuck it, then hire it. Don't buy it. That's me only philosophy," said this finalist in the Sexist-sloganed T-shirt competition. (His chest proclaimed "I'm a lesbian trapped inside the body of this big, fat, ugly bastard.") Mr. Cro-Magnon then introduced himself as Tony Tucker, an Aussie and the cameraman on the shoot.

"Um . . . charmed." But Shelly had spoken too soon because just then he peeled off a sock, causing the entire plane suddenly to take on the fungal humidity of a fridge you accidentally turned off while away on holiday. It was fair to say that Tony Tucker was a man of alternative body fragrance. The Bubonic Plague would take antibiotics before setting foot in this bloke's system. Thank God the hostess was demonstrating where the oxygen masks were located. Shelly tried to concentrate on the safety spiel, if only to drown out the cameraman's grunts and groans as he removed the other fetid sock. She found that she could just about believe the emergency advice until the stewardess pointed out the tiny whistle Shelly was to blow to attract attention should their plane belly-up in the Indian Ocean. But at this point in her life, off on her honeymoon after three years of celibacy but with no husband, and a camera crew tagging along to record her public humiliation for posterity, would death be such a bad option?

A honeymoon was supposed to be a time of orgiastic groping, serial bonking, champagne-saturation and endless oral sexual gratification . . . and that was just in the plane. She had expected to be joining the Mile High Club as soon as they switched on the "Unfasten Your Pants" sign. And yet here she was, marooned next to a grimy man with gray skin and thinning greasy hair, whose hand had just "accidentally" brushed her nipple as he readjusted his pillow.

Shelly was searching for her parachute and that whistle when Tony jabbed her in the ribs. "Here comes the Singlet." He pointed to Gaby who was approaching from business class. "I call the bitch that 'cause she's never off ya back. Can't direct for shit. She should just be off someplace loudly celebrating her womb."

"Has my cameraman grossed you out yet? Don't take his politically incorrect posing seriously. He's merely re-embracing Neanderthal behavior, then disguising his chauvinism behind the catchphrase of 'post ironic.'"

"I am?" Tony Tucker asked, bewildered.

"I did ask for a camerawoman but—"

"But the producer reckoned this shoot needed a man's brain," he boasted.

"Yes," Gaby retorted, seethingly. "And I just don't have the penis to keep it in. His nickname's Towtruck."

"Why?" asked Shelly.

"'Cause he's headed for a breakdown."

"Yeah. Too bloody right. Working for you, I am."

Gaby's eye was caught by the customs declaration form that Shelly was filling in on her fold-down tray table. For "marital status," Shelly had written with a shaky wrist, "Disastrous."

Gaby sighed with deep irritation. "I am not cut out for television. I just don't have a big enough capacity for alcohol," she lamented, wearily. "Look, Mrs. K., Kinkade is just playing hard to get. You and he are going to rekindle the public's jaded belief in romance and be very, very happy, even if I have to drug, beat and bribe you to do so!" She patted Shelly's hand. "One in three marriages ends in divorce. Yet arranged marriages have had a spectacular success rate down the centuries. And I will be there to capture it all for the nation—and win a promotion in the process. Okay?" She beamed.

As the inflight movies played and the meals came and went, Shelly felt herself rally a little. Perhaps Gaby was right. There was something peculiarly life-affirming about the reckless abandon of a whirlwind romance. And Kit had proposed so spontaneously—a delightfully chivalrous gesture in a world that distrusts romance. Maybe it was just the hideous journey that had deflated her spirits.

It was hard to pinpoint the worst part of the trip. Was it the turbulence over Saudi Arabia, which had rattled the passengers around like dice in a box, causing Shelly to breathe so deeply in an attempt to flood oxygen into the muscles around her heaving rib cage that she hyperventilated? Or was it Towtruck, cleaning out the gunk beneath his fingernails with a fork prong before eating with it? Or was it when the circumferentially challenged cameraman opened the little tomato sauce sachet with his teeth and squirted ketchup all over the white T-shirt Shelly had bought at the airport? Perhaps it was his scintillating conversation, during which he referred to his penis as "Kojak," his foreskin as "Kojak's roll neck" and the female genitals as "hair pie."

And what about the fact that Shelly may have landed and changed planes at the Seewoosagur Ramgoolam airport in

47

Mauritius and flown onto Réunion, but her bags had not. They were now, apparently, in a holding pattern above the Bay of Bengal—sent to Rangoon, instead of Réunion, which meant that she'd be meeting her groom in a fetching tomato sauce–splattered T-shirt for every day of their honeymoon. Or perhaps it was finally making it to Réunion airport, only to have a beady-eyed female customs officer rooting through her every orifice looking for substances banned under French law, i.e. manners, tolerance, compassion . . .

"Oh!" Shelly gushed sarcastically to the big-busted customs officer at the end of her strip search. "That was sensational! Now let me do you!"

The airport official pretended not to understand and proceeded instead to a cross-examination of the new arrival on her interest in visiting the French colony. How could she be here on her honeymoon—with no husband and no luggage? Surely she must have other interests on the island—business, political? Had she ever, for example, been a member of the Partie Communiste? Did she have any adverse views on French colonization?

Shelly was tempted to explain that being English she had no interest in the French . . . except perhaps to find out what would happen if you force-fed them McDonald's burgers and fries until it adversely affected their buoyancy level in a quicksand scenario. But she opted, instead, for the truth—her husband might be breathtakingly handsome, bold, daring and sexually dynamic, but he was also a rabid weasel, something she would be telling him the minute she got to the Grande Bay Hotel. Oh, her mother had been so right about men.

The customs officer insisted on checking up on her hotel reservation and left her in the interview room which reeked of urine, aviation fuel and men's armpits. Awaiting her return,

Shelly's thoughts turned to her mother. Guilt about her mum lay on her like a stain. Her mother had stayed beautiful right to the end, even when puffed up with steroids and chemo. No, her face hadn't fallen apart, only her hopes. If they'd just invent a romance botulism: not face-lifts but spirit-lifts. An injection to keep feelings frozen in time, then her dad would not have gone on the road in that regional tour of *Godspell* that stretched from three months to six months to a year until she realized he was never coming back. Her mother had been forced to live improvisationally—a recording session now and then, classical violin lessons occasionally, although, strangely, they were not in great demand in a Cardiff council estate, although there were a lot of house cleaning opportunities for £4 an hour. She'd taught Shelly the violin to Grade 8—only for her father's guitar genes to kick in, as predictable as the banalities of the pop songs he sang for a living. Her mother felt betrayed when Shelly gave up the violin for the guitar. Until her musical daughter began to excel, that is, as she picked her way with panache through the classical repertoire.

What would she make of her daughter now, though, riffing and whining away on electric for a living?

Even worse, Shelly realized with a jolt of horror as she readjusted her clothes, was that she'd accidentally married a sassy, brassy cocksure clone of her dissolute dad. As she laced up her running shoes, failure grimly dogged her. She gathered her disappointment around her like a cloak—not a good look in the tropics, she inwardly sighed.

Her miseries were interrupted by a moan from the adjoining interview room. Shelly peeked through the metal grille separating the cubicles. The adjacent cell was lit by one desultory lightbulb beneath which a French police captain and two officers in sunglasses were interrogating a Creole man in his mid-twenties. She watched as the captain nodded, a cue for one of the policemen to punch the prisoner so hard in the guts that he concertinaed to the floor. The captain nodded again, and the other cop kicked the suspect in the kidneys. It was choreographed and quick. The man was writhing about like a tropical fish that had flopped out of a tank.

Shelly's only encounter with men in police uniforms had been a birthday stripogram in the school staff room. What should she do? Tucking twenty pounds into the elasticated leg of some constabulary Y-fronts didn't seem quite appropriate somehow. Maybe if she stood there looking outraged and English they'd be deterred from making pâté de foie gras out of the poor bloke's private parts? What would a *man* do, she wondered? Now that she was thinking like a man, she supposed she'd have to *act* like one.

"Hey!" Shelly called out through the closely meshed metal. They wheeled around to stare. But while Shelly really did want to be an indignant champion of the common man, strangely a degree in classical music hadn't quite prepared her for hand-to-hand combat with fully armed gendarmes. And while a punch in the stomach is not the worst thing in the world it could definitely put a damper on a girl's honeymoon.

As the three baton-wielding police moved as one towards the grille, Shelly flung herself through the door and straight into the arms of her interrogator. But just when she was beginning to suspect that this entire holiday had been booked through Third World Shitholes Incorporated, the female officer ushered her through Customs and out into the friendly fug of backpackers, Gucci-ensembled globetrotters, bartering businessmen and weary mothers busily plugging their squawking babies' mouths with bottles. Moments later she watched in alarm as the police captain strode her way. He didn't need a badge to advertise his position. He walked with that certitude of official protection and privilege. Shelly was startled to see him flash her a Colgate smile of disconcerting amicability as he passed. His was a face she would never forget—a face that looked as though it had caught fire and someone had put it out with a shovel.

When she located the others she attempted to impart her frightening experience, but they were preoccupied with trying to steer their club-wheeled carts through the revolving doors. On the airport forecourt, elbowing aside taxi touts, she tried once more to report what she'd witnessed, but by then they were all too stymied by the heat to care. It was so overwhelming, spontaneous combustion was a definite possibility. The chickens on Réunion could only lay hard-boiled eggs, Shelly deduced, and the cows produce evaporated milk. Having burnt her hand on the taxi's door handle, she wedged herself sweatily between Towtruck, Gaby, the scrawny sound recordist Michael Moore, nicknamed "Silent Mike" because he never spoke ("He's in his own little world, but it's OK, they know him there," explained Gaby), and all their boxes of equipment, and set off on the last leg of their journey.

Another reason Shelly secretly hadn't really minded about her students submitting her name was that, outside of Cardiff, she had a feeling there might be a whole other popular place known as The World. And she'd like to see it. Although she considered herself to be cultured and well-read, thanks to her mother and four years of music college, Shelly's subsequent career performing in the rank and file ("wank and smile") of various orchestras and now full-time teaching to pay off her student loans had left her curiously under-traveled.

Reading between the lines of her Lonely Planet guide (so many of which filled the bookstores that it was hard to believe any part of the planet could still be lonely), she'd gleaned that most of the islands in the Indian Ocean had yo-yoed between the English and the French for centuries. For the Brits, this geographical tussle was invariably resolved when the indigenous people got to keep the island and the English got to go there to lose their virginity and get alcoholic poisoning. But when English became the language of the all-conquering Internet, the French, obsessively clinging to their fantasy of an empire, clutched even more firmly on to their few remaining possessions, Papeete, New Caledonia, Martinique, Dominica, Mayotte, French Guiana, Guadeloupe, Saint Barts, Saint Pierre and Réunion.

Réunion Island, between Mauritius and Madagascar and just off Africa, is really the tip of a gigantic submerged volcano. Shelly glimpsed the harrowing scenery as her taxi careered along the ocean road—the gashes of terrifying gorges, the sheer ravines fissured with spurting waterfalls and the three inhospitable cirques, vast natural amphitheaters formed as the volcano crater imploded all that time ago. Small towns clung to the edges of the island, huddling at the feet of these volcanic peaks as though terrified of slipping into the sea.

The taxi's steering wheel was so searingly hot, the driver had chosen to maneuver the vehicle with two fingers only. When the brakes whined impotently as they sped around a hairpin bend in the path of an oncoming police van, Shelly decided that not even Michael Palin could turn this journey into a witty anecdote. Even the tough-as-nails Gaby was apprehensive.

"Jesus! Do they drive on the left or the right side of the road here?" she shrieked, covering her eyes as Citroëns and Peugeots hurtled towards them.

"They're French," said Shelly. "They drive on both sides."

"Slow it down, dipshit," Towtruck yelled to the driver. "I

don't think it's an altogether good idea to go downhill in fourth fuckin' gear, ya know!"

But the Gauloise-smoking driver just grunted, making Shelly suspect that the local colonists—or "colons" as they'd been described in her guide—were as hostile as the landscape. Shelly didn't know much about the French except that they have a proud tradition of hating absolutely everyone. She also knew you could tell a French film by the amount of talking that went on in it. Conversation that Shelly could never understand, even in subtitles, because it was always so "deep." When they weren't being existential they were being elitist. On the bowel-clenching drive, the taxi had passed road signs without the customary warning pictures, just incomprehensible words like *"interdit d'entrée"* and *"fermé"* and *"sens interdit"*—French for "hard for the English to translate without pictures," but clear enough for Shelly to deduce that it would have been wise to fill out her organ donor card. She had a sneaking feeling that the only way to survive this honeymoon was to dread one second at a time.

But no, she wasn't going to wave a white flag just yet. It wasn't right to describe the tussle between men and women as a "battle" of the sexes. A battle only goes on for four or five days. And the genders have been at it since the dawn of time—which made it a war. She'd kept her side of the bargain by trusting Kit and tying the marital knot. (If only she'd realized it was to go around her *neck*.) And now it was time for Dr. Kinkade to negotiate his terms of surrender.

To celebrate the driver's discovery of third gear, the windshield wipers made a halfhearted salute to the sheets of tropical rain that suddenly deluged the car.

As they lurched around the treacherous coast road that cut into the flanks of the vertiginous mountains, a fatal plunge into the sea veering closer at every turn, Shelly tried to concentrate on how much she was looking forward to seeing her enigmatic groom. She had a vision of Kit Kinkade's high, freckled cheekbones, succulent, mutinous mouth and laughing, devil-may-care eyes: the complete, textbook Barbarian Raider look, now that she thought about it. Yep, she reckoned, as the taxi lurched perilously close to another cavernous gorge, a whole new world was opening up to her—like a grave.

The Differences Between the Sexes: Sex

Man: "Darling, am I the first man to make love to you?"

Woman: "Of course. I don't know why you men always ask the same silly question."

5 Rules of Engagement

The human species is far too irrational to be put off marriage by the odd century or ten of hideous experiences. Which is why, as Shelly approached her honeymoon hotel, she felt suddenly buoyed up with a sense of hope, or at least anticipation.

Back in London, the Metropolitan Police had been about to put out a Chastity Alert: SHELAINE GREEN: NOT WANTED, DEAD OR ALIVE. But Kit had wanted her. Her body was still giving her twitching aftershocks of pleasure to prove it. Which is why she was taking Kit's advice and surrendering to the Pleasure Principle. Why rail against men, when you could just act like them? That had been her mother's mistake. Men were always praised for "getting in touch" with their "feminine *side*." Well, *she* was going to get in touch with her "*masculine side*." Imagine the benefits! Car mechanics would tell her the truth! She'd be able to open her own jam jars! Four pair of shoes would be adequate for her whole life! The entire world could be her urinal! Liberated from the need to make a man fall in love with her, she was free to focus on the sex without any messy emotion getting in the way. Oh, there was nothing like a bit of equal opportunity objectification to lift a girl's spirits!

The cab finally roared down a dirt road to the opalescent ocean and skittered to a shuddering halt outside the Grande Bay Hotel. The headland stretched out into the sea like a bent arm with the bayside hotel nestled into the crook. The luxury resort was set in an acreage of billiard baize grass in which black gardeners toiled like bees. A Creole doorman—dressed, incongruously, like an Indian prince in a turquoise turban, yellow pantaloons and white gloves—eased open the cab door to receive them.

The T-shirt Shelly had bought at Heathrow read, "If nobody is observing this T-shirt, does it exist?" —just to get up the snooty noses of her Gallic hosts—but there was nothing existential about the wall of heat that hit her as she stepped out of the air-conditioned car. It was so hot the trees were positively whistling for dogs. The air was like a kitchen sponge.

Speaking of bloated, absorbent things, Towtruck was panting out of the cab behind her. "Christ. Me throat's drier than a fuck without foreplay," he said, with his usual eloquence. "Holy shit!" The vile man perked up, suddenly oblivious to all except the array of bikini-clad women showing a heroic dedication to achieving the perfect honeyed tan on the dark chocolate strip of volcanic sand before them. "It's Chuff Mountain! Babia Majora! Welcome"—he opened his arms expansively—"to Tuna Town!"

"What can I say?" Gaby grimaced. "The man's an ornament to the human race."

Shelly looked tentatively around her and felt instantly daunted. A pagoda housing the bar, restaurant and dance floor yawned to their left. Beyond stretched the pool, fringed with vine-leafed cabanas. To their right, hammocks lazed between palm trees on the lip of a turquoise sea.

She cased the hotel lobby expectantly, fairly certain that her groom would be there with an operatic welcome, complete with gift-wrapped apologies for his premature departure from Britain. But she was greeted instead by the hotel's entertainment officer, a sort of upmarket *gentil organisateur*. It takes a lot of personality, a lot of chutzpah to be an entertainment officer, and let's just say that Dominic was overqualified.

"Bonjour!!!!!!!!!!" His smile was as relentless as the tropical sun above them. Dominic had evidently escaped from a swimwear catalogue: he was wearing a pair of iridescent orange Speedos so tight he'd need an oxy-weld to cut free his genitalia. A navel ring glistened from his bronzed abdomen. The man was so tanned Shelly mentally christened him "Rôtisserie." After enthusiastically kissing them all, including the horrified, macho Aussie cameraman, Dominic set about organizing complimentary rum punches—plus a bottle of celebratory champagne for the "lucky bride," which gave him an excuse to kiss Shelly's cheeks all over again. As he flirted with the older female guests, who seemed to be in awed orbit around him, Shelly slumped into a rattan chair. There, while she timidly waited for her room key, the gauche high-school guitar teacher wondered mournfully if she'd be arrested by the Chic Police—"I'm sorry but you are just not fashionable enough to rub shoulder pads with French people"—until she noticed a famous but fading rock star passing the concierge desk. This was a breed she did know—they look irritated when you recognize them, and suicidal when you don't.

"Apparently, they're getting together material for an acoustic album," Gaby confided, salivating at the potential for cut-price-celebs-in-swimwear footage.

Shelly inwardly scoffed. All musicians knew that "getting together material for an acoustic album" was just a euphemism for "washed-up has-been."

These comical short-wearers were not the Glitterati, but the Gutter-ati. Grande Bay Hotel seemed to be offering High Life visas to every Low Life in town. Upon closer scrutiny, it seemed that the hotel's advertised guest list of Beautiful People merely boasted the usual collection of sex-exiles (otherwise known as Hollywood film producers), partners in advertising agencies (Ad Nauseam), ex-dictators, soap and porn stars and the type of shady businessmen who plead terminal illness to beat a corruption charge, only to be found a few months later enjoying themselves astride inflatable bananas in the shallow end of resort pools, celebrating their providential recovery. Shelly exhaled a breath of relief—she wouldn't be contracting A-listeria after all.

Impatient to find Kit, she hustled her room key from the clerk, swung her small black knapsack over one shoulder and ventured into the sun. Around the pool, more Euro-trash awaited her. Passing the wet bar, she was splashed by the kind of women who had dedicated the rest of their lives to letting their boyfriends know that they'd once slept with Mick Jagger. And broiling on the sand before her were their younger prototypes, those beach babes who tend to eat caviar off each other's buttocks in the beds of rich perverts. Everyone was topless, from teenage girls to grannies. It crossed Shelly's mind that she'd better hurry up and locate her Love God before an ageing heiress with her own heli-pad found him first.

Gaby prodded her in the back. "Just play it cool with Kit, okay? Think French. Be suave and laid back. Men fucking love that!"

Shelly was thoughtfully nodding at this sage advice when she spotted her muscled Adonis in a pair of minuscule black Speedos, lying supine on a sun-lounger. She marveled afresh at his sculptured abs and shoulders so broad she'd be able to shelve all her holiday reading right there, on him: from Jane Austen to Emile Zola.

Ignoring Gaby's urgent entreaties to "Wait! The camera's not set up yet!" Shelly positively gazelled to his side with a beam as broad as her husband's shoulderblades.

"Hello! I'm new to the area. Could you give me directions to your hotel bedroom?"

Kit peered over the tops of Secret Agent–type shades at his bride—with absolutely no recognition at all.

"It's me," Shelly said, crestfallen. "Your wife, remember?"

Kit was still taking a moment or two to place her.

"Seriously, where is our room?" Shelly entreated, more curtly now, as she shook the room key at him. "I'm desperate for a shower."

"They didn't tell you at the desk? I got us separate rooms," he yawned. "I mean, it ain't like we know each other all that well."

"Yes, it's not like we're *married* or anything," Shelly replied, facetiously. "Well, that's a real skill, Mr. Kinkade, avoiding commitment *while married*."

"Hey, Shell," he drawled, "I don't even jerk off over the same fantasy figure two nights in a row, in case she gets attached."

Shelly had never met a man who could so consistently short-change her conversationally. "Um . . . But I thought you were a romantic. If you don't believe in commitment, then, um, why the hell did you get married on TV before millions of viewers?" she demanded, standing over him. "Not *just* for the money, surely."

Kit gave a small, inconclusive smile and shrugged. "I didn't have a fondue set to my name," he improvised—his lack of candor obvious from the parentheses etched on either side of his tight-lipped smile.

Kathy Lette

"Besides," he replied cautiously, as if for a jury, "I've done everythin' else. Except anal sex. And I don't particularly wanna do that."

What on earth did this man have to hide? Shelly pondered. And, more to the point, who the hell was he exactly? This man she'd just—book me in for a lobotomy, sweet Jesus—*married*? If only he didn't look like the winner of a Mr. Romance Cover Model pageant. If only he hadn't just leant forward to take hold of her ankle, right where a slave bracelet goes.

She pushed him away, all the time thinking how good it would feel to pull him into her. But that wasn't on the carnal cards, not when he'd made such a point of taking separate rooms. Why on earth had he done that?

The possible answer to this question stirred at Kit's feet. For the first time, Shelly noticed the sleek, corkscrew-haired creature in a lime sorbet–colored bikini curled on a fluffy pink towel on the other side of Kit's sun-lounger. She was pouting up at Kit with lips like cushions, lips that just invited a man to lie down on them. She was also cradling an unstoppered bottle of suntan oil. And Kit's belly and chest did look so recently varnished . . .

Shelly's wrinkled shirt had stuck to her breasts in the humidity—or perhaps it was the heat of her embarrassment. "Well," she said crisply. "It didn't take you long to make friends." She tried to smile but it was more of a politely strained rictus.

"Oh, Shelly, this is Coco. Coco—Shelly. Coco's the singer with the hotel band. They're really hot," Kit enthused.

"Yeah, I'm sure. The new Beatles," Shelly responded, adding under her breath, ". . . except with five Ringos."

Shelly felt sure that Coco was the kind of woman who waxed off all her pubic hair. We're talking Farrah Fawcett *Minor*.

"*Salut.*" The singer gave Kit a concupiscent glance, before

62

shimmying to her feet. Coco's mouth was a sticky red bravado of lipstick. She pressed her petulant lacquered pout onto Kit's cheek before she and her lustrous black mane of hair and her no-doubt mown pubic pelt sashayed off to band practice. Coco possessed a perfection that inclined male observers towards the adjectival. Around the pool, men unused to superlatives had to tilt their heads backwards so that their eyeballs wouldn't fall out as the willowy goddess passed.

Shelly's heart plunged into her stomach. What the hell was he doing here with this manizer? On the surface Kit might appear to be the fly-button-jeans-with-battered-poetry-books-in-his-back-pocket kind of guy, but psychologically he was all paisley cravat and silk dressing-gown. My God! The man was positively Hugh Hefneresque. Oh, lust could seriously derange a woman's brain. It was time to stop thinking like a man and start thinking like a woman, which meant hopping on to the first plane back to Heathrow and into the first Häagen-Dazs ice cream container she came across.

But as she watched Kit roll casually onto his belly, propping his forehead onto a golden forearm, her blood gave a little insubordinate surge of desire. When Shelly saw those taut, brown buns in those skimpy bathers—we're talking the kind of pneumatic buttocks that had done more for female masturbation than Doctor Ruth—she made a noise not unlike someone forced to chew off her own foot.

"Beautiful, huh?" Kit drawled.

God yes, Shelly thought to herself. "Well," she said with mock nonchalance, "in those swimmers at least you'll have melanomas all over."

"The *island*," he clarified, mischievously. "The island is beautiful, you doofus."

"Yes, well, obviously *you* couldn't wait to get here," she baited.

"Oh, you're not gonna start actin' like a wife again, are you? Nag, nag, nag. Jesus Christ," he joshed. "Who the hell have I married? *Virginia Woolf?*"

"Yes. So be very afraid."

A hot rush of laughter escaped the autodidact's lips and Shelly relaxed a little as she watched him stretch, causing the muscles in his arms and back to fan out. That is, she relaxed until she realized that every other woman on the island—let's face it, every woman in the entire Indian Ocean—was also not only ogling in Kit's desirable direction, but preparing to leave their partners, pronto, and have his baby. They all watched as he caressed his chiseled abs with sunscreen, Factor Lust.

While Kit was cleaning his sunglass lenses with his towel, he blinked up at Shelly. It was then she noticed his eyelashes. They were long enough to tie reef knots. She sighed. Perhaps she could use them to tie him to the bed? Oh, but what bed? After all, thanks to Kit they were not sharing one. How could he be so alluring and so elusive at the same time?

"Kit, the separate rooms thing? I don't get it. I mean, what about yesterday in the limo?" Shelly prompted. "What about 'love at first sight'? What about arranged marriages being a centuries-old tradition?" Her voice sounded flimsy. "What about, 'If you rest, you rust'?"

"So." He leant up on one elbow. "Lemme get this straight. When you said, 'I do,' you weren't thinkin' about the money at all. You were just thinkin' with your pussy?" he asked, bemused.

"Well, partly." She tried to talk quietly but her voice was getting irascible with jet lag. "That's all *men* get married for, isn't it? Guaranteed sex. I mean, that's standard operating procedure for a guy! You told me that pleasure was part of the Y-chromosome bloke modus operandi. Why is lust so shocking in a woman?"

"So, just to recap." Kit tipped his shades down his nose to scrutinize her more clearly. "You only got married 'cause you couldn't get any casual sex?"

It seemed to Shelly that the entire poolside population swiveled in their direction at that point. You could have heard a jaw drop. She suddenly felt white-hot anger shooting off her like sparks. "Of course not! I don't like casual sex! I like it as formal as possible. Blood tests, CVs, the works. Especially with *you* . . . I wouldn't even *be* here, except for the fact that we were matched. By a computer. From God knows how many thousands of contestants. Our data was analyzed and we turned out to be the perfect couple! Reasoning powers superior to the human brain decided that we are uniquely suited. Doesn't that mean anything to you?"

"I don't need a computer to tell me about you." Kit laughed. "You're transparent, Shelly Green."

"I am not!"

He took off his sunglasses and appraised her with a cool eye. "You catalogue your CD collection by genre." Shelly raised an intrigued, though slightly embarrassed eyebrow. He was sounding her out with sonar accuracy.

"You have motivational tapes on your Walkman. 'I Must Kick Karma Butt—And How!'"

"I do not have motivational tapes!" Although, come to think of it, there were some self-help books burning holes in her bookcase somewhere. They should be reissued under "self-harm" for all the good they'd done her. "Don't kid yourself! No man can know anything about any woman." She was trying not to think of his hot mouth moving upon her only a couple of days before.

"We have different neural circuitry. While women ponder Life's Great Questions—Am I Happy? Is My Marriage Working? Am I a Good Mother?—the man is thinking, Have I got time to get laid and tune the carburetor before kick-off?" She noticed a drop of sweat on his upper lip and her pulse beat with an irrational pleasure.

Kit scoffed. "Ponderin' Life's Great Questions! Don't make me laugh!" He seized her wrist, right where a handcuff would go. "All you gals are ponderin' is why your idiot boyfriend won't put the toilet roll on with the serrated bit facin' out, rather than in."

"Ha! That's proof of how little you know! Men don't ever even put the toilet roll on! A man's idea of changing a toilet roll is to put it on the back of the cistern," she yelled back.

So much for the cute little joint message they'd leave on their answering machine. One hour into her tropical island honeymoon and sun-lounger hostilities were rivaling those of two Balkan republics. With all eyes still upon them, Shelly tugged Kit to his feet and frog-marched him past the pool into the nearest deserted structure—a shabby cabin with the grand name of Le Centre de Plonge, which she gathered from the army of black wet suits outside, their sleeves saluting in the wind, was the dive shop.

"So let *me* get something right," Shelly snapped. "All that stuff about waiting to be besotted, entranced, enraptured, iridescent with lust and longing—intoxicated by orgasmic bliss, was all crap, and you really only married me for the money?"

Kit smiled languorously. The man oozed sexual arrogance from every pore.

"Oh," she fumed. "My mother was so right about men. You're all low-down, lily-livered lying bastards hell-bent on making women miserable."

"What bullshit!" he bristled. "Truth is, you chicks have it so much better than us guys. We even die earlier than you."

"Typical. Leaving the cleaning up to a woman."

"We men die earlier because of stress. The stress of havin' to live with women! Always whinin' on about your period cramps and childbirth pains and the glass ceilin' . . ."

"Hey, bud, not only does the glass ceiling exist but women are paid four bucks an hour less than men to clean it."

"Oh, you gals are so superior, ain'tcha? I'd just like to sit in judgment when a chick asks, 'Will you go out with me? Will you sleep with me?'" Kit railed. "But women don't have to ask those questions, 'cause you already know the answers."

"Yeah . . . that men will sleep with anything," Shelly concluded, with bitter vexation.

He wrapped his fingers around her upper arms. "Is that what you think?"

"Yes." She caught her breath in an effort to recover from the thrill of his touch. "As long as it's warm and still breathing, men will shag it first—then count the legs afterwards."

"Will we now?" he said, with sly gaiety, squeezing her tighter.

"Because you don't give a toss about your emotional libido."

His lips curved into a lubricious smile. "Don't we now?"

"No." Lust skittered through her body. The air no longer seemed oppressive but sweetly charged with the perfume of jasmine and lemon, fanned by a warm wind laced with spices. "Men just don't get it—that love is between the ears more than between the thighs."

"Is it now?"

A sentiment that might have carried a little more weight if they didn't have their hands down the front of each other's pants.

"I mean," she shuddered, ground down by the delicious

weight of him pushing up against her, "how long did it take you to bed the French goddess Coco, for example? I'm surprised you even found out her name."

Just as Shelly was giving into the urgency of her pleasure, Kit pulled away from her. It was an uncharacteristically savage movement, rangy and impatient. "I thought you were jokin'. That's what you really think of me? That I'm nothin' more than a life support system to a cock?"

Shelly was speechless. "Well . . ."

"I have a, what's-it 'emotional libido' too, you know, Shelly."

"Oh really? I hadn't noticed."

"It seems to me that *you're* the one with no emotional libido. I mean, look at you. I'm nothin' more to you than a piece of meat."

"Oh, but such a delicious piece. Filet mignon, at the very least," Shelly teased, trying to coax him back. Every drop of her blood had sprung to attention. Her needs were melting her from sigh to thigh.

"Here you are whinin' on that a relationship can't be built on sex alone, and all the time you're just usin' me for my body. Yeah! I'm feelin' used," he said with sardonic amusement. "I feel, well, like a chick . . . In fact, I'm startin' to worry that my ass looks big in this."

But Shelly refused to be amused. "But you're the one who talked me into surrendering to basic sexual needs. With no messy emotion getting in the way. To be, well, like a guy! I fully intend to start timing my journeys any second now!"

"You could never be mistaken for a guy," Kit said, his eyes sliding down her body. "Figure it out," he punned. "But anyway, I wanna be appreciated for my mind and personality. Verbal togetherness, that's what I want. Yes, sirree. And I have this bad feelin' that we have nothin' in common——"

"Except for wanting to gnaw each other's clothes off with our teeth." She made another grab for him which he resisted.

"Shelly!" He pretended to be shocked. "Doin' it on the first date? I'll get a bad name!"

"You did everything else on our first date!" Shelly reminded him, piqued.

Kit threw his head back and released that hot gush of laughter that burbled recklessly out of him and made him so damn desirable. And yet his eyes, she vaguely noticed, remained sad—so at variance with his outward show.

"If we find that we get on in other ways—only then will I be ready to consummate," Kit declaimed.

"What?" Disappointment clung to Shelly like a wet shower curtain. Intellectually she could appreciate his logic, but it was a hard concept to explain to her libido, which was like a crazed animal hurling itself against the bars of its cage. "Kit, come on—"

But before she could elucidate that just because a woman could hide the primal engorgement of her libidinous organ, it didn't mean she didn't want to discover the supple hydraulics of his manhood *right now*, an avalanche of flesh engulfed her as Slothman heaved into the dive shop.

"Kids, kids, kids! Sounds like the romance has gone out of your marriage."

"It never went in," Shelly amended. "That's what we're working on."

"Thought you'd be off in Kit's Love-Lab by now, gettin' to grips with his crimson crowbar." With his balding head and close-set eyes, Towtruck looked remarkably like a crimson crowbar himself, Shelly thought. The repulsive man winked at Kit. Shelly noted that he even smiled fatly.

Kit gave Towtruck one of his slow, scathing looks. "Ain't I seen you some place before? Um . . . like *The Jerry Springer Show?* Who is this lowlife?" Kit asked Shelly, but Towtruck gave her no time to answer.

"Ya know, the Yank is right, Shelly. You birds have won, don't ya realize that? I feel so damn threatened by women I'm even training myself to stop saying 'cunt' as a swear word. But listen, kids, prattling on about equality makes shit television," he said, pointing out the hidden microphone taped under the flap of Shelly's rucksack.

Kit knifed to attention and seized the cameraman by the scruff of his neck. "You've been secretly tapin' us?"

"Strewth! Gaby's been drooling through the telescopic lens. She reckons if she'd known you were gonna look this hot in a pair of cossies she'd have had her nipples plucked."

"You've been filmin' us too?" Kit's face was now shoved so closely into Towtruck's that he seemed to be glaring into one volcanic pore.

"Too bloody right."

Shelly felt a wave of nausea in the pit of her stomach. "Documentary voyeurism has just been raised to new depths," she announced, sarcastically.

"Read your contract. Youse can be filmed at all times except on the dunny or shagging." Towtruck's grin revealed tombstone dentistry. "Now smooch up a bit, will ya." He pointed to the camera perched on its tripod in the shrubs. "This is the Honeymoon Capital of the World. There are hymens everywhere. You can buy hymen souvenirs. Mounted hymens. Macraméd hymens." He prodded Shelly in the chest. "You can go topless too, ya know, love. You'll be on after the watershed."

Most men have learned to tread warily through the semantics of modern feminism. But, marveled Shelly, not Towtruck.

"Bugger New Men!" He flashed his terra-cotta teeth. "I want tits with everything!"

"Forget it. For you my cups do not runneth over," Shelly retorted.

"Oh yeah?" So saying, Towtruck produced a ten-pound note from his back pocket and slapped it onto the dive desk. "Betcha ten quid I can make your tits move without touchin' 'em." Without waiting for a reply, he leaned over and squeezed Shelly's nearest boob. "You won!" He spluttered into incontinent laughter, before winking conspiratorially at Kit. "That'll loosen her up, mate."

Kit slapped a twenty-dollar note onto the same table. "I bet you twenty bucks I can make your balls move without touchin' them." Then, faster than you can say "countertenor," he kicked Towtruck between his huge and hairy legs. "A painful death awaits anyone who tries to film me again without my permission," Kit simmered. "Have you got that, you needle-dicked sonofabitch?"

"You . . . you *cunt!*" was Towtruck's not exactly Wildean riposte.

As Kit stomped away towards the beach, Shelly ran after him. Heat beat up from the pebble-dashed path. Cicadas hummed, playing castanets with their wings.

"Four million years of spectacular human evolution and what the hell do we have to show for it? Reality goddamn television," he fumed, when she caught up with him.

"I know. Reality TV is just people who haven't got anything to do, watching people who can't do anything! How thought provoking."

"Yeah, and the thought it's provokin' is, 'Why the hell am I watchin' this shit?'"

"See?" she enthused, "We have one thing in common already. How much we hate the show . . . So, shall we just go and make a withdrawal from our bonk account?" Shelly cringed. Dear God, she was sounding like Towtruck! While pausing to empty sand out of her shoes, roll up her jeans and regain her decorum, Shelly stole a surreptitious glance at her husband, who was quietly appreciating the curve of her posterior as she bent over.

"So?" She gave him a coquettish smile.

Contradictory feelings scudded across Kit's face like clouds on a windy day. Beneath his ebullient surface seemed to lurk another life, like the hidden reefs below a calm, blue sea. Shelly was finding him impossible to navigate. Who was this man?

Kit hesitated, wavered then decided on his course of action. "Sorry, I just ain't that kind of boy." He flashed her a smile so luminous you could read by it at night, then broke into a run.

The sort of person you choose to go on holiday with says a lot about you. Vacationing with a husband who won't sleep with you says that you're an A-grade shmuck, Shelly wailed inwardly. Everybody is so obsessed about sex before marriage. Well, what about sex *after*?

She'd finally taught herself to think like a man, only to find her man thinking like a woman.

"He wants *what*?" screeched Gaby, panting up behind her on the beach moments later, frantically waving Kit's contract.

"He wants to increase our verbal togetherness."

"Yeah, right. Can you imagine nearing the end of your life and wishing you'd had less sex? Listen, Mrs. K., I've only given two blow jobs in my life and this directing job is one of them. Don't fuck it up for me."

"But he hates the camera."

"Well, he's signed a contract, okay? Look, I'll give you the rest of the afternoon to win him over. No cameras. But after that, I start filming again. Got it? Verbal togetherness, my ass. He's continuing to act nonverbally with that French slut from the bloody band, I bet."

If Kit *was* sowing his wild oats with Coco, Shelly could only pray for a crop failure, and the best way to do *that* was to find out what they had in common. The computer had matchmade them from thousands of applicants. They must be on the same wavelength. Certainly the sexual signals he broadcast could make her hum. Surely the only thing they had in common couldn't be that they had nothing in common . . . could it?

The Differences
Between the Sexes:
Excitement

Men get excited by beer, football, blondes, food and the Playboy channel.

Women get all excited about nothing—and then they marry him.

6 State of Siege

One of life's great mysteries is why people are divided into those who like the outdoors and those who like the indoors, and why they invariably end up married to each other.

On the first morning of her tropical paradise honeymoon, Shelly discovered that her groom was otherwise energetically engaged, parasailing, hang-gliding, waterskiing, aquaplaning, whitewater rafting. While Shelly's natural habitat was the concert hall, it turned out that Kit was the type to toss a tent casually into his back pocket and disappear, at a jog, up Everest for a week or two.

Shelly had been known to run too—but only when her apartment was on fire. Her mother had once entered her for the London Marathon, in aid of Single-Parent Families. People thought she'd won . . . until they realized that she was just finishing *last* year's race. Her main anxiety in life was that the evil prick who thought up aerobics classes might be thinking up something else right now, that sadistic bastard!

Having found her beach-side, thatched-roof bungalow with its Beatles haircut, she showered, then raided the hotel boutique for overpriced bikinis and sarongs. Shelly was now ready to make a brief sortie in search of Kit. But when she discovered he was waterskiing (the art of knocking down a jetty with your face, and hence the mainstay of neurosurgeons worldwide), she declined his offer to join him, saying she wanted to exercise her mind instead . . . But all she could think about was why should he do all this healthy exercise when orgasmic infrequency increases a man's mortality rate by 50 percent. She rushed off to inform her husband that sex was also a very effective way of enhancing the cardiovascular system, but by then Kit, in tight shorts and T-shirt, was limbering up for his pool laps.

"Are you comin' swimmin'? You do like swimmin' at least, don'tcha?"

"Oh yes! I just have one problem—buoyancy." It came back to her in a wave—the clammy heat of the local swimming pool and the sickly chemical smell. She gave an involuntary shiver. "The trouble with swimming is that one gets so wet."

Kit laughed, before executing a perfect parabola, fully clothed, into the pool.

The gelatinous-thighed women in Dominic's aquaerobics class made hamster squeals of delight as Kit surfaced among them. The sight of his wet shorts clinging to his baguette-sized bulge caused a high-speed pile-up during the "lunge and return" segment. It also caused the entertainment officer to flex his carefully hewn 600-sit-ups-a-day six-pack torso in pique and turn off his quadraphonic blaster.

"What's the matter, Dom?" Kit laughed, one of the ladies' long thin pink flotation devices between his powerful thighs. "Havin' trouble with your noodle?"

When he wasn't exercising, Kit liked to spend his time basking beachside, slathering himself in sunscreens as his skin caramelized into a golden brown.

Shelly was acutely aware of her own curds-and-wheyish white skin, which had begun to curdle in the sun. (The woman needed to tan for six months to go *white*.) She didn't like the adhesive quality of suntan lotion either. No matter how she lay on the sand, she quickly became coated in cigarette butts, bottle tops and unwanted locals selling indigenous nose flutes. She preferred the solarium and booked in for a sunbed session, which required claustrophobic entombment in an ultraviolet sarcophagus. While she was at the salon, she also got talked into a pedicure and manicure and cellulite-cure and . . .

"Jeez Louise! I thought you liked the natural look. You don't need all that crap on your face. I had no idea you were so vain," was Kit's response when she appeared hours later, all bouffed and buffed. He flicked his towel free of sand with the grace of a matador. And Shelly did, indeed, see red.

"Vain!" she retorted, crushed. "Men are much vainer than women. I mean, you people don't think you need makeup!"

They had their differences in dress sense too.

"Why don't you go and sit over there near those Germans," Kit teasingly suggested over pre-lunch drinks on the beach balcony. "The best thing about Germans is that they're even more badly dressed than you are."

"You don't like the way I dress?" Shelly, who favored the cheap and cheerful end of the tailoring spectrum, glanced down at her boutique-bought denim clam diggers and floral flip-flops.

"Well, it's a look. For a *wino*, maybe."

Everything Kit wore looked divine, of course. His clothes seemed to worship every contour of his body as though they, too, couldn't wait to caress him. They were clothes that Shelly thought would look even more divine crumpled up in a heap on her bedroom floor.

"I thought it would be logical to dress badly so that a man would want nothing more than to *get me out of these annoying clothes*," she muttered behind his back as she followed him into the dining room. "You know what would look good on me? *You*."

In the restaurant, Kit preferred the smoking section, while she liked nonsmoking. If there'd been a non-mobile phone section she'd have sat there too, as Kit's phone was constantly chiming with calls from Coco to join her for dessert.

Food was an equally divisive topic. Kit liked his fast, whereas Shelly was definitely not an all-you-can-eat-buffet kind of person. Though she rankled at the term "organic fascist," she did try to ensure her tuna was "dolphin and surfer-free." Still, in an effort to convince Kit of their similarities, she lined up at the smorgasbord. The table groaned beneath a feast that could feed Somalia. But watching carbo-bloated tourists coming back for seconds, thirds and fourths rather killed her appetite.

"Why is it that people on holidays eat as though they've got seven rectums?" she found herself complaining. "Each meal leaves you feeling like a boa constrictor, post-pig. But instead of lying around digesting the meal for, oh, say, six months or so, what do they do? Simply go and consume another meal just like it three hours later."

"You see? Completely incompatible," Kit laughed, before sauntering off to pile up his plate even higher. By the exotic fruits, Coco nibbled his neck in greeting. The Frenchwoman obviously had a very unusual eating disorder—she liked to devour other people's husbands. Whereas Shelly was Kit's *pièce de résistance*: the man resisted every piece of her. Shelly cursed herself. What she'd meant to say to him was: "If it's true that we are what we eat, I could be *you* by morning."

Then there was food for thought. Over lunch they discussed books. Shelly liked reading: George Eliot, the Brontës, Byron, Keats.

Kit picked up her copy of *War and Peace* and spent five minutes reading it cover to cover. The man considered Doonesbury cartoon strips to be right up there with the Dead Sea Scrolls. So, as it turned out, did Coco, who had popped off to the hotel shop to buy him papers for their joint perusal. The only thing Coco had ever read cover to cover were diet books. *For Whom the Calorie Tolls, Wuthering Bathroom Scales, War and Wheat-free.*

But Shelly and Kit would have to have sex soon, because they'd run out of conversation. Having completed an Open University course on Freud with her mother, Shelly found Kit all too easy to psychoanalyze. He would never need to regress to his childhood, because he'd clearly never left it. Hence his predilection for restaurants with giant wall-mounted salad forks and crappy sports programs like, well, "baseball," which, now lunch was over, he was rushing back to his room to watch. But when he reappeared, hours later, and she asked him about the game, he became all mistrustful and remote. "What game?" He leaned back moodily on the chaise, jeans undone just enough to reveal the tops of his briefs.

"If you haven't been watching the baseball, well, where've you been all afternoon then? I mean, this is a rare sighting. You're like the lesser-spotted tit," his wife said dryly. "I know you're not supposed to see your husband *before* the wedding, but nobody said anything about not seeing him *after*."

Kit grinned suddenly and became as warm and gregarious as he'd just been dark and distracted. "Oh yeah, the game," he winked. "Gotta get back for the last inning. New York is one up on L.A." And he was off again.

Shelly took mental notes. They read: "Never Get Married Again."

"Come on!" urged Gaby, buttonholing Shelly over afternoon tea. "This marriage consummation is the most keenly anticipated one in modern history. Bets are being taken. The whole world, well Channel Six anyway, is waiting with bated everythings to see whether you bonk or not."

Towtruck flung himself into an armchair, his shuttered camera sitting mutely accusing at his huge and hairy feet. "I should be fucking filming with an endoscope, 'cause so far I've got shit," he whinged.

"What can I do?" Shelly protested. "Kit's spent the whole afternoon in his room. I can't make him want me."

"No, but you can stalk him relentlessly until he eventually panics and caves in."

"I've tried everything, Gaby, bar having myself delivered by room service on a bed of bloody lettuce."

"Wait! Maybe that's it!" Gaby epiphanied. "Obviously Kit's had enough sexual uninhibitedness. What he's craving is sexual inhibition. Maybe you should try being more subtle? Guys don't like a chick who plays easy to get. Just stop wearing your fanny on your sleeve, okay?"

Only trouble was, subtle took so long. Shelly tried to assuage her frustration by leafing dispiritedly through the cocktail menu. But even these were libidinously named. Choosing between Knee Tremblers and Lime Licks did little to take her mind off Kit Kinkade. Above her pastel cocktail umbrella she watched disconsolately as pair after pallid pair of newly betrothed paraded before her, a conveyor belt of happy couples. Ordering another piña colada seemed her only option.

It's easily understandable why beach weddings have become

so popular—no off-key harmonium playing Handel, no impersonation of big white meringue. But this was an epidemic. The evening of the first day on her honeymoon island, Shelly witnessed so many wedding ceremonies she started to suffer from confetti-fatigue.

There were happy honeymooners to the left of her, life-jacketed and squealing as their giant green rubberized alligator wobbled over the wake of the speedboat that towed it. There were happy honeymooners to the right of her, bonding with other happy honeymooners in a spot of postnuptial hammock lounging. The tidily eyebrowed brides compared the shiny rings on their pearl-pink, nail-polished fingers. The grooms got sunburnt while indulging in wedding-one-upmanship. "*We* rode off down the beach in a horse-drawn carriage while white doves were released from heart-shaped cages." "Oh yeah? Well, *we* left the Casino on a white Harley Davidson to the strains of an orchestra playing the theme song from *Titanic*." Hell, there were even happy honeymooners above her, their entwined legs dangling over the turquoise sea in tandem from airborne jellyfish as if parasailing in from some James Bond movie. Everybody seemed happy, except her. Even the bend in the local bananas made it look as though they were smiling from their bowls. All Shelly could do was contribute a toast to their happiness, again and again and again and . . .

"Hey, Shell." How the melodious undulation of Kit's voice made her tingle. "Well, the game's over. What d'ya feel like doin' now?"

Shelly was trying to remain urbane, but Kit's fingers accidentally brushed her arm and she was twitching like a junkie. "I dunno." Ice cubes clinked musically in her glass. "What about holding your head under the spa pool until you decide to have sex with me?" she said, *subtly*.

83

Kit scrutinized the number of cocktail glasses piled up around her on the Sunset Balcony Bar. "Or maybe I should just help you back to your bungalow," he hinted.

"Yes! Let's go back to my place and do all the things I'm gonna tell all my girlfriends we did anyway." God, she congratulated herself, did she know how to play hard to get or what? "So, exactly what was that limo ride?" Ice cubes chimed as she took another slurp from her cocktail. "Are you just a clit-tease, Kinkade?" she drawled with the vocal force of an air-raid siren, drowning out the band and drawing the attention of everyone in the Sunset Bar. "Don't you find me"—she burped—"attractive anymore?"

Kit's gaze was impassive. "Oh look," he said sarcastically, pointing at Shelly. "See this woman sound asleep in a pool of her own saliva? That's my wife!"

"Waiter! More drinks. A Harvey Wallbanger for the man and strychnine for me. I am going to kill myself if you don't make love to me." She hiccoughed. "Would it help if I just got down on all fours and licked your feet?"

Kit leveled a steady gaze at her. "I think it would help if you stopped drinkin' and let me help you back to your room."

"Why bother? I should just auction you off to the highest bidder. 'Brand-New Husband! Never Used!!'" Shelly tapped on the side of her glass with a spoon and lurched to standing. "Attention, Ladies and Jellybeans," she drawled.

Kit, who had just noticed Towtruck's camera trained on them both from across the bar, tried to rescue Shelly from further humiliation by dragging her into the fierce frottage on the dance floor, where he moved with erotic grace into the beat of "La Cucaracha."

Now, despite being musical, Shelly Green was to dancing

what Al Qaeda is to World Peace. She definitely moved to a different drummer. But unfortunately the cocktails had affected her critical abilities to the point where she thought she could dance. Which is why, moments later, Shelly found herself scraping all the skin off her nose on a disco glitter-ball, having mistimed a pogo dance step as only a gal from Cardiff can.

Kit carried Shelly over his shoulder back to her bungalow. "Have a little snooze and I'll see ya later," he suggested kindly.

"Where are you going *now*?" she managed to mouth.

"There's another game on. Chicago against Detroit." Kit bit his lower lip and looked away.

Even in her alcoholic haze, Shelly suspected that he was lying to her. "I'll see you after that then? What, about nine?" she slurred.

Kit cocked a caustic brow. "I think sleep is what you need right now, Shelly."

"No! No! No! I don't need sleep! Women need love! Ask any syndicated advice columnist! Hey, don't leave me!" she called out after him. "Couldn't you sleep here? We could just sleep. I promise nothing will happen. I won't touch you." It was what men always said. Then *he* could see what it was like to wake with the imprint of an erect clitoris in the small of his back.

But he left her, quite literally, high and dry. How long was a football match? she wondered. At nine P.M. she opened her door wearing nothing but baby oil—to greet the porter delivering her missing suitcase full of designer wear.

By ten o'clock on the first evening of her honeymoon, Shelly was so bored she was counting her armpit hairs. All evening she lolled about in the La Perla underwear supplied by Channel 6 watching remedial cable television with CNN X-Generational hosts specifically chosen for their inability to read an autocue. By eleven P.M. she had TV bends. By midnight she realized that she was Miss Havisham. "I may as well sit in a dusty room for the rest of my life wearing a macraméd hymen, clutching our wedding album," she confided to Gaby over the internal phone.

"Men are scum. Just go ransack your minibar for something insertible," was Gaby's advice. "I'm making do with a small bottle of gin, although it ain't proving much of a tonic."

By one A.M. the next morning, Shelly deduced that she obviously possessed the sexual magnetism of a half-thawed rissole. Why else was she flying right under his romantic radar?

By two A.M., as she tore off her erotic underwear, she realized that Kit was a marital mirage, little more than a hormonal hallucination. If only he weren't so damn attractive—Kit Kinkade could excite passion in a large geological granite formation—she could forget about him.

She tried to put him out of her mind but everything reminded her of sex, a phenomenon repeated when she ordered mussels from the twenty-four-hour room service menu. She'd never thought of them as vaginas-of-the sea until the waiter placed the plate of pouty pink labias on the white tablecloth before her. She prised them free from their shells with her tongue. God. Even her meal was getting more action than she was. Hey! she thought drunkenly. She'd pulled a mussel! Was it any wonder that the poor woman had a libido the size of Paraguay?

Beyond her bungalow balcony, a lime tree avenue swept away to the voluptuous Fountain of Love—the milky-white marble of carved female flesh gleaming libidinously against the dark volcanic rock. Even the interlaced limbs of the frangipani trees seemed to mock her. Just to ridicule her further, a line of black ants had marched across the floor to her discarded La Perla knickers. They were busily ringing a tiny drop of her juice—an entomological wagon train.

At three A.M. the bedsprings mourned as she rolled over. Her nightie had twisted as she'd tossed and turned until she was as wound up outside as in. Kit had proven himself to be a Sex Object all right—she wanted sex and he objected to it.

At four A.M. she stared out at the beaten silver sea. White satin bands of clouds drifted towards the dark horizon. The moon rose, its light lying over the ocean like a bridal gown. Shelly slumped onto her lonely sheets, her spirits squashed flatter than roadkill, the bottle of celebratory champagne unopened in the ice bucket, and synchronized her sighs with the sea.

It was obviously a case of premature cohabitation.

The Differences Between the Sexes: Support

Men: Behind every successful man is a wife . . .
Under every successful man is a mistress.
(Otherwise known as a mattress.)

Women: The only thing supporting a woman is her
Wonderbra. (So called because when you take it
off, you wonder where the hell your tits went.)

7 Aquatic Maneuvers

Sex with Kit was amazing! Shelly marveled, waking the next morning . . . but how much more amazing it would be if he had actually been with her at the time.

Only one word was insinuating itself between Shelly and happiness: abstinence. But it seemed that Kit was not going to be the cure. Fine. She was no longer going to waste time pondering the tit-tweaking, clit-clenching, ovary-twisting, womb-worming question as to why her husband wouldn't sleep with her. She would just leave for London. Straight after breakfast—although she wasn't all that hungry having consumed slices and slices of humble pie throughout the night. What had she been thinking? This whole ridiculous escapade was so out of character. Shelly Green was *not* the type to sleep her way to the bottom, goddamnit.

Kit had told her he never ate breakfast unless he'd worked up an appetite doing carnal calisthenics so Shelly slouched, exhausted and hungover, into the thatched dining area known as

La Caravelle, alone. It was better this way. Now she wouldn't have to do the old "marriage takes its toll, so please pay at the booth" Good-bye and Good Riddance speech.

"Not the look of a woman who got lucky," Gaby surmised, collaring her at the breakfast buffet. "What are you planning, woman?" The director admonished her with a fork. "An an*nul*ment from the *Pope*?"

Scowling, Shelly retreated to a secluded corner of the pagoda. She was just tucking into her cereal when her eyes lit upon Kit . . . breakfasting with Coco—a sight so surprising she accidentally swallowed the little plastic giveaway toy that had been hiding beneath a bran flake.

As Shelly staggered to his table, spluttering and wheezing, Kit greeted her with a casual "hi" and nonchalantly sipped at his café au lait. "Coco's just been tellin' me all about the history of colonization here on the island. How the friggin' French enslaved Africans to toil on the coffee plantations and then later for the sugar barons." He was noisily chomping his way through a basket of brioches. Now what could have given him an appetite like that? Shelly wondered bitterly.

Coco looked up at Shelly with molten-chocolate eyes. "Ze French, zey are like parents—zo bor-ring," she volunteered in a lilting Parisian accent. "You know 'ow you outgrow your parents and start to 'ate zem and zen you need years and years of therapee to get over zem? Well, eets just like zat." (Shelly inwardly scoffed. Not exactly a Che Guevara revolutionary theory.) "I ask you a simple question?" Coco continued.

Do you ever ask any other kind? Shelly was tempted to say, but shrugged instead. "Sure."

"As a, you know, ambassadeur of ze British Empire, where do you stand on ze issue of colonization, Nelly?"

"It's Shelly. And where do I stand?" On *you*, would be my first choice, Shelly thought to herself. "I think anyone born on this island is the winner in the Lucky Sperm Competition. I mean, they *could* have been born on a dung pile in Guatemala or on the streets of Bombay . . . or in public housing in Ebbw Vale," she said tetchily, her face burning—and not from the sun either.

"Kit, he understands, don't you, *mon chou*? Many people, zey walk in and out of your life, but only true friends leave footprints in your heart." The singer's smile was as sickly sweet as her cliché.

It wasn't foot but *finger*prints Shelly was more concerned about—as in *Kit's*, and all over *Coco*. But before the ideology-addled French bimbo could launch into another pat spiel, Shelly's attention was drawn to a man, impeccably kitted out in white leisurewear, who'd swaggered into the breakfast area and was now striding towards them with menacing intensity.

Coco gave him a scornful glance—but a wide berth, immediately gliding to her feet and moving off in her lamé hotpants with an insouciant catwalk sashay which set not just Shelly's teeth but every part of her body on jealous edge.

"Monsieur." The man doffed an invisible hat and glanced at Shelly's hand. "Madame. You must pardon ze staff 'ere. Zey are not allowed to fraternize wiz ze guests. Especially zat one," he pointed in the direction of the disappearing Coco. "She came 'ere, a good French girl, but as you English say, 'went native.' Though why?" He shrugged. "I do not know. Before we came along and civilized ze Creoles, zeir main form of transportation were vines, *n'est-ce pas?*"

As he paused to light up the ubiquitous Gauloise, Kit and Shelly swapped a glance. It was immediately clear to both that this was a man who suffered from *high* self-esteem. It was only now, when he removed his sunglasses, that Shelly recognized him as the brutal police chief from the airport. How could she forget that face? The man was so ugly it was a wonder he wasn't in a bottle somewhere in a science lab.

"Christ," whispered Kit. "I think his mum must've fed him with a slingshot"—an image underscored by the man's cheeks, which were corrugated with acne scars. Even more visually alarming was the police chief's tonsure, which involved three strands of badly dyed maroon hair combed over a sun-ravaged cranium. His huge feet bulged sockless out of his alligator loafers. Hovering above these pregnant reptiles, stocky legs had been squeezed into ironed white jeans. And above these fat albino sausages, a belly, which had known too much Perrier Jouët and pâté de foie gras, strained at the buttons of his Pierre Cardin shirt. He was intimidating and powerful, but in a compact sort of way, like a lapdog on steroids. That's what he was—an attack Chihuahua.

"Ze blacks, zey are so lazy. Ze problem is, we pay zem too much. Because we French, we are too liberal. Too generous. We pay zem less?" He shrugged. "Zey work 'arder."

Shelly felt her blood boil. "Really? I thought the enlistment of labor on a subsistence basis was now forbidden—except in marriage." (It was something her mother had always said.)

But the police chief had already taken a small bow and barreled off in pursuit of his pulchritudinous prey.

Shelly swiveled towards Kit. "You're right, you know. Commitment is a load of crock. You men only get married to colonize women. Just like the French have colonized these poor Creoles. When women are restless, we burn holes in our credit cards, get a new hairstyle, eat chocolate, whereas you males colonize another country. English and French men just barged around the world, fought each other for possession of every island they could find, not even bothering to wipe their feet first—and then getting slaves to clean up after them, just like *wives* do."

"Ah! So you do agree with Coco." Kit gave a victorious, snaggle-toothed smile.

"No. Yes. All I'm saying is, yes, blacks have been discriminated against, but so have women. My mother wouldn't be dominated by her father or my father—my dad wanted her to give up her music, you know. So she ended up raising me on her own in public housing. You should see a Welsh housing project. Then you really could believe that the world was created in only six measly days. She was a second-class citizen for most of her life. Most women are. Husbands have this terrible habit of turning into Victorian patriarchs. One wedding bell and they're off. 'Do you really think you should wear such a short skirt in public?' 'Do you really think it's appropriate behavior to ask my boss why lesbians wear strap-on dildos if they hate men?' You blokes may no longer make us cover up piano legs to curb your sexual excitement, but you're still putting us in emotional crinoline and not taking us seriously."

"So, um . . . why do they?"

"What?"

"Wear strap-on dildos? The dykes, I mean," he said, not taking her seriously.

"Have you been listening to a *word* I've been say—"

"Kinda, until my brain got the bends. I can't have such deep conversations. Not when I ain't got my scuba gear on yet. Are you comin' divin', by the way?"

"Scuba diving is proof of mental illness. Besides, I don't own the correct sort of vile, luminous outfit."

"Wet suit. It's called a w-e-t s-u-i-t." Kit spelled it out remedially. "Come on! Don't be such a wimp, you Euroweenie!"

"Read my lips. NO scuba-diving. Have you ever wondered why fish don't need cocaine? Why they're just naturally jumpy? *Because something much, much bigger is always trying to eat them.*"

"Ain't there any sport you do like?" beseeched Kit.

Shelly shrugged, demolishing Coco's uneaten croissant. "Golf?"

Kit sprayed half-masticated brioche across the table. "Golf? Golf is a sport for folks who aren't fit enough for anything else."

"I rest my case."

"Along with your fat ass." And he playfully slapped her bottom, like a marauding pirate set on pillage and plunder.

Shelly blushed hotly. "Do you mind? I am *not* some remote island in need of development. Do not try and colonize *me*, thank you kindly," she stropped.

"That's the trouble with you Brits. You never do anythin' spontaneous."

"I'm planning a little spontaneity, maybe tomorrow." Shelly's face burnt with embarrassment. "When I kill you, Kit Kinkade."

It was the sort of parting line that required orchestral strings and a sunset . . . but Shelly had to make do with the aquaerobics Muzak throbbing from the entertainment officer's ghetto blaster. But who was she kidding, Shelly thought as she booked her flight back to London. Retreat is nothing more than a strategic maneuver by the combatant who has lost the battle.

When Gaby located Shelly checking out at reception, she went ballistic. "What about your contract? What about the twenty-five thou you get to collect at the end of the week?" Her voice buzzed insistently in Shelly's ear. "Look, I agree that one-eyed Cyborgs that eat human flesh are less alien than *men*. But can't you just stick it out with the arrogant fucker for a few more days? What about my bloody ratings?"

"I'm sorry about your show, Gaby. But I'm sick of being humiliated. This is not me—chasing a man. I am just not like this. Besides, it's pointless. Kit's too busy getting in touch with his 'feminine' side."

"Yeah. On another female."

"What do you mean?"

"Coco just got a job crewing for the afternoon on the dive boat."

Now while Shelly had been reconciled to the fact that she could only feel her oats but not sow them, she was damned if any other woman would reap the horny harvest while *she* went to seed.

Which is why, one two-hour lesson at the bottom of the swimming pool later, Shelly was producing three forms of ID to get a beach towel. She stared out with trepidation at the Indian Ocean, which was still occasionally visible between oil slicks of suntan lotion, lilos, speed boats, parasails, glass-bottom boats and squadrons of jet skis, buzzing like aquatic mosquitoes back and forth across the bay as they touted for trade.

A swarm of locals, balancing a basket of conch shells on each hip, with the odd sari-clad granny disporting a fruity turban of ripe pineapples, immediately descended on her, squawking, "You buy?" Which is why she didn't spot Kit until some ten minutes later, lying there on his belly on a swathe of black volcanic sand alongside the pellucid sea. A baseball hat covered half his face, leaving only his luscious lips which had fastened themselves wetly onto a mango. Oh, lucky fruit. When he paused in his devouring to extract a mango fiber, caught pube-like between his teeth, it was positively pornographic.

Shelly swallowed hard. "So, where do I get my wet suit then?"

Kit cocked his head sideways to squint up at her. "You're comin' on the wreck dive?"

What she wanted to say was: It's number one on my Things I'd Least Like to Do Before I Die list. What she said instead was, "You betcha!"

"Are you certified?"

Certifiable, yes, after the big fat lie which was about to squeeze out of her mouth. "Uh-huh," she improvised.

Shelly had determined to win back the affections of her Love God, even if she had to break every bone in her body to do so . . . which would be quite easy, of course, floundering around a hundred feet deep in the sea.

An hour later she was green-gilled with nausea, teeth-chatteringly butt-frozen and clutching the seat of the thumping dive boat for dear life as it slapped through irritable waves way out past the headland of the choppy bay and into the open sea. The 80-horsepower boat seemed far too flimsy for such deep waters. The aerated vessel was called a Lomac and looked as though they'd merely strapped an outboard motor to Coco's lips. When the engines finally cut, Shelly realized with rising panic that there was no land in sight, only the licorice-like bodies of the twenty wet-suited divers, flippered and masked and edgy with excitement.

Just to put the cherry on the angst parfait, Shelly now noticed that not only were Towtruck and Silent Mike on board, but also the police commandant, the man so clearly separated from Napoleon at birth. Napoleon? Who was she kidding? *Napoleon* would have had a *Commandant* Complex.

"What's his name, the police chief?" Shelly asked the irrepressible entertainment officer. Dominic was busily (and oh so enthusiastically!!!!!!) organizing his aquaerobics ladies, all trying to look younger than they were in leopardskin thong bikinis and fake tans, into their snorkeling gear.

Mwah! Mwah! Shelly's cheeks had to go through the usual

saliva Jacuzzi before Dominic would finally answer. "Simeon Gaspard."

Simeon? It sounded to Shelly like a bad wine.

"Zere are people who 'ate him for his Impunité Zéro—Zero Tolerance policing. Since 'e arrived from Paris, 'e has been so tough. Cops—so many cops on ze streets, 'ard sentencing, routine rounding up of *putains* and anarchistes and undesirables. In France 'e is a big deal. They call him Super Flic. But zere was scandal, *ma belle*. He is 'ere, 'ow you say, on loan, until events, zey calm down."

"On loan? I'd be more inclined to guess that what he's *on* is the run from the International War Crimes Tribunal." But what was he doing *here*, she wondered, on the hotel dive boat?

"Where is your cameraman, *ma belle*?" Dominic asked hopefully, pulling one foot up behind him like an exotic flamingo in a thigh stretch that sent all his aquaerobics ladies into an overheated swoon. They demanded he return to zip them into their wet suits, proffering up thighs that looked like clotted cream raked with forks.

Shelly noticed Gaspard shoot a venomous look at Coco. With her languid, sensuous grace she was effortlessly upstaging every other female on board, an advantage exquisitely enhanced by a silver lamé bikini so weeny it was more like a molecule than a piece of swimwear. Shelly knew instinctively that this was not the type of woman to wear "period pants." No, it would be nothing but the best lace lingerie day in, night out; not a woman to trust, in other words—a woman who has tattoos in painful places. Even her tootsies were perfect, Shelly noted, with their pink nail polish and gold ankle chain and turquoise toe rings. She looked down at her own unpedicured feet—the chapped, unmoisturized heels resembling slabs of the parmigiano reggiano she'd had yesterday for lunch—and stuffed them quickly into her flippers. Although, sadly, who would notice?

"Feel free to leave your valuables on ze boat," Gaspard announced to the other divers once the captain had dropped anchor. "Ze Creole crew?" He chuckled. "Zey will be going through your wallets, directly." He glared pugnaciously in Coco's direction. The police chief's cronies laughed dutifully. If Coco heard his comment, the great Revolutionary didn't even flicker one mascaraed lash. Not exactly a Garibaldian response. Wasn't she supposed to be in Mao Mode? Oh, move over Ulrike Meinhof!

Shelly hauled on her wet suit, which seemed to have been created from a fabric made from recycled breast implants. The trainee Dutch diving instructor whom she'd last seen on the safe cement bottom of the hotel swimming pool hooked on her buoyancy jacket, pulling the straps claustrophobically tight. "You okay?"

"Sure," Shelly replied. "Loss of feeling in the legs doesn't always indicate a brain tumor."

"Just remember your international underwater signs, okay?" He made an O with his thumb and index finger.

Shelly tried to return an "Okay" sign but as she attempted to move, the bulky air tank banged painfully against her coccyx. She lost her balance, keeling backwards and flailed about uselessly on the boat deck like a stranded beetle. By the time she'd been maneuvered upright again by her instructor, divers were plopping backwards over the edge of the boat into the choppy gray sea like wet-suited lemmings. All too soon the instructor propelled her towards the back of the skiff and it was her turn to go over the side. This was a prospect Shelly approached with such reluctance that her flippers left skid marks down the deck visible from the Mir Two space shuttle.

"Nervous?" Kit asked, amused, as Shelly overbalanced once more and crashed into his side. He gave her a sleepy, sun-drenched smile, a smile that made her shiver with desire, despite how angry she was with him.

"Nervous? Who—me? About jumping overboard into that shark-infested watery grave? Gee, I dunno . . ." Shelly said, her voice pitched an octave or two higher than a coloratura's top C.

Kit gave her a quizzical stare.

"It's just I'm not used to open-water dives," she ad-libbed. "I'm more your coral-reef kind of a diver, you know?"

"Towtruck's the only friggin' predator we have to worry about around here." Kit hooked a thumb in the direction of the cameraman. Two crewmembers were attempting to stuff his flesh into a wet suit. It was like watching a Great Dane trying to get through a cat flap. "And what about that sound man? Does he ever talk? Or *wash* even?"

"He has a few problems, yes, but the medicated shampoo should take care of it," Shelly said, in an attempt to appear more sanguine than she felt.

"Oh good." Kit laughed. "Anyway, the way to make sure you don't end up in the jaws of a three-thousand-pound killin' machine, is not to act like bait, okay?"

That should be easy enough, Shelly thought despondently. Kit hadn't exactly taken her hook, had he?

"Sharks are dumber than pit bulls; meaner too. Don't panic or splash. You'll look like a wounded seal. Go deep. I usually move to the bottom and make like I'm a rock. If the shark does attack, punch it in the gills. That'll make you too much trouble to be lunch. Who Dares Lives." Kit winked, before lowering his mask over his sun-kissed face. "Oh, and don't pee in the water. Sharks love piss. I'll be right nearby if you need me."

"Need you? Don't flatter yourself, Kinkade!" Shelly said, trying to sound both casual and courageous. It was reassuring however to know that she was diving with a qualified doctor. Oh, how Shelly yearned to experience his bedside manner, preferably *in her bed*.

Kit smiled knowingly, placed his regulator in his mouth, held his mask in place, then slid, soundlessly, into the sea.

Shelly's entrance into the briny was a tad less elegant. It was more reminiscent of a walrus giving birth. After she'd spluttered and flayed on the surface and drunk a gallon or two of sea water, the instructor gripped the top of her tank and dragged her backwards through some weed towards the anchor rope.

Descending notch by notch, counting to ten at each knot while holding her nose to pressurize her ears the way she'd practiced in the hotel pool—Shelly reminded herself that in all her favorite poetry, gods swim with naiads and nymphs. Pan, the wildest of the gods, who does he dance with? The sprites of the pools, that's who. Water, she reassured herself, was good, natural, beautiful. She hummed Handel's *Water Music*. Yes. She was confident, she was safe, she was fine—besides which, Kit was a trained medical expert. She was in the best possible hands, or at least she soon would be, once she had faked a diving accident requiring mouth-to-mouth resuscitation from the Good Doctor.

The instructor signaled for Shelly to let go of the rope, an invitation she treated with the same amount of warmth she'd give to a suggestion of unanesthetized surgical removal of both breasts. The currents tugged at her from all sides. This wasn't so much a sea as a giant blender. The Dutchman motioned once more for her to follow. Why was it, she wondered, that the more potentially fatal a pastime, the more it is deemed pleasurable? A direct trip to the Congo seemed like a better alternative to letting go of this rope in the middle of the open ocean.

The instructor made the international diving signal Shelly had been taught in the pool for: "Are you okay? Is there anything I can do for you?"

Shelly, hyperventilating, wondered what the signal was for: "What about a complimentary souvenir lung transplant?"

The instructor impatiently prised Shelly's fingers free and gestured for her to swim towards the murky shadows. Through the eerie gloom, bursts of bubbles indicated the tanks of the other divers, their dark legs scissoring as they cut effortlessly through the water below. The weight of the tank was making her roll drunkenly from one side to the other, but somehow she floundered closer to the dive group. To her alarm she saw that they were about to enter a sunken vessel, some kind of cargo boat by the look of it, encrusted to the sandy seabed. One by one, the divers disappeared through a barnacled porthole. Shelly made the international signal for "no fucking way" to her instructor, who shrugged, then finned off with the others into the mucky interior.

Shelly tried not to panic at being left alone in the depths of the Indian Ocean. All was silent, except for the sound of her own rapid breathing.

It was a lunar landscape down here—empty, but for a school of Mick Jagger impersonators technically known as cleaner wrasse and the odd stingray with its theatrical cape and stage-villain grin.

Tentatively, she finned to the back of the sunken boat and, emboldened by her success at swimming with an overgrown milk bottle strapped to her back, kicked towards the starboard side of the stricken vessel in the hope that her companions would soon emerge through a corresponding porthole.

Rounding the corroding rump of the cargo ship, her heart lurched up into her throat. Instead of a familiar face, she found

Kathy Lette

herself staring into the glazed eye of a large dead dog. The bloated carcass bobbed there, suspended in the current by the rope around its neck, weighted to the ocean floor by a stone. The creature seemed to be surveying Shelly with mild curiosity.

Raw panic gripped hold of her now. Okay, a dead dog was better than a live shark, but wasn't a dead dog exactly what a live shark would be looking for?

Splashing out for the port side of the wreck, she tried not to see sharks in every shadow—until she did see a shark, that is. It was a mistake of nature to camouflage sharks—I mean, who are *they* hiding from, hmmm? Shelly had a split second to wonder, before the prehistoric predator, as gray as the sea surrounding it, sliced through the water towards her with such speed that she didn't have time to pretend to be a rock. No. Shelly immediately acted like bait. She thrashed, she splashed, she peed her short wet suit pants. She attempted to hit her flotation button to get to the surface but deflated instead, plummeting to the ocean floor, losing her mask, scraping all the skin off her shins and getting a periwinkle up her bum in the process. The rapid, ramshackle descent also knocked her regulator out of her mouth. Holding her breath, she blindly flailed around for it, felt the rubber in her hand and snatched it towards her face. She thrust the regulator into her mouth and inhaled frantically, forgetting to hit the button that would clear the salt water from the hose. As the sea water ejaculated down her throat, she spluttered and choked, feeling terror seize her chest. She found herself wondering if the captain kept the number of the Intensive Care Airlift Rescue Service on speed dial? A dangerous lightness seeped into her. Her mind was floating in a way in which her body was definitely not. What was the French for blood transfusion? she wondered. But no! Dear God. Don't let them take me to a French hospital! I don't speak French! I could come out with a sex change! she thought erratically.

Her brain detonated and all was suddenly black. She could feel someone's arms around her. She was obviously hallucinating from lack of oxygen, because it seemed that a blurry version of Kit was placing his regulator in her mouth. She felt the rush of cool, clear oxygen surge through her bloodstream and realized that it *was* Kit. Gently, so as not to startle her, he removed the regulator and drew deeply on it, before squeezing it back between her blue and trembling lips. Now he replaced her mask, miming a demonstration of how to clear out the sea water, the way she'd been drilled in the pool. Shelly hadn't realized that sharks hunt in packs until she saw Towtruck, in an absolute feeding frenzy, capturing her humiliating ordeal on scuba-cam. He filmed her with Kit, buddy-breathing all the way to the surface, wrapped, finally, in each other's arms.

The fizzling dazzle of sunlight was the loveliest thing Shelly had ever seen. Her lungs scrambled for fresh air. For the first twenty minutes she lay on the deck, her body all torqued, arms flung wide, busily converting to religion.

"Has anyone ever told you how beautiful you look coughin' sea water up outta your lungs?" Kit's voice was like a quenching cool drink in the heat.

"*Mon dieu!* Your life. It flashed? Before your eyes?" Coco asked, squatting beside her wearing a bright, hostess look. "Ohhh. Maybe you have some bad karma, no?"

Shelly blinked up at her, salt water streaming from her nose. "I used to believe in karma, but that was in a past life," she spluttered.

She could see her remark parting Coco's lovely black hair as it went right over her head. Kit showed his appreciation for

Shelly's wit with a loud chuckle—but Coco's racy inner-thigh tattoo was not lost on him either, Shelly noticed with dismay.

"I just knew somesing bad would 'appen today! I feel it in my bones. You know I'm psychopathic?"

The hubbub of conversation ebbed a little. Shelly looked at Coco, sharply. Could this be the disgruntled owner of one dead dog?

"I know what will 'appen to people," Coco elaborated, "you know, before . . ."

"You mean *tele*pathic, not *psycho*pathic," Shelly corrected, snatching the towel Coco had just given Kit and tousling her own seaweed-braided hair. "Then I don't need to tell you to get the hell away from my husband," she muttered, under her breath.

Gaspard stopped toweling off and looked mistrustfully at Coco, his stocky legs astride, hands on flabby hips, his manhood leaving nothing to the imagination in a skimpy French G-string. Coco pursed her lovely lilo lips and hurried towards the front of the boat to fetch beers and sandwiches from the coolbox. Gaspard coughed flatulently, then followed her.

"That woman is living proof that to become a Love Goddess you don't just need pneumatic breasts and silken thighs, you need stupidity too," Shelly whispered, spitefully, salt water still riveting attractively from her snoz.

"Dumb? Coco? Actually, it's kinda dumb of you to think so."

"Come on, Kit. You're not still deluding yourself that she's a political activist, are you? The woman flunked out of the University of Life. Although she could have got an A-level in flirtation and applied bikini waxing." Kit's eyes strayed in Coco's near-naked direction. "Here." She shoved a towel into his hands. "You're supposed to wipe my fevered brow. It's in the *Husband Handbook*, you know."

"Hey, you seem to forget that I did save your ass down there. Speakin' of which," Kit raised his voice, "why was there no dive master and only one trainee instructor? That was so goddamn dangerous. Actually, all the sports activities are kinda understaffed. Where are all the staff?" Kit directed this question to Gaspard, who'd reappeared at their end of the boat, beer in hand.

The police commandant shrugged, then fired up a cigar. "You know what zese Third Worlders are like." He spoke with an air of amused *ennui*. "They've probably found ze face of ze Virgin Mary on a *coco de mer* and decamped *en masse*." His hateful, peevish eyes looked at Coco, who was helping a black crewmember maneuver another coolbox out of storage. Gaspard's sullen, abrasive tone made Shelly's skin crawl. Along with Milosevic and Attila the Hun, Gaspard would be eliminated early in the heats for Mr. Caring and Sharing. "I imagine zat zey are all at an animal sacrifice." The police chief dragged on his cigar. "At our local zoo zey 'ave a description of ze animals on ze front of ze cage, and underneath? The recipe."

"Hey, what's Creole for 'eat shit and die, asshole'?" Kit loudly enquired of the black crewmember.

Gaspard swung around in Kit's direction as if to punch him, but Coco clasped Kit's hand. "*Mon dieu!* You 'ave a coral cut!" she gushed, before rummaging through her first aid kit for aloe vera and echinacea. Coco was obviously the sort of gal who has raspberry enemas and befriends tumors. Her approach was nothing short of Nouveau Voodoo. She obviously *had* gone native with all that homeopathic gobbledygook.

"Hello? Drowning victim here? In need of medical attention . . ." Shelly sulked.

Towtruck finally shook his gigantic body out of his wet suit, his doughy gut wobbling. Droplets of water flew, as if from a

Labrador, in all directions. "Hey, Jacqueline Cousteau." He hoisted the camera onto his shoulder and approached, umbilically attached to the sound recordist. "At least you can say you finally went down on your honeymoon! And it's all captured on celluloid for the audience back home."

"Don't film me now! I look terrible," Shelly pleaded.

"Ah, but ze poetry of your soul, eet eez in your eyes!!!!"

Even if Shelly hadn't recognized the chirpy, acrylic tones of the entertainment officer, the wet lip lock fastened onto her cheek told her it was Dominic. He wrapped himself around her, then beamed into the camera. The man seemed to be able to spot a lens at fifty paces. He also seemed to enjoy wandering around shirtless for far longer than strictly necessary. While Kit wore his masculinity effortlessly, Dominic's looked store-bought. His biceps (the size of research submarines) and bulging lats (strapped to his flesh like shoulderpads) suggested hours of gym-junkying.

"The poetry of your soul is in your eyes? . . . Isn't that just French for you're ugly—but I'll shag you anyway?" Shelly shrugged his arm off her shoulders and swaddled herself in her towel. Her humiliation had left her vivisectioned, exposed, sliced open for the world to see. "I just had an off-day, that's all," she soliloquized for the camera. "Tomorrow I'll show you all what a waterbaby I really am!" A plume of sea drool slapped her full in the face as the boat lurched to life, drowning her dishonest remark.

Now it was Kit's turn, contractually, to comment to camera. What did he think about Shelly's diving accident, Towtruck wanted to know. "I think if at first you don't succeed, then scuba divin' ain't for you, hon." There was laughter in his voice as Kit peeled a strand of seaweed from her hair.

Shelly craved a stiff drink, but all that was being poured was scorn. Oh, and beer at the boat's prow. "Towtruck, Mike, look, mother's milk!" With the crew successfully distracted, Shelly hissed at Kit: "Are you laughing? Is that laughter I hear? I should have known that you'd use this dive to humiliate me."

Kit snorted. "Hey, Shell, it wasn't much of a challenge! You said on the questionnaire that you liked outdoor activities, 'specially water sports," he chastised. "So, what else have you lied about?"

She hadn't lied, her *pupils* had. Still, she admitted dismally, Another Bloody Point to Kit Bloody Kinkade.

Speckles of warm light broke through the low clouds and her spirits lifted as Dr. Kinkade gently raised her wrist to check his patient's pulse. The sun on her upturned face was warm as a kiss. She felt lulled by the soporific drone of the boat's motor.

"Look," he added, kindly, "if you do wanna dive again, you gotta go back to basics."

But Shelly didn't want to go back to basics, she wanted to go back to his hotel room and get naked.

"I wanna keep you under observation, girl," he said, huskily. "You could go into shock later. You gotta keep warm and quiet and drink plenty of fluids."

"Yes, sir. At least I've finally discovered something we have in common—an allergy to karma and all that hippy shit Coco goes on about. I mean, you don't believe in any of that rubbish, do you? For a doctor, belief in reincarnation is not a reassuring sign, right?" she winked.

"Dunno. I ain't no doctor."

"What?" Shelly felt a hot prickling sensation all over her body. "But on your form you said you were a doctor."

"Did I?" Muscles twitched beneath his chiseled cheekbones. "Oh, well, I did play a male nurse once in a TV soap, stateside."

"A TV soap?"

"Not very glamorous, I know. Still, it was better than playin' the guy who slaughtered the giant squid alien in *Beyond the Universe, the Final Frontier,* which is my only other dismal claim to TV fame. Didja ever see me?"

She was sure she hadn't—hell, her tongue would still be attached to the TV screen. "I thought I was diving with a doctor. That's the only reason I went into the water. I thought I'd be safe. I nearly got killed out there!" Shelly's stomach contents roiled, and not from seasickness. "Honesty seems to have the same effect on you as sunshine on a vampire!"

Kit began to reply, then bit his lip and turned his face away with a look of wistful resignation. Despite his outdoorsman bonhomie, Shelly detected a subtle complexity in her husband. He was all major/minor chords, unsettled and haunted. His sudden black mood clashed with the azure sky and sapphire sea.

Shelly now felt persecuted by the pitiless sun, persecuted for her gullibility. "I'll expose you," she threatened, "as a fraud!"

"I think you're exposin' enough already, don't you, love?" Towtruck scoffed, beer in one hand, pointing to her thighs with the other. Shelly glanced down to discover that she was indeed having a bad hair day. A small pubic kiss curl had escaped from the leg of her swimming costume. "You could stalk stags in that bikini line, darl."

Shelly nearly blurted out that Kit liked it but then realized that, actually, she wasn't sure what Kit liked anymore. Or who, she thought, watching Coco hand him a beer after pressing it refreshingly into the small of his back.

Towtruck swung the camera into action to complete Shelly's soliloquy. Shelly tried her best to look poised but just at that moment the boat listed in the big seas, as did Shelly, who nearly tumbled overboard again. Groping for purchase, she placed her hand in the bait bucket and recoiled, shrieking.

"I can thoroughly recommend a holiday here." She played up to the lens. "Yes, do come! Enjoy the superb emergency medical services on offer! Highly recommended! You too can be shark bait!"

The shark, everyone tried to reassure her simultaneously, was only a gray nurse, not a man-eater—the magnificent creature was just curious about the dead dog. Shelly was curious too—about how that dead dog got there in the first bloody place—but nobody seemed to know or care.

"Sharks. Zey are more scared of you zan you are of zem," Coco homilied.

But it seemed to Shelly that sharks were notoriously unbashful. That cliché was just another one of life's Big Fat Lies. Along with, "Hi, marry me . . . *I'm a doctor*!!"

Kit suddenly grinned. "It was all that splashin' and thrashin' that was irritatin' him." He laughed along with the others as Coco toweled off his beautiful body.

But Shelly knew the real reason the shark was so irritable—because they mate for life.

The Difference Between the Sexes: Housework

"Home cooking" is just that place where a husband thinks his wife is . . .

8 War Footing

Matrimony would be easier if you could be strapped into a marriage simulator to experience the terrors and exhilaration, and see if you have what it takes. Shelly *definitely* didn't have what it took.

Day three of her honeymoon and with still no prospect of consummation, her blood pressure was reaching thermonuclear levels. She would never, ever confess it to a living soul because Good Girls Don't, but she was masturbating so much she needed terry toweling sweatbands on her wrists. She had the most exercised right hand in human history. There hadn't been digital action like it since Proust wrote all seven volumes, longhand.

There was a pounding at her hotel door. It wasn't opportunity knocking, but Gaby, Silent Mike and Towtruck.

"Oh, it's *you*," Shelly said despondently. "So what sporting horrors have you got in store for me today?" She groggily shielded her eyes from the glare of the fluorescent sun. "Rhino slaying? Volcano abseiling? Castrating the odd elk, perhaps?" A sneeze rattled through her. She had a cold from the previous day's oceanic ordeal and a severe if odd case of sunburn from thigh to toe and bicep to fingertip; a painful, melanomic outline of her tropical wet suit.

"Mrs. K., it's time you put your vagina where your mouth is, so to speak." Gaby pushed her specs up the bridge of her nose, then waved Shelly's contract in her face. "I need some footage!"

"Forget about shooting footage and just shoot me. This whole TV marriage has to be the most stupid bloody thing I've ever done. Including that perm in the late eighties."

Shelly shook her head with bewilderment, remembering the sudden, reckless moment in the back of the limousine where the sensation of a man's lips had altered her whole life. "I'm a miserable, pathetic failure and I'm off to join a monastic order immediately where I can dedicate myself, mind, body and soul, to my whittling." She crawled back inside and into her bed, and shoved her head under the pillow.

"Well, as your hubby doesn't seem remotely interested in ya, if ya do crave a bit of luncheon-truncheon"—Towtruck patted her posterior beneath the sheet—"I'd be only too happy to slip you the sausage. I mean, ya don't want it to seal up, now do ya? What do you say to that, Shelly-kins?"

Shelly looked up at the heffalump in floral board shorts. The man could be suspended from a rope and used as some sort of wrecking ball. "What on earth can I say to him?" she beseeched Gaby.

"I dunno. 'Eat my panty-liner, dick-breath' kinda hits the spot really. How can you possibly think any woman you haven't inflated could be attracted to you, Towtruck? If *you* went to a computer dating service you'd get matchmade with Belgium. Now piss off."

"Thank you, Gaby," Shelly sighed once Towtruck had stomped from the room.

"That's okay. Men are like high heels—so easy to walk on once you get the hang of it. So come on, let's think. You're crap at outdoor stuff. We know that now. But what about *indoor*? You're cultured, right? So that's what you'll do. Wow the prick with sophistication! There's a twenty-five-thousand-pound incentive. Now get up off that bed, you slut, and into some hair gel!"

Shelly looked at her director. It was useless. It was insane. To put any more energy into this marriage would be to prove that she was the only living brain donor in Britain.

But there was that second installment of prize money at the end of the week . . . And she did owe Gaby a favor. Plus there was the added bonus of seeing Kit in his swimming trunks once more.

No! She reprimanded herself. Where was her self-respect? But self-respect didn't kiss a girl's eyelids. Self-respect didn't get your earlobes nibbled. Self-respect didn't make you come like a frigging freight train.

In the sex war a woman's uniform is not jungle fatigues with a belt of bullets slung across the chest, but an LBD (Little Black Dress). Her face is not smeared in camouflage paints but in Clinique and Clarins and thus attired, some hours later, Shelly stalked in high heels into Rendezvous, the most exclusive restaurant in the resort. Kit's response of "Yowzah!" didn't exactly put him at risk of breaking the savoir-faire barrier. But it did give her hope that this time she might finally make it on to the man's menu . . .

Dinner began with a little French cheese, which Shelly had graded in order of smell. Performing as a student at Hampstead soirées had taught her to appreciate milk's leap towards immortality, especially with a hearty Merlot.

Kit looked dubiously at the incontinent cheeses dribbling down the sides of the porcelain platter. "Pong gradation?" Kit raised one sculpted brow before seizing the elbow of a passing Indian waiter. "Could I please move to another table?"

"Yes, of course, sir. Where exactly?"

"Um . . . on another island?"

It was now Shelly's turn to accost the waiter. "Would you mind bringing my companion a packet of crayons so he can color in his place mat? Thank you so much!"

"Hey, *I'm* not the one being childish," Kit said. "*You're* the one who doesn't realize that cheese is nothin' more than butter gone bad."

Remembering Gaby's instructions, Shelly bit her tongue and tortured her mouth into a smile. "May I titillate your palate with anything else then?" she pushed on bravely, trying to sound as posh as possible. "Châteaubriand, steak tartare, cassoulet, foie gras en croute?"

"Ah, I kinda thought I'd just have a fish burger and fries."

"Kit. What's the point of being on a French island, if you don't try the cordon-bleu cooking?" she said, exasperated.

"French cuisine? Oh yeah. That's where they serve everythin' in pools of congealed phlegm, ain't it? French food exists chiefly to be criticized by refined palates. And I definitely do *not* want to gnaw ecstatically on radicchio and gush arrogantly about Normandy endive. Okay?"

"It's not that the French are arrogant, Kit. They just happen to feel superior to *you*. And who could blame them? Americans. God, your culinary highlight is a dip-enhancer."

"Oh, you're soooo right. Our food's not nearly as tasty as your traditional English dishes of cock-a-leekie-dick-in-the-spotted-hole, or whatever the hell it is you people eat. Cats have formed the bases of every English curry I've ever eaten."

"At least we don't have themed restaurants where the toilets are marked Hooters and Hangers, or Flip Dry and Drip Dry. At least our palates can fully appreciate haute cuisine."

"Hey, just 'cause the French give snails a fancy name like *escargots*, you really and truly think we should eat pondlife? Hey, garçon!" Kit snapped his fingers and fog-horned. "Could I please have a snail and a frog in a mosquito marinade?"

The waiter approached and flicked open his notepad. Shelly placed her order, ostentatiously rolling the French syllables around her mouth as though they were wine.

"And for you, sir?"

"My friend here will just have some mastodon," Shelly answered for him. "With some pterodactyl on the side, because his tastes are so prehistoric."

"Fish 'n' chips. And gimme a drink, will ya?" Kit demanded, lunging for one of the two wine bottles open on the table.

Shelly stayed his hand. "They're vintage. I'm still letting them breathe."

"Breathe? What are they? Asthmatic?"

Kit slopped vintage vino into his glass and skolled it in one long gulp.

"Dr. Kincade's meal opened with a 1992 Diet Pepsi"—Shelly commentated in the hushed tones of a TV lifestyle announcer—"which was allowed to stand and breathe first, of course. To blend with its heady bouquet, cherished by the epicurean palate, this seasoned gourmandizer recommended the batter cunningly fused with marginally aquatic foodstuffs configured into a geometric design called *le fish burger et les frites*."

"Tell me, have you always been such a pain in the ass, Green, or do you take lessons?"

They were sitting there, silently fuming at each other, when Gaby appeared, striding purposefully towards them in her uniform of khaki pants, espadrilles, baseball cap on backwards and tank top featuring various slogans for assorted esoteric movies usually never seen outside film festivals. It was Gaby who should have been nicknamed Towtruck, Shelly thought, as she was always dragging along that wreck of a cameraman.

She gave them the thumbs-up. "Fucking romance at fucking last! I don't believe it! This is the kind of stuff that rates! And advertisers love it too—tapping into the Pouilly Fumé pound. So how's the date going, kids?"

"We've momentarily stopped attacking each other with our entrée forks," Shelly reported, grimly. "So that's something."

Gaby's face fell. "Well, what about a little less talking and more dancing?" The producer directed their gaze to the dance floor where Coco's Sega band was busy demonstrating that knowing only three chords need not be a bar to a career in music.

"No way." Shelly rubbed her glitterball graze. "The music is so loud on the dance floor that I wouldn't even be able to hear myself say that I can't hear myself think," she said as the band lurched from "You're The One That I Want" to "Sexual Healing."

"Come on!" teased Kit. "Doesn't the music get to you? This is my all-time favorite Top of the Pops." He tapped his foot and broke into a lazy, broad grin. "Marvin Gaye's so damn catchy."

"Yeah, well, so is gonorrhea," sulked Shelly, gnawing her way through the basket of sliced baguettes.

"Hey," Kit said, "if God hadn't meant us to have rock 'n' roll He wouldn't have given us padded jockstraps." He indicated the Fading Rock Star Here to Get Together Material for His Acoustic

Album, who had just risen from an adjoining table and was now strutting towards the stage.

"Believe me, a rock band is nothing more than five people who think the other four can't sing. What about Bach? Rachmaninoff? Mozart? Why can't people get interested in real music?"

But Kit was more interested in Coco singing his favorite song with a slow, seductive African rhythm—similar, Shelly reflected, to New Orleans blues. She was also singing it directly at him, gyrating with the sensuous movements of the traditional slaves' dance. "It's called the Maloya," Kit told Shelly, entranced. "The slaves adapted the dances of the white settlers, like the quadrille, to their own African rhythms, Coco reckons."

"Do the band take requests?" Shelly asked, sweetly.

"Yeah. Why? Whatya want 'em to play?"

"Monopoly."

"Dance with him, for God's sake," Gaby hissed in Shelly's ear. "Take his mind off Coco. My God, that woman has a trick pelvis. It could pull a rabbit out of a hat!" She scurried off to set up her romantic shots.

The wine was kicking in and the music was thumping entreatingly. Perhaps just a little tentative hip-jiggling then. Leading him onto the dance floor, Shelly had just started to muse on the fact that pumping your hips into the buttocks of a complete stranger wasn't all bad—being the closest you can get to extra-marital sex without the syphilitic sores—when the band segued into "La Bamba," a song she had been teaching the kids at school. None of her pupils could execute the chords. "CFG, CFG," she'd encourage, hour after excruciating hour. "Da da da da da da—oh shit! Da da da da da da—oh shit!" they'd reply, hour after excruciating hour.

Shelly felt her intestines tighten. "No, no, sorry. Not this song. I just can't." She tugged Kit back to their table. "I teach this kind of trash."

"Like I said, you Brits are so lackin' in spontaneity. What do the French call it when they put name places around the table?"

"A *placement*."

"Well, you Brits would have a *placement* at an orgy!" Kit laughed, sliding back into his chair. "And write thank-you letters later. 'So glad you came!'"

"Well, it would be nice if you Yanks showed a little restraint and forethought now and then—especially when it comes to spontaneously dropping bombs on urban areas. What a society! The constitutionally guaranteed freedom to have stupid T-shirt slogans and sexist bumper stickers and moronic presidents. Whoopee," she said, winning her man's affections in her usual subtle and charming way. "The three most important men in America at the moment are called Bush, Dick and Colon! What does that tell you about a country?"

"Hey, at least we have a constitution. What's your constitution? The right to be miserable. The cold baths, the warm beer, the worst ocean—just a giant toilet—the worst Olympic record, the worst weather, the worst male pick-up lines. For Chrissakes, an Englishman just points at his dick and cries." Kit picked up some utensils and used them as drumsticks to play on the crockery.

"Do you know why America even exists?" Shelly said above his rhythmical racket. "It just gave us British a handy place to dump all our god-bothering religious maniacs."

His cutlery drum solo got louder, leading Shelly to conclude that the computer must have been severely malfunctioning the day it predicted that she and Kit Kinkade had anything in common. Unable to restrain herself any longer, she leant over to seize and then realign his cutlery in the correct order on the salmon-colored tablecloth. "I know you're probably used to eating with your feet, but in *Europe* we try to eat from the outside in," she condescended.

"God," he moaned. "You English have PhDs in cutlery. You're a utensil-rich environment, j'know that? Why all the old-fashioned rules? For your info, this is the twenty-first century. Husbands and wives no longer separate after dinner."

"No, they separate at the end of the evening to go to their respective lovers," Shelly snapped, nodding in Coco's direction, just in time to see her pushed aside by the Fading Rock Star Here to Get Together Material for His Acoustic Album so that he could vocally assault a Rolling Stones classic while thrusting his groin into the mike stand in a grisly simulation of a carnal encounter. "Are you sure you still need proof that rock stars really are lower on the biological scale? Like animals they have to wear bright colors and display their genitals to attract females. I mean, look at that idiot!"

Gaby was now stomping back towards them. She threw her hands up in despair at her TV subjects' romantic intransigence. In doing so, she collided with a passing waiter who dropped his load of crockery with a shattering clank. The French maitre d' was at his side in seconds, livid about the accident. Even without a fluent understanding of French, Shelly realized that the poor Creole had been sacked on the spot.

Instantly Towtruck and Mike pointed lens and microphone towards the commotion. Within seconds, the omnipresent police chief had barreled to their table, his designer sunglasses (despite the dark) perched on his bulbous nose, cashmere sweater (despite the heat) knotted casually around his neck. He commandeered the camera, ejected both battery and tape, then flung them into the ornamental fishpond.

"Filming ze workers, it is *interdit*—forbidden." He shoved the microphone boom aside and scowled at Mike.

"At least if he arrests the sound recordist he'll have the *right* to remain silent," Shelly whispered to Kit.

"Yeah, and at least in a French jail in addition to your one phone call you get a nice glass of *citron pressé*. And before a strip search, dinner and a show," Kit added.

Shelly started to laugh until Gaspard slammed his hand down onto their table, making the glasses quake.

"Tourism supports zese people. But zey are too stupid to understand zat. For what we have done for zem? Bah! Zey are not grateful. Before we came 'ere, it was just some fungal jungle in ze middle of ze Indian Ocean. Wizout us, it would go back to ze land of savages. I 'ave zis friend from Durban. You know what he calls a black in a tree? A branch manager!" He threw his head back to guffaw.

Kit decided that this was the perfect time to talk to Shelly about why Paris is still so pretty architecturally—something along the lines of how the French rolled over and spread their legs for the Nazis. "What do you call a hundred Frenchmen with their hands up?" he added for good measure. "The army."

The lizardy lids of the French police commandant half-closed, while he smiled warmly the whole time—the same look he'd worn at the airport, Shelly recalled with mounting dread.

"Forgive him," she giggled nervously. "He is, after all, an American. Allowances have to be made. Even their president said that the trouble with the French is that you have no word for entrepreneur! Right?"

Just in time the manager, his hair parted in the one o'clock position, made his entrance into the restaurant. He was wearing the jaded look of all veterans of the public relations industry—an expression that was meant to be geniality but was more reminiscent of a man who'd just heard a big explosion and hadn't got his hearing back.

"We'll see what the manager has to say about this!" Gaby seethed, flouncing off towards him.

Gaspard shrugged then sauntered back to his Gallic guests. Shelly watched him sprawl in a chaise longue in the bar area as if he owned the place. Which perhaps he did, since he was always here. While it was clear the man had a penchant for the five-star lifestyle, Shelly couldn't help but feel there might be a more sinister reason for his permanent presence . . . When a pretty black waitress leaned across him, he gave her posterior a proprietorial pinch. In return she blew him a surreptitious kiss. The Super Flic then turned sideways and kissed the hand of a frumpy, middle-aged woman who, by the way she greeted him with a detached yet dogged acceptance, Shelly deduced to be his wife. So much for suave French sophistication and the primitive Creole. The policeman was swinging from mistress to spouse with all the grace of an orangutan.

Towtruck, complaining bitterly to everyone who would listen how tired he was of taking orders from a "jumped-up Sheila producer who was a few pieces-to-camera short of an autocue," harrumphed back to his bungalow for a new battery and tape, calling for Mike to follow. And so it was for the first time on their honeymoon, the computerized, matchmade couple found themselves utterly alone. Allied against the police commandant, a momentary armistice descended over their own hostilities.

"I can't believe what you said to that cop's face. Standard procedure for the French police is to hit first, ask questions later!

You're so brave!" Shelly said, fondly. "You're so sure of yourself, Kit. I bet you even do your crossword puzzles in *ink*."

"You think I'm confident, huh?" Kit asked absently, concentrating on the metronomic movement of the swizzle stick he was oscillating through his cocktail.

"God, yes. The only reservations *you* have are in posh five-star hotels—thanks to my computer profile selecting you, that is!" She smiled. "A hotel with big, gorgeous fluffy double beds," she emphasized for good measure.

"Well, my hotel bed has reservations for no one at the moment, I'm afraid. Not until I've found my, what's it, emotional libido," he bantered, but only halfheartedly.

Shelly took a gulp of wine. "Look, Kit. I didn't mean it when I accused men of having no feelings. It just doesn't suit you wearing a 'Do Not Disturb' sign on your Y-fronts."

"But I'm still gettin' in touch with my feminine side," he smiled, roguishly. "I've found I'm obsessively anxious about food, weight, complexion, fanciability and cellulite." Despite Kit's surface jocularity, his fingers were now tapping out a fretful rhythm on the tabletop.

"Kit, why are you being so mysterious? If you're not a doctor, then what are you? And why did you lie? You're always scurrying back to your room. You even eat there. Except for yesterday's dive, you won't go farther afield than a two-minute sprint from your bungalow. Why? Are you an android, recharging batteries? Are you transmitting messages to your Mother Ship? Spying for Mossad? What?"

"I have things to wax," he said, playfully, in a high-pitched voice. But his fingers gave him away. He was fretting at them, bending and stretching them as if warming up for a piano concerto.

Shelly placed her hand over his. "What are you really playing at, Kit? Come on, talk to me. If ever you want to scream into a sympathetic ear, I have excellent hearing." They'd ordered escargots for her and fish and chips for him, but what was eating Kit remained a mystery. "What's up, Doc?" she smiled.

Kit looked at Shelly's compassionate face. "Hey, the things I'm worrying about I couldn't even confess to a priest, let alone my poor, bewildered bride," he said gloomily.

But Shelly wasn't buying it. Her husband reminded her of the Rodrigo guitar *Concierto de Aranjuez*. She'd nearly given up on that too, but in the end she'd bloody well cracked it. She tried another tack. "All right, let's change the subject. How about we get to know each other's philosophy of life?"

Kit turned his head away from her, put on his sunglasses and gazed out of the restaurant window on the pretext of watching the last of the sun bleed into the sea. There seemed to be a place in him he kept secret. He retreated there in solitude, unaware that Shelly was even watching him.

"Kit?"

"My advice for life? Um . . . if you've got foreskin rings, don't wear nylon undies—you'll electrocute yourself. Oh, and never eat hotdogs from a roadside stand. 'Specially if it's owned by your folks."

Shelly reared her head suspiciously. "*Folks*? I thought you said your parents were dead?"

"Did I?"

"Yes, you bloody well did." She drilled him with a stare.

"Well, they're living in a trailer park in a town called Purgatory sellin' junk food—so they are dead, all but legally," he ad-libbed.

Shelly's face burned with indignation. "Would you just stop lying to me? Enough with the International Man of Mystery Routine. Who the hell are you exactly?"

The turned-up collar of his black shirt and his dark shades made him look more than ever like a spy.

"Shelly." He said her name in a low, resonant tone. Some sadness strained his face. "You're a good kid. And I'm sorry I've been such a prick. Thing is, I ain't been entirely straight with you."

"Oh, no kidding."

He touched her cheek tenderly, removed his sunglasses and gazed into her eyes. "There's somethin' I need to tell ya," he said, intriguingly.

Shelly braced herself for the truth. "I'm listening."

"Ooohhh! I am so 'ungry!"

Coco and her shimmering Lycra mini shimmied into the empty seat at their table, where she proceeded to pick at the cheeses.

Shelly regarded the lead singer with resentful amazement. "You're *eating*? If you swallowed a bread crumb you'd look pregnant. You French women usually just order one crouton for lunch. Then share it."

Kit laughed and tweaked Shelly's cheek. "Who's bein' a bigot now? You're bein' as racist about French women as Gaspard is about the Creoles, you Frog-basher, you!"

Shelly felt her face break out. "I realize that I'm generalizing here, but as is often the case when I generalize, I don't give a damn," she blurted. As she was already splotched floridly with sunburn, she hoped they couldn't see the fierce blush burning her cheeks.

"I lurve *all* ze pleasures of ze flesh," Coco purred, with an innocent blink of her iridescent eyelids. "Unlike *some* women"—Coco glanced meaningfully at Shelly—"I *am* very careful about what I eat." She patted her bare, taut midriff, which made her breasts, nestling in their bra cups, jiggle invitingly. "Your body, eet eez a temple."

"Yeah, well, there's no services today," Shelly muttered under her breath, in an effort to avert her husband's eyes as they slid into Coco's creamy cleavage.

"Zere is a shiatsu point to lessen appetite. I show you, Kelly?"

"It's *Shelly*. And no, thank you," Shelly fumed.

Coco turned to Kit. "And zere are erotic shiatsu points too. I find zem for you?" she simpered, pouting her magenta lips.

"What we'd like you to *find* is your way back on stage," Shelly suggested.

This wish was fulfilled by the arrival of the first course. Coco, a vegetarian, grimaced at Shelly's plate of *escargots*, then ran gagging back to the stage where she launched immediately into an unusual set of African rhythms, reggae, sega and maloya, all sung in Creole.

This bowl of *escargots* doesn't look anything like congealed phlegm, Shelly told herself queasily. Put that thought right out of your mind immediately. With Kit's amused eyes upon her, she plunged into her meal, spooning up the juice with gusto. She impaled what looked like slug pupa on her fork prong then swallowed, proving her superior sophistication, urbanity and general worldliness over the anorexic, tofu-eating band singer, whose culinary highlight probably involved massaging her bowel with bran flakes.

Finally! A point to Shelly Green, she congratulated herself.

But her triumph was short-lived. Shelly felt the chili burn in the back of her eyeballs before she became aware that her throat was on fire. She grabbed at her larynx, going cross-eyed in her agony and mimed for bread, trying to semaphore to Kit that her gastric enzymes were no longer on speaking terms with her tonsils. Chili in *escargots*? The menu had said nothing about chili. She was producing a coughing attack worthy of a pleurisy unit. Guests swiveled to watch her contort and clutch at the tablecloth during her digestive discotheque. As usual, Towtruck and Silent Mike had arrived just in time to catch her degradation for posterity.

"*Ma pauvre chérie!!!!!!!*" It was Dominic, his voice a car alarm whine, wrapping his arms around her. Being hugged by Dominic was a bit like being mugged by a golden retriever. He immediately set about administering spoonfuls of soothing yogurt. "Oh! You ate piments? Chilis? Of course, you know, in Réunion, ze very best method for"—he stroked his neck— "calming ze throat is ze sperm gargle," he purred, winking at the camera.

But Shelly's agonized cries were drowned out by an even louder noise. At first she presumed it was the bartender's cocktail blender on overdrive. But then she realized that the emotive twang of the electric guitar had turned into a shrill, discordant screech. The whole audience gasped in the direction of the stage where Gaspard had Coco manacled by the wrists. Gun-waving gendarmes leapt upon the other band members, knocking over mike stands and snare drums, then strong-armed them all out of the restaurant. A substitute singer scrambled on stage and began an adenoidal rendition of "*La vie en Rose.*"

"What the hell's goin' on?" Kit demanded of Dominic.

"The band, eet eez under arrest. Zey sing some freedom liberation sega song—ze work of a local Rastaman."

"So what?" Anger was making the veins in Kit's neck stand out like cables. "Lemme guess. Gaspard thinks Freedom is some kinda friggin' tampon brand."

Dominic shrugged. "It's a breach of ze *ordre public.*"

"Where are they bein' taken?"

"'Otel de Police."

"Ain't anybody gonna do anythin'? What about their civil rights?"

Dominic gave a hollow laugh. "Under Super Flic zey don't 'ave any. Zere is a scandale and ze authorities in Paris, zey hold zeir noses and kick 'im out to Réunion. Now 'e must prove 'imself."

Kit smoldered like a lightning-struck tree, a tree that could flare at any moment. "We have to help her, Shelly. Coco alone with Gaspard—Christ, it's like facin' up to Darth Vader with a butter knife. And it doesn't look like anybody else is ridin' to her goddamn rescue." Kit glared accusingly at Dominic. "I'll just leave you here then, to organize the telethon, shall I? Oh and Shelly, have you got any Euros? I might need to borrow some for bail."

Having Coco under lock and key seemed like a splendid idea to Shelly at this precise moment. Once she regained her power of speech, she was definitely going to say no. She was also going to advise Kit that a neck is something that if you don't stick out, you won't get in trouble up to. And most importantly, she would also make him finish that sentence that Coco had interrupted. What Donald Rumsfeldesque bombshell was he going to drop on her now? she wondered.

But then Kit's hand was on her arm, and it was so warm that she let it steer her first to her hotel room safe and then into the taxi. And in the taxi he put his arm around her shoulders and so there she was, melted once more in the equatorial warmth of his embrace. The briny air was tangy with expectation. Shelly thought they must be near the airport. But then she realized that it was just her heart taking off.

The Differences
Between the Sexes:
Communication

Women: So, you will call me tomorrow?

Men: Sure . . . I'll call you a bloody idiot for ever believing that I'd call you to-bloody-morrow.

9 Cease-fire

There is only one fixed rule when traveling in a foreign country. Armed police are right about everything. Break this rule and you could find yourself bullet-riddled. Her first sight of the forbidding police headquarters, laced in barbed wire and bristling with machine gun–toting cops, brought Shelly's soaring 747 heart to a grinding halt. But before she could reach the panic button and activate her emotional ejector seat to bail out, she was inside the Hotel de Police, a hotel where the guest is always wrong.

Two riot police were smoking, their helmets lifted up onto their foreheads like frogmen. They watched Kit and Shelly enter the Ministère de l'Intérieur with bloodless indifference. The police dogs at their feet were absorbed in genital grooming. A fluorescent light sputtered and stuttered and music seeped from a small radio. A giant photograph of a smug-looking Jacques Chirac, Président de la République Française, dominated the room. The Declaration of the Rights of Man on the opposite wall had been put to ominous use as a dartboard.

"Listen," Kit said, sotto voce, as they waited for Officer Gaspard. "I've seen the *Battle of Algiers*. Whackin' you in the face with the butt of his pistol is French for 'hello.' So lemme do the talkin', okay?"

"Just be careful," Shelly heard herself saying, then to disguise this display of feeling, "I mean, you are my only husband, after all. It's not as though I've got husbands to squander, you know."

There was a piercing caterwauling and they all turned to peer out of the open windows into the courtyard where Gaspard seemed to be feeding a stray cat to a police dog. The man obviously didn't take milk with his human kindness. When the Super Flic strode into the station, the police stood to attention like a firing squad.

"Bonsoir, Commandant of the *Fromage*-Eating Surrender Chimps." Kit took a small bow. "So what's new in the world of crime and punishment then? I've been meanin' to say to you"— he screwed up his nose a little as though recoiling from a bad smell—"don'tcha think a bidet really is too small a bathtub to wash your *whole* body in?"

Shelly cringed. If that didn't get a French Hello, she didn't know what would. Gaspard assumed an expression that suggested severe hemorrhoidal tribulation. Her heart drilled in her chest. "Don't mind him," she laughed fakely. "Do you know how to condescend to an American? Speak in English!"

But before you could say "freeze and assume the position," it was *Shelly* whom Gaspard ordered to be escorted into his office. The commandant indicated the hard-backed chair in which she was to sit. In classic cop cliché, he perched on the desk, looming over her. Behind him on the windowsill a fan labored, swiveling its large face lethargically this way and that, as though sleep-deprived from interrogation. The walls, she noted, were nuthouse, institutional beige. Shelly broke into a sweat. There was nothing she liked more than the combination of a locked door and a deranged psychopath.

"So, Mademoiselle . . . oh pardon, *Madame* Kinkade, you 'ave 'eard of our law of sedition? Our law of 1881 which makes it a serious crime to insult our ministers and officials and our policemen?"

"Yes, but I really don't think Coco is a flag-waving malcontent," Shelly began.

"Zat song, eet eez the anthem of the pro-independence movement here on Réunion. Eet eez very nasty about our government in Paris. She 'as, it would seem, 'er concerns." Gaspard spoke from lips that seemed to be no more than a slit between chin and nostrils.

"Concerns? With respect, Commandant, I think all Coco is concerned about is whether her jewelry matches her toenail varnish."

"Coco—her comrades call her La Tigresse—eez a very dan-ger-ous woman," he said, with the pinched, practical demeanour of a debt collector.

"Dangerous?" Despite her nerves, Shelly laughed. "She's a pop singer. She uses her head merely as a place to prop the headphones of her Sony Walkman."

"You are being naive, madame. Women zey are used by ze communist terrorists because by zemselves *les femmes* do not arouse suspicion. Zey can go anywhere."

"Communist? Mr. Gaspard, the only party Coco is interested in is the dinner party, I can assure you." Having just gate-crashed mine, Shelly added mentally.

"Now zeze female recruits, zey are scaling ze chain of command."

"The woman *sings* scales, yes. I'm sure the silly cow didn't even know that the song was revolutionary. The woman's wonderbra has cut off oxygen to her brain. I mean, what kind of evidence do you have against her? Just that silly ditty?"

"She has been caught—what you say—spray-painting graffiti pro-*révolutionnaire*."

"She's twenty-two. We were all a bit ideology-addled at that age. She's yet to learn that spray-painting the word 'fuck' on a toilet wall does not really enrich the lives of those who see it."

"Coco she has, you know, what you call—she is mad about black cock," Gaspard explained, smirking, his dentistry fluorescent-white and ill-fitting in his sour mouth.

Shelly thought this was a good time to study the constellation of cigarette burns on the linoleum floor.

"Three years ago, one 'otel, zey employ 'er as a singer. Then she fell in love and never go back to Paris. 'Er black boyfriend, 'e was in the pro-independence movement, 'e is shot dead. In a riot. One year ago. And zat is when she swear 'atred of ze French police."

"If you don't mind me saying so, that is ridiculous. The only thing Coco's boyfriends are likely to shoot are pictures of her naked for *Playboy*."

"And now she is the concubine of his successor. You tell your 'usband to be careful. 'E is getting involved with things 'e does not understand. You should keep 'im under control."

The man's voice made her scalp crawl. "Um, just because we're married, doesn't mean I own him." (Christ, she thought, I can't even get him to eat cheese, let alone change his passionately held moral beliefs.)

"Coco, she got a job in Grande Bay 'Otel as part of a sleeper cell."

"Well, that I *can* believe. The woman seems to like to sleep with as many husbands as possible, if that's what you mean."

"Yes, madame. Zat eez exactly what I mean. She seduces men and then squeezes money from them for the independence movement. This 'usband of yours," his voice was prodding, metallic—cold as a gynecologist's speculum. "You think 'e is faithful?"

"Yes," Shelly lied. "I trust him completely."

"Well, you watch 'im. Zese terrorists, zey are ticking bombs. Intelligence is our most important tool. Zese black militants are difficult to catch because zey all have the same DNA. Zis also explains why they are so *stupide*."

Shelly couldn't understand why these pro-independence activists were proving so hard to extinguish. Surely the French could just *smug* them to death?

Gaspard presented his card with a furtive flick of his Rolexed wrist. "If you see anything suspicious, report to me immediately."

"You want me to spy on my own husband?"

"Spy, eh, that is such an aggressive word. *Protect*, zat is what I am thinking." His tone shifted down into a more avuncular gear. "Protecting 'im from 'imself . . . and from ze charms of La Tigresse." He smiled. But his smile never reached his dead eyes. "Otherwise"—he stood abruptly and spoke wrathfully— "your marriage? It will be very short, madame."

Gaspard's icy monotone was as final as a cell door slamming. Shelly rose to her feet. She thought she'd better get out before he had another mood swing.

Shelly blundered back into the smoke-hazed front office where Kit was threatening to call lawyers and thumping the desk, demanding to know where Shelly had been taken. When she reappeared, he almost hugged her with relief.

"God"—Shelly waved away stale Gitane fumes from in front of her face—"they could just wipe out their revolutionaries with passive smoke inhalation."

"Yeah, or bore 'em to death with a crack team of French existentialist philosophers spreadin' *ennui* and despondency about the futility of human action in the face of infinity." Kit lowered his voice. "Are you okay?" She nodded. "What did the sonofabitch want? Wait, we'll talk in the cab." Kit made a move towards his back pocket and three cops immediately cocked their guns, gesturing for him to put his arms up in the air.

As they were frisking Kit, one of the gendarmes pulled his wallet free with such force that it flapped open, fluttering out his money, receipts . . . and a small photo. Shelly picked it up. It was a snapshot of a haughty, beautiful blonde. She had one of those sculptured, high-cheekboned profiles used to advertise five-star hotels.

"Somehow I don't think this is your mother," Shelly managed to say. "You seem to have neglected to tell me that there was another woman in your life." Perhaps it *was* time to spy.

Kit seized the photo, shredding it violently. "Not anymore, there ain't." He turned his stony attention to the bail form. "I'll have to name you—'cause you're stumpin' up the bail money. I just didn't wanna waste time at the hotel, changin' pounds into Euros. So, how should I describe you? Partner? Significant Other? Defacto? . . . Pal. I'll say pal." He started writing.

How about, This is the woman who regularly invites me back to her *chambre* so we can rut like randy rabbits? Shelly thought. Why was this man, who'd leapt out of helicopters with skis on his feet, parachuted into the ocean in full scuba gear and given cheek to police prone to making penis pâté, so completely and utterly terrified of getting close to a woman?

When they'd signed the form and Shelly had handed over a

thousand pounds of her precious prize money—it was all she'd changed into Euros—Coco floated towards them, wearing the bewildered look of a hunted minx. Shelly had never seen anyone who looked less like a terrorist, an impression only enhanced when the bimbo spoke.

"Obviously I 'ave not taken good care of my chakras," Coco decided, taking Kit's arm as they pushed out of the police station. "Did you know zat you can change your life through meditation?" She turned his face towards her, so that he was looking straight down her cleavage. "I could teach you to visualize goals."

Somehow Shelly doubted this was a reference to Chelsea United.

"Kit," Coco earnestly entreated, gazing up into his eyes, "'ave you read *The Road Less Traveled?*"

That would be the road to my bedroom, Shelly mused, trotting along behind them. Not even a road really. Just a path.

"When ze band played . . . why so much fuss?" Coco smiled, innocently. "I thought it was a lovely folk song," she sighed, before waving good-bye and wafting off down the road. She no doubt had a play date with her inner child to make Creative Things With Play-doh, Shelly surmised. Her own inner child, meanwhile, wanted to throw up.

"Okay, the woman is into a few isms—tofuism, Taoism," Shelly said to Kit as they got into a taxi. "But communism? La Tigresse? Pul-lease! We're talking Rebel Without a Clue."

"So, you don't think a Tigresse can change her spots?" Kit gave Shelly a sidelong, mutinous look, which she couldn't quite fathom. . . .

The taxi whisked them back along the beach road. In the harbor a majestic sailing ship, a replica of the old French clippers that brought the first colonialists to these islands, tacked across the bay.

"So, tell me about Gaspard—what the hell did he want with you?"

"Oh, isn't it beautiful!" Shelly verbally sidestepped, pointing to the boat. "It's for tomorrow's re-enactment ceremony. *To celebrate settlement of Réunion by the King of France in 1642*," she parroted from the promotional pamphlet she'd read in the hotel reception.

The taxi driver, a Creole, snorted derisively. Shelly flinched, sensing—correctly—that she'd cued a diatribe about indigenous rights.

"Pah! We have nothin' to celebrate. Except la degradation of African people over ve last three hundred and fifty years." As she'd feared, the temptation to rage at length was not resisted. "Our forebears were slaves, makin' ve British on Mauritius and ven ve French on Réunion rich—while keepin' us poor."

The driver swung up a back street leading away from the harbor, his car scattering alley cats which squealed like rusty hinges. The tropical vibrancy of the main square with its bougainvillaea-vined, white-shuttered colonial mansions was immediately extinguished. Here, jumbled hovels leant arthritically onto each other, exhausted by their effort to stay erect, like prisoners left too long on the parade ground. The general air of degeneration was made more pungent by sewage stink and rotting garbage. Shelly wound up her window, quickly.

"Vis island is part of Africa," the taxi driver railed. "We want self-determination and independence. We want our own ambassador in ve UN. We want to keep ve wealth for ourselves and not send it back to Paris. Colonial Re-enactment? Pah! It just rubs salt into our wounds."

His lecture and his vehicle were halted by a police roadblock which found him pulled over to the side of the road. "*Desolé,*

Monsieur. You will 'ave to walk to your 'otel from 'ere." He pointed up the beach.

For Shelly it was a relief to escape the car. As they walked along the shore the sound of the tropics lapped around them. From the forest came the most exotic chorus. Birds caroled, frogs baritoned, insects percussed in a hot hum of excitement. A breeze scented with cinnamon and nutmeg tickled her face. Palm fronds were waving at her in a friendly way. Upon their approach, sherbet-winged parrots took flight from the trees. They paused to shuck off their shoes.

"Thanks, Shelly." The sand creaked beneath their bare feet.

"For what?"

"For lendin' Coco the cash. You're the first chick I've ever met I can rely on, d'ya know that?"

Shelly wished she could say the same thing about him. "So, the woman in the wallet . . . she really hurt you, huh?"

"Oh, no more than your average lapsed Satanist," Kit said.

Once more, Shelly could glimpse, beneath his bravado, something heartbroken in him. But whenever she probed, steel filled his voice and the psychological portcullis slammed down. What was the combination to his lock? she wondered.

"Okay, I know we both lied on the quiz applications, but let's be honest now. And so," Shelly said, in an American game show host's accent, "Contestant Number One? Tell us a little about yourself. The truth this time."

"As in, the facts?" Kit gazed at Shelly reflectively. "Well, I hoped to play football professionally, but an injury ended all hopes of a sportin' career. So, I became a first-class gate-crasher on the L.A. party circuit. Went anywhere there were free drinks. Tagged along with a buddy for his model agency interview, but they picked me instead. Next thing I know I'm on a giant billboard at the corner of Sunset and La Cienega. The ad, for Calvin Klein underwear, caused traffic pileups and prompted a shitload of complaints."

Shelly would bet anything that for women drivers it would have been the most painless traffic accident ever. Oh, how he would have filled those briefs. Whiplash me, baby, one more time.

"Anyways, after that I was like—no more ads. Started up a bad band, drifted into actin', then went travelin'. Was a victim of a cocaine sting in Bolivia, got struck by lightnin' in Malaysia, nearly stepped on a land mine in Sierra Leone, lost my dog to a gator attack in Mozambique . . . you know. The usual."

The usual? Shelly listened to him, enraptured. Ambushes, tornadoes, infernos, avalanches—usual for Indiana Jones, maybe.

"And now, what about you, Contestant Number Two?" he challenged. "What've been the highlights of your life?"

"Um . . . well, last year I conducted a concert at school and nobody farted during the solo. That was pretty amazing."

"Okay, next question. Why do you always feel with life that the glass is half empty, never half full?"

"I suppose you don't need to be Freud to know that it's got to do with my dad," she disclosed grimly. "My father who never came to see me. Too busy playing in bad bands in pubs called The Slug and Lettuce. Or The Phlegm and Testicle. His latest ensemble is called The Four Skins—only the bass guitarist has just left and The Three Skins just doesn't have the same ring somehow."

Kit shook his head, bewildered. "How could he leave his darlin' little girl?"

The silver sea shivered beneath the moon. And she shivered too, but not from cold. "No matter how often my mum repeated it was nothing to do with me, how can a kid not feel rejected and unlovable?"

Kit smiled. It was a compassionate, warm smile, and it was just for her. When he smiled at her like that, her world was an infinitely warmer and more wonderful place. Her blood raced then idled through her heart. Her feet sank into the wet sand as they made their way along the water's edge to the hotel, their legs pacing together metronomically. It was all she could do not to hold his hand. She felt herself opening up, like an oyster.

"And then?" Kit asked gently.

"And then, when my mum died, well, my entire world died with her. My mother always used to say to me, 'Leave a note and I'll know where you've gone.' When she died, all I could think of was, Where is the note? Where has she gone?"

Kit was still. "Damnit, Shelly. You just got to my emotional libido." This time when he smiled at her there was a flare of expectation in his eyes. "What a shame you're only still interested in me for my body."

"Oh no. I'm not remotely interested in you for your *body*. Now that you've let down your guard, I'm only interested in your *mind*." A wave surged high up the shore—the water rushing sibilantly around their bare feet.

"Oh. Then this will have no effect." And he leaned down and kissed her neck. At the feel of his lips Shelly gave a swoon worthy of a Beatles concert circa '66.

"Not at all," she lied, living in the kiss, gazing up past his face at unfamiliar stars. So much for holding his hand. It was now proving very hard to stop herself from lunging at his groin.

"Really?" He nuzzled the words into her ear. "And what about if I do *this*?" He flicked his warm, caramel-tasting tongue into her mouth and kissed her for a full five minutes. "Whatya say to that, then?"

Fuck me now would be good, she thought, or perhaps a more formal inquiry as to whether or not he felt like a little rambunctious entwining on a sand dune somewhere. "I'd say you were employing biological warfare. I'd say you were using your pheromones to take my hormones hostage."

"Ah, the sexual Stockholm Syndrome. So, are you ready to befriend your captor?" Kit's face, lit by a rhomboid of moonlight on the water, looked playful and wicked. "Are you ready to admit defeat? And be punished for your crimes against humanity?" He said it hot and growly in her ear.

"Are *you*, you mean?" She bit his lip, hard enough to draw blood. "For your crimes against femininity?"

This state of sensual siege Kit ended with armed intervention, by pinning her against a dark boulder on the beach and pressing his hungry hips into hers. "So, Shelly Green, are you ready to be disarmed?"

Night purred around them. The sea lapped like a cat. His fingers were light as a breeze on her skin. Shelly was startled by the warmth spreading through her like sunshine in the dark.

He lay her back on the bed of powdery sand, then covered her like the most delicious sauce, all warm and everywhere.

He smoodged his way under her ruched-up dress and mouthed her breasts as though they were the most delicious marshmallows. She twisted under him, feeling the gratifying weight of his body. As he stroked between her legs, an aching throb built up in her blood; the lace of her panties dissolving in his fingers like candy floss. He eased her open with measured caresses. She moaned, her muscles clenching his fingers.

Then suddenly she was tugging at his jeans, the zipper rasping impatiently against the denim. A hot sigh was on his lips and a shout of joy in her dry throat. Her heart was banging away like a Protestant's drum in the Ulster marching season—which is no doubt why she didn't hear, beneath the beech trees behind them, the shark-shaped car stealing out onto the sand. She had no idea they were being watched until the shadow of Gaspard fell upon them like a net.

In retrospect, knowing the exact location of all vindictive policemen in the immediate area is obviously the minimum precaution one should take before exposing one's genitalia to the elements. Shelly tried to swim back up through her waves of pleasure, but when she finally came ashore, she was still tingling and only half in the world.

"*Atteinte à l'ordre public.* Indecent exposure is a prosecutable offense." Gaspard shone the malevolent beam of his torch onto their bodies, which twisted as they grappled back into their clothes. The car's headlights flicked on and Gaspard, sniffing around them like a dog, laughed derisively. "Caught wiz your pants around your ankles. How crass you Americans are. 'How gauche it with you?'" he mocked, in an exaggerated Texan accent for the benefit of his gendarmes, who were emerging, snickering, from the police car, their semi-automatics slung casually over their shoulders.

"Hey, Shell," Kit said loudly, "ever noticed that the higher the caliber of gun, the lower the caliber of intellect?"

"I am watching your every move." Gaspard was a night-hunting snake, invisible infrared sensors at the ready. "You and Mademoiselle Coco." He puffed on his ever-present cigar.

"You know, Gaspard, I really think it's wise never to smoke a cigar bigger than your dick. It will only invite acerbic asides from former girlfriends."

Shelly cringed. Kit had his foot in his mouth so often it was a wonder his toenails hadn't developed taste buds.

But Gaspard's car was already skulking back into the darkness. Kit threw a rock after it. "That guy has *corrupt cop* written all over him: the sailin' tan, the Rolex watch, the fuckin' manicured hands—on a cop salary? I smell a whiff of sewage in the police ranks." His mood had become turbulent and volcanic. He was as explosive as the brooding mountain behind them.

Kit then stomped off in the direction of the hotel. Shelly had to run to catch up with him. She placed urgent hands around his waist and turned him towards her.

"Look, I know we can't do anything about all the misery in the world, but that doesn't mean we have to add to it personally. I mean, isn't it our job to have as much fun as possible?" she suggested, a little desperately.

"Why is he always at the hotel?" Kit brooded. "That dipshit has his entire *arm* in the till," he said—and she knew she'd lost him. Gaspard had rained on their passion parade. "I gotta get back." He removed her hands with absentminded agitation. "Sorry."

"Why?" She couldn't see his face in the shadows. His bent, averted head was dark against the moonlit sea.

"I just do." The man played his cards so close to his chest only his nipples knew what was going on. "Tomorrow, we'll pick up where we left off, okay? I wanna do it right, Shelly. I'm just not in the mood now."

"Well, at least tell me what you were going to say"—she cupped his face in her hands— "in the restaurant."

"I was just gonna tell you that your eyes are so blue a guy could drown in 'em. He could fall so deeply, so fast, before he even knew he was gonna stumble." And then he was gone, as quick as a cat burglar.

Shelly tried to run after him but only caught one last glimpse as he retreated towards his bungalow. His shoulders, stooped beneath some mysterious anxiety, made him look like a question mark in the dark.

And she realized with a jolt that she wanted to be the answer.

Coital marital interruptus left Shelly wound up tighter than a Taiwanese toy. Normally she avoided La Caravalle bar—glittering with gold chains, perma tans, tailored teeth and too tight leisurewear—but now she definitely needed a drink.

As soon as she entered the smoky enclave she regretted her decision, because, as always, there was no escaping the tentacular presence of Gaby and crew.

"You're alone?" Gaby wailed. "Oh no! You struck out *again*?"

"Christ!" Towtruck guffawed to the sound recordist. "It's not *that* hard to set a one-eyed trouser-snake snare."

"Kit just feels we should do it right," said Shelly, primly, "and—"

"*Feels*? You didn't ask him how he feels, did you?" Gaby cringed. "How can a man explain his feelings when he doesn't know he has them?"

Mwah! Mwah! It could only be Dominic. "*Chérie !!!!!*" The man had honed his cheerfulness to talk-show perfection. He then bent over her hand and kissed that. "Would you care to dance? You *must* let ze entertainment officer entertain you. You are not allowed to 'ave a bad time 'ere. There are spies lurking be'ind every cocktail umbrella making sure you are Enjoying Yourself. Eet eez time, you and me, we did some serious bonding."

Shelly gave a mirthless laugh. "Serious bonding? Sounds like something you read on a card in a phone booth in Soho. For Serious Bonding, call Simone . . . "

"You are a beautiful woman, Shelly. You need a man who can really appreciate you." He talked softly so that she was obliged to lean closer to hear him—Technique Number 1 from the *Don Juan*

Handbook. "Eet eez a mystery, why you are alone on a night as beautiful as zis. If I were your lover, I would be"—he paused while his mind seemed to run through a checklist of his clichés—"ze wind beneath your wings," he said—a sentiment as insipid as a Hallmark card. "Tell me, *chérie*, what is your star sign?"

"My sign?" Shelly said, sternly. "*My* sign reads Do Not Disturb."

"In France, we know 'ow to take care of our women. Come back with me to my place, *chérie*."

"Gee, I don't know. Will two people fit under a rock?"

"Ze lake of your desire will overflow," the oleaginous Frenchman oozed. "Shelly," he said, with indefatigable enthusiasm—and, also, his hand on her ass. "Tell me, is zis seat taken?"

"Um, it seems to have slipped your attention, Dominic, that I am a married woman." Shelly removed his hand as though it were a dead roach.

"Ah, so where is your 'usband, *chérie*?"

"Ah. Zis information I can provide." The police commandant slid into view like an eel from a crack.

Shelly looked at him aghast. "Are you stalking me, Inspector? My husband is—"

"Down on ze beach." He turned his clinical eyes upon Shelly. "With 'is tongue down ze throat of that *salope*."

Shelly looked at him, with his professionally polished skin and buffed fingernails and aftershave imported from Marseilles, and she felt her fear evaporate from the heat of her anger. "You know you really are starting to look underdressed without a straitjacket, Mr. Super Flic."

Gaspard gave her the sort of smile a piranha would give if a piranha could smile. "Zen come and see for yourself," he said with contemptuous suavity.

He propelled her down the steps onto the beach and through

the palm trees. She followed the direction of the police commandant's pointed finger to the far end of the cove where, once her eyes adjusted to the light, she discerned two figures embracing.

She could hear her own stark, jagged breathing, at odds with the gentle implacability of the waves on the beach.

"That could be anyone," she said bravely, despite the doubts buzzing as insistently as cicadas in her brain.

"Allow me." Gaspard thoughtfully produced a pair of field glasses.

What a way to spend your honeymoon, staring longingly at your beloved—through binoculars, Shelly despaired, as, almost hypnotized, she held them up to her eyes. As the lenses focused, her vision was jumping from overgrown jet skis to speedboats snuffling at their moorings. Then she swung more to the left and finally snared on the handsome shape of her husband with (she twisted the lenses for a sharper image) his arms wrapped around the lithe body of Coco.

Grief, like a knife, sliced into her heart. She jerked away as though she'd been slapped, dropping the binoculars as if they'd scorched her. A tear crawled down her cheek and then she tasted it in her mouth.

Gaspard pressed another of his cards into her hand. He seemed to have arranged the evening's events as carefully as his three strands of comb-over.

"What were you saying about trust?" He laughed harshly with all the charm of a death squad.

Shelly was sprinting away down the beach before she realized what she was doing. Her whole life seemed to have become a 747 in a nosedive, with her "hubby" as the pilot. Back at the bar, she slumped, furious with herself, in front of her cocktail—although a Molotov cocktail would have been more appropriate. She'd been intrigued, fascinated, obsessed even, by this dashingly handsome daredevil, but typically he'd turned out to be just another fraud—a zircon hero, artificially dazzling; a self-absorbed, selfish prick like her dad. Rejection hovered like a headache. She was captain and crew of SS *Delusion*.

So much for the cease-fire in the Sex Wars. To dump her for that freebie-loving fellatrix, for whom he'd forced Shelly to stump up bail, was an act of war. It was time to put this marriage to the sword. Shelly tried to assuage her humiliation by diving into a Loch Ness–sized glass of Jack Daniel's bourbon (it was her father's favorite drink, known as "the rock and roll mouthwash") and downed half of it in one draught.

Kit was wrong. It didn't matter if the glass was half full or half empty. Because what it contained was arsenic on the rocks.

The Differences
Between the Sexes:
Fidelity

Women: Unless crossed, the female of the species tends towards fidelity and constancy.

Men: There are a few species where the male stays faithful until he dies, mostly as a result of being eaten by his partner after mating.

10 The Cold War

Shelly awoke the next morning lying in the beach bar, and nursing a hangover the size of Réunion itself. Thanks to the sumo mosquitoes on the island, she was also polka-dotted with itchy bites. Oh well, she thought, the hangover could occupy the head she obviously wasn't using last night. Why on earth had she opened up her heart to that two-timing clit-jockey? She listened to the clear glissando of a mockingbird mocking her for being such a bloody idiot. Welcome to Dumpsville. Population one.

"I just heard." The voice was Gaby's. "Call it sick, call it twisted, call it male. I'm sorry, Mrs. K.," she commiserated, handing Shelly a glass of fizzing Barocca which Shelly declined because she couldn't stand the noise.

"Well," Gaby prodded, tentatively, "how are you?"

"Put it this way, I think it's time someone removed my belt and shoelaces."

"That bad, huh? So what are you going to do?"

"Actually I was thinking about staggering off into the

wilderness to die. God, I feel so sick. If only I could make myself throw up . . . I know! Show me my marriage video again!"

In the bay, the glorious French clipper they'd seen the night before, called in fact the *Glorieuse*, was preparing for today's Colonization Re-enactment Ceremony. Watching it maneuver back and forth made Shelly even more nauseous. She squeezed her eyelids shut in the hope that this might at least stop her brain from leaking out of her orbs. "I'm sorry, Gaby, but today I can only undertake leisure activities that are within staggering distance of a toilet."

Gaby mopped the dank hair from Shelly's pasty face. Due to this small unexpected act of kindness, Shelly suddenly let out a sob that sounded like a hamster being strangled. "How could he?" she wailed. "With her?"

"Talk to me, Green. I'm on your side, you know."

"I mean *Coco!* The woman holds the world record for having a conversation without saying one thing worth repeating. What does Kit see in the sort of hippy-trippy dipshit who can make a two-minute conversation stretch over twenty-six years?"

Gaby was about to answer when she was interrupted.

"Sure, there ain't a lot upstairs, but fuck a duck! What a balcony!"

At the sound of this gravel-voice, Shelly froze. She hadn't been aware that Towtruck, all florid nose and vermilion splotchy cheeks, was behind them, swigging on a Bloody Mary with one hand and filming Shelly with the other, Silent Mike technologically Siamese-twinned beside him.

"You're filming me *now*? How could you?"

"Towtruck! Turn that bleeding thing off immediately!" Gaby demanded. "I have a woman on the brink of a nervous bloody breakdown here! Now piss off and get some footage of that French re-enactment boat. The ceremony will be starting any moment. I'm so sorry, Shelly, about that pissant, but don't worry. I'll wipe the tape completely, okay? We girls have got to stick together. The Sisterhood, an' all that."

"Thank you." Shelly, squinting into the sun, watched the awful man tacking his way against the wind on to the beach and disappearing with his camera in the crowd of dignitaries. The majestic clipper had been moored at the dock and was now straining at its anchorage in the choppy seas. The Maire and other French officials were huddled on the dark volcanic sand. Incongruously dressed in suits and ties, their hands were laced behind their backs in perfect Prince Philip impressions. The naval top brass wore their Grand Blancs—impeccable military uniforms complete with white gloves à la Minnie Mouse. They struggled to keep their peaked white caps from blowing off in the gale. Behind them straggled a clapped-out military band emitting a tinny "*Marseillaise*."

"So, the romance? It's completely dead?" Gaby quizzed anxiously.

"Well, not dead exactly. Just unable to breathe unaided by ventilator."

Mwah! Mwah!

Oh, just what she needed—more liquid.

"*Chérie*, you are hungover, no? Try my noodle!!!" Dominic thrust the long, thin, neon-pink-foam flotation device into Shelly's hands. "Join my aquaerobics class after ze ceremony! Get, 'ow you say, in ze swim, no?"

"Swim? In *there*?" Shelly asked, hooking a thumb over her shoulder at the container of dead skin cells, hair and bacteria otherwise known as the hotel pool. For some inexplicable reason, she really didn't fancy doing laps in children's pee. "Only if you seat me in the nonurinating section."

"Exercise, eet eez ze only way to 'ave closure after emotional abuse, *chérie*." Although French, Dominic spoke the language of Californication—all touchy-feely. "And zen a little fun too. Tonight, you must come to ze fancy dress ball wiz me!!!"

The man was always so up. Shelly wondered if he had personality priapism. "Don't you ever feel a tiny bit down?" she asked plaintively, her throbbing head begging for a little charisma detumescence.

He bowed before her, took her hand and kissed it so ardently he nearly sucked her nail polish off. "I'd be 'onored, *ma chérie*, if you would be my partner."

Shelly was so unused to men being attentive to her that she didn't know how to react. "Um, Dominic, are you just visiting from the thirteenth century, or are you planning to live here indefinitely?" But he was already gone, sauntering towards the ceremony.

"Maybe my reality doco hasn't bitten the romantic dust after all." Gaby tapped her pointed chin thoughtfully. "A girl should never waste mascara crying over a man, but just shout 'Next!'"

"Gaby, no. He's so young. What is he? Twenty-one, -two?"

"Young, dumb and full of cum. Mmm. What could make shit-for-brains more jealous? I mean, have you seen Dominic in his swimwear? We're talking DOD . . . Dick of Death, darling."

She strode after Towtruck to explain her new televisual tack. But all Shelly could think about was the slippery softness of Kit's beautiful mouth. His beautiful *lying* mouth. Where was that scummy bastard anyway? She was desperate to see him again, just in order to tell him that she never wanted to see him again. But Shelly was so alcoholically poisoned that she was finding it hard to differentiate between a waffle and a doorknob, which is why she didn't register, through her gritty slits of eyes, the image of her wayward spouse approaching.

It wasn't until Kit leaned up against the bar, cowboy-like (one leg up on a stool rung, left hand slipped casually down the inside of his jeans, thumb hooked lazily through a belt loop, 100-watt beam switched in Shelly's disheveled direction), that she registered his arrival.

While Dominic's effulgent charms were as flashy as the gold and diamond chains glittering around his neck, Kit just effortlessly filled up a room with his presence in nothing more than a pair of denim fly-buttons, torn just below the butt, and a cobalt blue shirt with a Cadillac-finned collar. His skin was deepening into a violin color and his dark hair was bleached blonde on the tips . . . The only thing missing was the "666" tattoo for his forehead. Even his *smile* was crooked. Kit was tall, dark and obnoxious.

"What's with this wind? It's like bein' in a bad Italian rock video. Have you guys noticed how strong that goddamn breeze is blowin'?"

"No. Only the hot air," Shelly replied curtly.

Kit glanced at her inquisitively. "Emotional Weather report: cold air mass approachin'. If I didn't know any better I'd say you got out on the wrong side of somebody's bed this mornin'. What's up, kiddo?"

"Nothing! I'm just hunky dory. Apart from a stinking cold, a killer hangover, agonizing sunburn, mosquito bites and now an allergy hive on top of my sunburn which is soooooo timely because it means I CAN'T SCRATCH THEM."

"Allergy? To what?" he asked, kindly. "It's probably just a twenty-four-hour thing."

"Oh yes, well, *you'd* know. Being a *Doctor*," said Shelly derisively. "I diagnose an allergy to you, Kit Kinkade."

Before Kit could cross-examine Shelly as to why, overnight, she'd taken on the demeanor of a hostile witness, the hotel manager appeared, wearing an agitated expression.

"Hey, bud. Where's all the staff?" Kit demanded. "I've been tryin' to order room service for two friggin' hours. I think you should erect a monument to the brave vacationers who died tryin' to place a food order here."

"The chef is not well today but I can cook pancakes," he anxiously volunteered.

"Mmm. Pancakes for breakfast, lunch and dinner. I name this Pancake Appreciation Day! And what's with this damn wind?"

"Oh, just a brisk sea breeze, monsieur," the manager said with the rehearsed chivalry of a diplomat. "Excellent for sailing."

He tried to smile but the livid semicircles beneath his eyes belied the laid-back façade. When a hotel manager starts slicing the bread, setting the tables and cleaning the rooms, then playing the maracas for the evening entertainment, you've got to start to suspect that something is seriously up. They watched him scurry off to tie down the sun umbrellas and rescue capsized beach loungers that had blown into the sea.

As if Shelly didn't feel sick to her stomach already, she now noticed Coco sashaying towards them, her glossy black locks feathering into her face in the squall. Men adored Coco's thick, corkscrewed hair. Shelly, however, thought the gorgon tendrils resembled a sack of copulating snakes.

"Zere is no band rehearsal because of my appearance zis afternoon in the Cour d'Appel. So, we go windsurfing, yes? I don't 'ave to sing tonight either because zere is a classical concert planned. A requarium."

"A requarium? Hah! What is it? A concert for fish? A coral concert?" Shelly gave a brittle chuckle.

Kit shot her a reprimanding look before correcting Coco. "Um, I think it's called a requiem."

Coco shrugged and undulated towards her cabin in the women's staff compound to get her bikini.

Shelly rounded on Kit before he had a chance to chastise her for being condescending. "I can't believe you conned me into forking out for her bail," she said, her throat on fire with misery. "And all because you think she's a female Castro. Castroenteritis is definitely what she's giving me right now."

"Don't underestimate her, kiddo," Kit reproved. He would have looked perfectly at home propping up the bar with Bogey in Key Largo.

"The only politics she's interested in are sexual. She has every man she meets wrapped around her clitoris in seconds. I've seen car bumper stickers which read, 'Honk If You've Had Coco.'"

"Just because she dresses like a whore doesn't mean she can't think like a pimp," he said sternly.

"Huh! That woman doesn't *think*. She's got a 'lick me' tattoo on her inner thigh," she insisted.

Kit fell into a truculent silence. Shelly felt once more that sense of dangerous heat in him. Why did she become so jittery in his presence? She felt angry that she allowed herself to be so unnerved.

"So, while I'm writing our thank-you letters for all those wedding gifts, would you like me to write and thank her for the venereal diseases she's no doubt given you?" Coils of anger loosened from Shelly's tongue. "I believe crotch lice are nature's way of promoting monogamy, you know, Kinkade!" A volley of words was firing out of her. "'Devoted husband' is obviously oxymoronic!" she said between shuddering intakes of breath.

"Hey, let's just flag down that bullshit taxi you're drivin' there for one goddamn minute! I haven't touched another woman since we got hitched."

"Well, it didn't look that way on the beach last night. That woman's body isn't a temple, it's a bloody amusement park!"

Kit's strong brows knitted in annoyance. "What in God's name are you yakkin' on about?"

"Gaspard told me not to trust you! He told me to keep an eye on you!"

The face Kit presented to his wife was a knot of opinion, all of it unfavorable. "You were spyin' on me? Last night?"

"He told me you'd fallen into bad company. I just didn't realize how far you'd sunk."

Kit gave her a scalding look. "And you'd take the word of that brutal scumbag over mine? Christ! When Gaspard enters a room, plants wilt on the vine. Doesn't that tell you all you need to know about the slimeball?"

"I saw you with my own eyes! When you told me you 'wanted to do it properly,' I took that to mean in the 'you bring the crème fraiche and I'll lick it off' sense. Then seconds later you're in some passionate clinch on the beach. But hey, you know, don't hug her too hard—she'll leak silicone all over your shirt."

"Do you wanna know the real reason I was holdin' Coco? 'Cause yesterday was the anniversary of her boyfriend's murder. After you and me left the police station in the cab, Gaspard followed her. He thinks she might lead him to some kind of rebel reunion. Only Coco went to the cemetery with flowers. Gaspard was furious. He demanded that she take him to rebel headquarters. When she wouldn't, he roughed her up. She pretended to help, then escaped through the graveyard. That's why he was on that deserted bit of beach with his headlights off—lookin' for her."

"Oh really? Why hasn't she reported it then?"

"Who to? The *police*? Get real, Shelly. In France a bread roll is called a 'brioche' and rape is called a 'liaison.' "

"You'd believe anything that woman told you. Though God knows why. Coco's the sort of singer who lets a man look up her skirt—then complains that she's not being taken seriously as an artist. Now I know why the French call you dumb Americans." Her words hung there, horrible and irretrievable.

"You're right, Shelly. I must be stupid because look who I married!"

"Go to hell," Shelly spat.

"Hey, do I get travel expenses?" Kit spun on a Cuban heel and strode off towards the re-enactment ceremony, elbowing aside French journalists and photographers and top hatted-and-tailed dignitaries, who were trying to keep their toupées and bouffants intact in the wind. The men held out their palms and looked skywards as the first drops of rain fell, unlike the women, who ducked their heads and ran stiffly, like distressed ostriches, for shelter. But not one female kept her head in the sand as Kit passed by. They forgot the rain and paused to smile appreciatively. One look at Kit Kinkade and women went as limp as a perm in a sauna.

"This marriage is over!" Shelly called out after him, trying not to perv on his peachy, taut posterior. It was her fault for believing she was worthy of a man who looked like that . . . and for believing that a man who looked like that could ever develop into a well-rounded, nice human being and not remain a total, arrogant, lying, lowlife bastard. Men like Kit should come with a warning. "Too sexy for his own good. Danger. Do not approach. The management cannot be responsible for broken hearts, hymens, etc."

Why, she wondered, do humans celebrate marriage before it's had a chance to happen? Usually you celebrate *after* something.

Oscars happen after the movie. A christening, after the birth. Olympic medals, after the race. And do you know why people celebrate a marriage before it's happened? Because there's fuck-all to celebrate later. Oh, how quickly it goes from "Till death do us part" to "What the hell did I ever see in you, you asshole?"

It was then that she saw Coco up close. Shelly had retreated into the poolside changing rooms to grieve unobserved, only to find Coco readjusting a sarong and T-shirt over her leopardskin bikini—but not before Shelly had glimpsed her upper arms, which were aubergine with bruises. She had a cut on her neck, a tobacco-colored fingergrip mark on her inner thigh and an angry contusion on her back.

Remorse flooded into Shelly like sea water into the *Titanic*. Coco covered up quickly and left before Shelly could say anything. Oh Christ. Why had she believed Gaspard and not her own husband?

Shelly sprinted through the dignitaries who were now saluting the frantically flapping French flag as it was hoisted heavenward by the mayor. There was a clatter of birds' wings as the cormorants, disturbed by her panicked arrival, swooped and arced up into the sky. Shelly seized hold of Dominic's shoulders. "Did you see where Kit went?"

"Canoe," replied Dominic, who seemed to be developing "air lip": a blistering around the mouth due to the air-kissing of too many guests. "To ze island, no?" He gestured to the honey-colored strip of crushed coral that fringed the palm tree–fronded islet, about a mile out into the lagoon at the tip of the reef.

Oh great—back into the shark-intensive strip of aqua. And in *this* weather. But she had no choice. If Kit and Shelly's fledgling marriage had been a car, they'd just broken down in a dangerous neighborhood. . . .

The Differences
Between the Sexes:
Change

A woman thinks, okay, her man has a few flaws but with time she can change him.

Men know that the only time they've ever been changed by a woman was out of their diapers.

11 Biological Warfare

"What the hell are *you* doin' out here?" Kit was treading water next to Shelly's pedalo, which bobbed erratically in the choppy waves around the small island a mile from shore.

"Oh," she replied, "just trying to spot a whale that doesn't have a Friends of the Earth activist strapped to it."

"You came to spy on me, I s'pose, for that prick Gaspard."

Shelly felt a stab of embarrassment. "Look, about this morning. Turns out you were telling the truth about Coco. I'm sorry I didn't believe you. Just because Coco's flirting with you doesn't mean she's sleeping with you as well. I mean, does a dog actually plan to catch the car it's chasing? No, it's just habit."

He shook his head at her choice of analogy and rolled his eyes. Waves lapped percussively against his face as his legs scissored in the deep water.

"Climb aboard." She extended her hand. "It's like swimming in a washing machine in there." It was true. The wind had whipped up the water. The tidal rush hissed at the hull of her flimsy craft, jerking her violently this way and that.

"Can't."

"Why?"

"Buck naked."

Lust jitterbugged in her gusset. *Yes*, she thought, there *is* a God! "So?" Shelly feigned nonchalance. "We are married, after all. What happened to your trunks?"

"When I kayaked over here that shit-weasel Towtruck followed me in a motorboat. When I went for a dip, he sneaked out from behind those palm trees there and stole not only all my goddamn clothes but the freakin' canoe too, right off the beach. He's back there on the island, camera rollin'. Waitin' to get some shots of my bare ass. Just pedal around the point, I'll swim after you. Then that sonofabitch won't get the satisfaction of any footage."

Once out of view of the island's sandy cove, Kit hauled himself up out of the sea and on to the seat beside her. Shelly marveled afresh at his magnificent body. *All* of his magnificent body.

"I thought the marriage was kaput? I thought I was a lyin', cheatin' bastard?" He leaned back, legs akimbo. The man had an effortless sexual confidence. He wore it like a scent. Shelly of course had an amorous odor too, a little something by Chanel called Desperation—Eau de Désespoir. She tried to fake insouciance and stop stealing surreptitious glances at Kit's appendage, which looked as though it should have been on a launch pad at Cape Canaveral. If only a perfume house would put out a suggestive scent that said to a man, "My tongue will trace the contours of your abdomen, flicking and flexing and pushing into the hollow of your glistening navel, *and then bonk you till your brains fall out*." Was that so much to ask, hmmm?

168

"I know you can never underestimate the male ability to fuck up, Shelly, but you seem to be mad at *all* men. For what they've done. For what they *haven't* done. For what they *might* do. For what they might *not* do. For what they've *said*. For what they've *not* said. And most especially, no doubt, for sayin' this to you."

"That's nothing. You should have heard my mother's standard lecture on male inadequacy. It made the Neolithic period look like a brief spasm of history. Woman, gentle gatherer. Man, wildebeest–slaying warrior. And"—Shelly shrugged—"it rubbed off, you know?"

But having the World's Most Sexy Man completely naked by your side did tend to recalibrate a girl's feelings about the inferiority of men somewhat. Shelly blushed. She squirmed. She broke into a torrential sweat.

"You can't stay hunched under the weight of your mum's anger towards men for ever," Kit was saying seriously.

True. Her mum had drilled into her that marriage was an open prison. But being single? That was solitary confinement. She didn't want to become like her poor mother—all feelings freeze-dried and vacuum-packed. Female emancipation was one thing—dying all alone in the bath and only being discovered because of an Indian summer and a fly swarm was quite another.

"Truth is," she found herself confessing, "I pretended to be angry that my pupils had entered my name into the competition, but secretly I was glad. I couldn't have faced another blind date."

"Why not?"

"Kit, if a friend set you up with a blind date and said, 'She has so much personality,' would *you* go?"

Kit smiled his familiar lopsided smile, the one that was supposed to be a whole big smile but got waylaid by some secret sadness on the way.

"And then, when it was you I got set up with—well, it was like going to the doctor and being told that you needed to put *on* weight. I felt like Bottom waking up in the arms of Titania and thinking, 'Thank You, Jesus!' And also—a computer did matchmake us. There must be some kind of scientific reason it did that."

"We were probably the only two people who didn't say their hobbies included moonlight strolls on the beach, workin' for World Peace and a passion for Deepak Chopra—which sounds *so* like a vegetable, don't you reckon? And not to forget havin' a GSOH," he said.

Shelly, proving that she actually did have a Good Sense of Humor allowed herself to feel a flicker of joy. But Kit was surveying the horizon anxiously.

The rain had stopped but the air was still leaden with humidity. Clouds sloshed across the sky like drying gray laundry. Birds skimmed and wheeled haphazardly over the water. "What the fuck is goin' on with this weather?"

Shelly took his hand. "You know that cold air mass you predicted earlier? Well, um, it seems there's a warm front approaching." And she placed it on her breast. He looked into her eyes while his hand cupped her tenderly, fingers squeezing her nipple through her dress. When he took his hand away, she felt her skin glowing where he'd touched her.

"You really are a very sexy woman, Shelly. I think under the circumstances even your mom would permit me a mildly appreciative, post-feminist *phwoar*! Don't you?"

"You see, Kit, the trouble is, I've now had a wide-on for" —she checked her watch— "exactly 120 hours—so it's no wonder I've been a little bit irritable, okay?"

Kit's sea-deep green eyes took a long, slow unnerving look at her. "You do have the hottest, sweetest pussy, j'know that? I keep expectin' to see Maggie the Cat on a hot tin roof down there, swiggin' Southern Comfort, and smokin' a cheroot."

Hot and sweet, but what about wet? Shelly felt sure they could hold aquatic sports in her knickers. People could kayak down there, goddamn it!

His warm fingers moved slow as Albinoni's "Adagio" up her leg. "So, what's your Cavewoman Within sayin' now, Shelly Green?" he asked, huskily.

"She's saying Fuck Me Now, You Big, Hairy Hunter."

They locked eyes for a heartbeat. Then his mouth brushed her neck and, just as she was contemplating the impossibility of struggling half-naked on a pedalo in a storm without getting any seaweed up any orifice, his fingers were tangled in her hair, his tongue was around her tonsils and her legs were around his waist.

Orgasm was hovering like a thought on the tip of her tongue as her body juddered and writhed while she desperately tried to shed her dress. The slippery softness of their lips inspired in them the fantasy that the surrounding world had dissolved—an illusion cruely shattered when their pedalo hit a rock, smashing the propeller, not to mention the piquancy of the moment. They floundered there in the open sea as the tide burbled bad-temperedly around the rocks. The somber clouds were bloated with rain. Birds bickered as they raced for shelter. The seagulls wailed like alley cats. And the tide was propelling them out into the open sea.

"Shit. We're driftin'. We'll have to swim to the island."

"Without flippers? I'll drown."

She was already drowning in a cross-current of emotions. She was in way over her head. These feelings were dangerous. They could wash a girl way, way out to sea. Shelly looked at the man next to her. What was he? Shark or lifeboat?

"You won't drown 'cause I'll be with you. Hurry up. Climb on to my back and hold on to my shoulders." Kit slid into the water, steadying himself with one hand on the pedalo. The other he held out to her. "Come on. You can kick breaststroke-style to help me."

"Um. Let me see. How can I put this? Um . . . no!"

"You have to trust me, Shelly. How can we ever have a relationship without trust?"

He hauled himself half up out of the water and kissed her mouth. And oh, woman overboard! SOS. Mayday, Mayday. She was lost. She inhaled a ragged breath, then lowered herself into the percolating sea.

But it would seem that there is nothing like the Houdini contortions of making love on a beach or on some precarious craft to attract onlookers. Just as the heavens opened, turning the sea into a bubbling cauldron, a powerboat throbbed around the point. It surged towards them in a coruscation of spray, driven by Coco who idled the motor as she approached so that they could scramble up the ladder out of the boiling foam. They took shelter beneath the boat's canopy, then swaddled themselves in towels they found there.

"You are lucky I can drive a boat. All ze staff zey 'ave walked off ze job in protest. A famous Rastaman 'e 'as killed 'imself in custody after, ze radio said, 'voluntarily confessing to terrorist acts'."

"A voluntary confession?" Kit snorted. "No doubt obtained with electrodes to the testicles. I think it's safe to say that this was an assisted suicide."

Coco shrugged. "I am not political. I do not know about such sings. But I do know *one* sing, though. If I 'adn't come"—she pointed to the abandoned pedalo, already drifting out beyond the reef—"you would 'ave arrived in Africa even wizout zese tickets." She rummaged in her bag to produce two airline tickets. "For tomorrow's plane to Madagascar."

Kit gave a cheerless smile. "I appreciate your discretion, Coco."

"Madagascar?" Kit had punctured Shelly's helium-filled happiness with that one word. A cormorant creaked low across the water before crash-landing. Shelly knew just how it felt.

"Well . . ." Kit hesitated before he looked brazenly into Shelly's face. "I was thinkin' of takin' a little holiday from my holiday. You didn't mention this to anyone else, did you?" he demanded of Coco as the boat engine gave a croupy cough and lurched into life, making them all grab instinctively onto some part of the pulsating deck.

As the boat jolted, Shelly snatched the plane tickets from Coco's hands. Though Kit made a frantic lunge, Shelly was already dangling them over the froth of their wake. He froze.

Anchoring her body against the swell, she quickly cast her eye over the ticket. She noted with dismay that Kit had exchanged his own London–Réunion–London return ticket for *two* economy one-way tickets from London to Réunion—*no return*.

"You came here with someone else?" she asked in dismay.

Kit examined his toenails with forensic absorption.

"And what about *this* part? Two non-return tickets to Madagascar?" She tried to steady herself by clinging one-handed to the railings of the thumping boat. This marriage was like some sick carnival ride. "What's going on, Kinkade?"

But Kit kept up his Trappist Monk routine.

"Now is not the time to get all Pinteresque on me, okay?" she shouted above the roar of the engine.

Still silence. If only the tradition of calling people by their defining characteristics hadn't gone out of fashion, Shelly thought. Hagar the Horrible, or Ivan the Terrible—what convenient sociological shorthand. Kit the Chronic Lying Bastard.

'If you don't tell me what's going on, I'll say terrible things about you on the *Desperate and Dateless* documentary," she triumphed, rain running into her mouth.

Kit's Adam's apple yo-yoed up and down like a tiny elevator in his throat as he swallowed his emotions.

"Really terrible things. On prime-time television. To the nation. I'll say that I do like you, I do, despite the shoulder-length ear hair. And that maybe the halitosis is only temporary . . ."

"And if you don't give me back my goddamn tickets I'll say *you* have a homemade Star Trek uniform."

"And I'll tell them about your overwhelming urge to wear women's underwear. Would you really risk having your sex life exposed, tabloid style?"

"You're the one who'll be tabloid toast, kiddo. Especially when I reveal how you could only get your rocks off when I sucked your toes—which was kinda unappetizing, considering your persistent foot fungus."

"Oh, don't be so childish. I really can't stand children, *especially when they're adults*. At least kids can't help shitting on you. But grown men shouldn't have unpredictable defecatory habits."

"*You don't like kids*? That just proves what a coldhearted, selfish, snotty-nosed British bitch you are."

"Selfish? *Me*? Let me just remind you that *I* won half this hideous honeymoon too. And *I'm* not the one running out on it. Christ! If only the computer had selected one of the other finalists. That nice criminal solicitor, for instance."

"I think you'll find 'criminal solicitor' is a tautology."

"He graduated from Eton, I'll have you know."

"Yeah. In Advanced Sodomy. Only he failed first time and had to take it again. If it weren't for *me* you wouldn't have won any of this goddamn honeymoon, 'cause *I* chose *you*," he confessed angrily.

"What? I thought the computer matchmade us?" The boat pitched and rolled ominously as it left the shelter of the island.

"Don't be so green. One of the producers is a pal. He owed me a favor. I needed some dough quickly so . . . welcome to the Wonderful World of Graft and Kickback." Kit gave a joyless chuckle. There it was again, beneath the bonhomie, something bruised and melancholy.

"*Desperate and Dateless* is *rigged?*"

"They're *all* rigged. *I'm sorry, ladies and gentlemen,*" he said in a singsong American accent, "*but the game show you're watchin' is fixed.*"

"You could be prosecuted for deception and conspiracy! But tell me this." Hope pulsed irrationally through her heart. "If you could choose any woman you liked, why the hell did you choose me?"

Coco, hunched over the hot outboard motor, was steering for the wharf. Kit, saronged in a towel, tossed the looped rope onto the dock then leapt ashore after it to secure the boat to a pole. "'Cause you seemed so, well, harmless."

"Harmless?"

"I mean, you know, nice. Nondescript. Bland. Predictable." His hand guided her on to the deck. "Safe."

"Nice?" Shelly was shattered. Kit used her perturbation to snatch the tickets back from her limp hand.

"Nondescript? Bland? Predictable?" Shelly looked up at the gray, clotted skies to stop herself from crying. "Is that really how you see me?"

But he was gone, along with her fledging hopes—vaulting over the edge of the wharf and away up the beach in the rain.

An end to heterosexual hostilities? Not bloody likely.

Her mother was right after all then. A girl should never approach a man with an open mind. It only lets the flies in.

The Differences Between the Sexes: How to Impress

How to impress a woman: tenderness, caressing, talking, devotion, trust, truth, togetherness

How to impress a man:

a) turn up naked

b) bring a naked double-jointed supermodel who owns a brewery and has an open-minded twin sister

c) wrestle in mud

12 Declaration of War

Shelly wasn't sure how she looked dressed as a Love Slave in fishnet tights, a leather bustier and a zebra skin genital thong, but she was pretty sure it wasn't safe and predictable.

If Kit was shocked by Shelly's Sex Goddess transmogrification, he certainly didn't show it. The man didn't even blink when he caught sight of her in the poolside cabana hammock curled up with the entertainment officer. To her disappointment, Kit said nothing, just cocked his head, as though listening to the rock 'n' roll seeping out from the Fancy Dress Ball inside La Caravelle. The music had been so loud it had made Shelly's vital organs do cartwheels (one should always be suspicious of music which sounds better drunk than sober). But here, in the cabana, the cacophony of people dressed as Teletubbies and Tina Turner, singing "Love Me Do" and dancing the "swim" and the "hitchhiker" in silly, satirical ways had been thankfully drowned out by the racket of the tropical storm.

"You do realize Dominic's only usin' you to get his ugly mug

179

on TV," Kit finally called out. The flaming torches around the cabana sputtered in the fierce wind, as if indignant on Shelly's behalf.

Dominic flared his Gallic nostrils. "*Pardon, monsieur.* Our friendship eez best described by the great essayist Montaigne. 'Because I was I and she was she.' And now, as a seal of authenticity, I must give you what ze English poet Keats calls slippery blisses," he said, brushing Shelly ever so lightly on the lips. Shelly immediately shivered, whereupon Dominic shed his leather jacket and tucked it around her.

"You see?" Shelly snuggled into the jacket. "This is what lovers *do*. They give you their coats when you're cold," she lectured Kit as he approached. "They quote *poetry*. They *woo* you. They are suave and charming and thoughtful and intellectual. The opposite of *you*. *You*, Kinkade, are just an animal."

"Hey, the animal kingdom is an improvement on the vegetable kingdom," Kit said, staring pointedly at the entertainment officer. "Listen, Love Slave"—he reached under the jacket and tugged on Shelly's thong—"I need to talk to you, privately."

"*Need?* Well, I have needs too. Which are being met, thank you very much, for the first time since I bloody well got married." She turned her back on Kit and nestled into Dominic.

"Well, thank God I arrived in time to save you from havin' a whole range of hideous bacterial organisms introduced into your reproductive system." Kit rolled Shelly back to face him—and not gently either. "When Dominic says that he's a liberated male, fully aware of women's intellectual, sexual, emotional and economic oppression, and totally embarrassed by his fellow Male Supremacist Chauvinists—that's just a long-winded Frog way of sayin', 'How 'bout it, babe?'"

"What's it to you, anyway?" Shelly swung her feet onto the ground and faced him.

"Um, we are married, you might recall. All this time you've been questionin' *my* fidelity, when *you're* the one who's bein' unfaithful."

"*Me?*" Shelly pulled Dominic's coat around her shoulders. "Well, do the math. You have *two* tickets from Heathrow and *two* to Madagascar. Explain that for me."

Kit glanced anxiously at Dominic to ascertain whether he had absorbed this information. But the entertainment officer was busy trying to sip his Montrachet while balancing himself on one elbow in the hammock.

"Oh, are you sure that wine is *chambréd?*" Kit asked him sarcastically. "That's how Shelly prefers it, you know. Room temperature." And then he tipped the hammock with his foot, spilling wine all over Shelly's paramour and capsizing him floor-wards.

"Oh, sooooo sorry."

"*Merde!*" Dominic replied before stomping off to Le Centre de Plonge for a beach towel.

Shelly sighed. "It would be so much easier if you men had antlers. It's a real design fault, don't you think?"

"I came lookin' for you to explain about the tickets," Kit said quietly. "I'm sorry I scammed you. But I've been broke for so long. Yep, I finally found out that there actually is somethin' money can't buy—*destitution*. Truth is, I had to use the prize money to pay back pals and loan sharks. Which is why I cashed in my return ticket for two economy singles, then sold one ticket to some guy on standby. And why I didn't have any cash for Coco's bail."

"Then what about Madagascar?"

"A surprise for you. A real honeymoon. A honeymoon from our honeymoon. Where we can get to know each other without the pryin' eyes of Gaby's camera and the whole United Kingdom gawkin' at us. It's true that in the beginnin' all I wanted was the money. Hell, I didn't wanna like you. God knows I've had enough woman trouble in my life! And Christ! You are so infuriatin' . . . but you're also kinda funny. And hot. Every time we kiss, I get this, like, endorphin-high. Jesus. You've made me feel so high, so often, I can now qualify for frequent-flier points. Truth is, I've never met anyone quite like you, Shelly Green . . . and, well, I wanna know more."

His face was chiaroscuro in the light from the flaming torches. Shelly couldn't quite read his expression. But she liked what she was hearing. "Go on," she said, tautly.

"You just keep makin' the mercury level rise on my romance-o-meter. But I didn't wanna tell you until it was all arranged. Especially on the boat, in front of Coco. Until I was sure you wanted to go. And sure that you wouldn't say nuthin' to nobody. You haven't, have you? . . . Said anythin'?" he asked, a beseeching look in his irresistible green eyes.

Shelly shook her head in answer to his question. She also shook it in disbelief at his story. She viewed the notion that Kit Kinkade really had feelings for her a little the way the world viewed Michael Jackson claiming he hadn't had cosmetic surgery. The guy had more nerve than an unfilled tooth. There was no way she would ever again fall for any of his vagabond's lies. No bloody way.

"Really? The ticket's for me?"

God! Who was scripting this marriage? Why did she keep forgiving him? Well, it could have something to do with her previous boyfriends. The cellist from the Academy, whose instrument was between his legs more often than she was. The sensuously lipped flautist from school . . . but a girl can't survive for long with a man who plays the descant recorder first thing in the morning. Then there was the dating tumbleweed that had been blowing through her life since then. And the horror of going back to blind dates, with their god-awful, orbital loop of cocktail small talk, those endless conversational ringroads with no destination in sight. That must be why she wanted so hard to believe Kit. Like all lonely women suffering from affection deficiencies, she'd tried to read the writing on the wall—but it seemed to be in Sanskrit.

"Really? You want me to go with you?" she heard herself saying again, her voice wavering. (Warning! Moth; think flame.)

When he touched her arm, she felt anointed by his attention and her resolve melted like butter in the tropical sun. Hey—why interrupt her journey to the center of Self-Annihilation? In the limo, Kit had asked her what she had to lose. Oh, nothing much, she reprimanded herself now. *Only self-respect, life savings and sanity.*

Shelly shrugged off his hand abruptly. "Sorry, but I've just checked the old mercury level on our romance-o-meter and actually we're legally dead, boyo."

Dominic reappeared now, wearing his costume for the ball—a matching His 'n' Her S&M ensemble including leather trousers and studded dog collar. To his amazed pleasure, Shelly pulled him down into the hammock and nuzzled his neck with vampiric enthusiasm.

Kit threw his eyes up to heaven, and in so doing spotted Gaby and crew bustling through the rain beneath umbrellas towards them in the cabana.

"Fuck me naked." He flinched. "This is *all* I need."

Bursting into the cabana, Gaby shook the water from her hair. "Shelly! Dominic! There you are! I've been looking for you lovebirds everywhere." She beckoned Silent Mike to come closer with his phallic boom. "So, a rather surprisingly erotic twist to my doco, sorry, my disaster movie, don't you think, Kinkade? Do you have anything to say to the nation?" She motioned for Towtruck to swivel his camera onto the rejected groom.

"Yeah, well, I kinda do get the feelin' my wife may be losin' interest in me."

"Oh? What makes you say that?" Gaby probed.

"Well, she seems to be lickin' the jack boot of a leather-jock-strapped sexual dominator with gold nipple rings—on our honeymoon."

"Forgive him, viewers," Shelly said straight down the lens. "After all, the man does have double standards to uphold."

"At least I *am* a man. That thing you're kissin' is practically pubescent. What are you gonna do—date him or adopt him?"

"There's nothing wrong with going for a younger man . . . As you men never mature, it doesn't really matter anyway, does it?" Shelly retaliated.

"Look, I really need to have a heart-to-heart."

"Really? But what are *you* going to use?"

"Privately," Kit urged, ignoring her barb and the televisual voyeurs.

"No fucking way," cried Gaby. "Ms. Green is wanted on set. She now has a new part to play . . . a romance in which the man is not the pigeon and the woman the statue!"

"For old times' sake," Kit pleaded.

"Huh!" Shelly scoffed. "What 'old times'?"

"It's just a quick chat, Shelly. It's not like I'm askin' you to test-pilot a stealth bomber."

"That would be easier," she moaned with annoyance, but eventually harrumphed up out of the hammock.

"You'll come with me then?"

"Of course I'll come with you. How else can I hit you over the head with a coconut, push you into the pool and make it look like a drowning accident?" Shelly had begun to understand that there is indeed a very fine line between sexual frustration and homicide.

"My passport, plane tickets and all my money's missin'," Kit blurted once they'd relocated to the far end of the cabana. "There's only one person who had a key—Coco."

"Coco? You gave Coco a key? Why would you give Coco a key?" Usually there was only one reason a man ever gave a woman a key to his room—and it wasn't to hem a curtain.

Despite the poor woman's bruises, Shelly had become addicted to hating Coco. Until tonight she'd only hated her in social situations, but from now on she'd be hating her up to one hundred times a day. Put it this way: if the Taliban invaded the island and nobody told Coco and she happened to decide to take an unsuspecting saunter down the main street in a micro mini, *I wouldn't much mind,* Shelly confessed to herself.

"She needed to hide from Gaspard. But the bitch has ripped me off. There's no other explanation. I know right now she's in the hotel gym. I can't get past security to the women's staff quarters. But *you* can . . ."

"Was Coco the person you were going to take to Madagascar?" Shelly said with sudden, sad insight. "God. That's the only reason you're pretending you wanted to take me, isn't it? To dupe me into getting back your bloody tickets." Kit wasn't a Trojan Horse, he was the Trojan Man. She'd allowed him to be wheeled into her fortress, thinking he was a gift, only to find him full of tricks.

185

"Shelly." He held her by the hips and turned her towards him. While Dominic was all polished poise and practiced seduction, Kit had a languorous, instinctive charm. If only she could stop thinking of that agile tongue of his, the sort of tongue that could lick insects off leaves. And of the way he'd devoured her with such salacious rapture, just as he'd eaten that mango on the beach.

"And why would I want to help you anyway?"

"Well, to get back your bail money for one. Charges against Coco were dropped in court. Your cash is in my friggin' wallet."

"Oh shit," Shelly responded eloquently. Only three days of this horrid honeymoon to go, she thought, steeling herself: unless I get lucky and *die*.

"I'll explain everythin', okay, but only after you find my stuff. There's no time now. Just believe me. It's a matter of life and death."

Kit spoke with such urgency, his face working with emotion, that Shelly felt her determination give out, like elastic in your oldest cottontail underpants—the kind of underpants Coco wouldn't have, of course. It also crossed Shelly's mind how satisfying it would be to prove to Kit that a man should never trust a woman who has no period pants—which was why, ten minutes later, she was in the women's staff quarters, hiding behind her Love Slave sunglasses. She tried not to laugh at the sign on the gate, which read: "Because of the impropriety of entertaining guests of the opposite sex in the bedrooms, it is suggested that the lobby be used for this purpose."

The lone sentry pointed out Coco's cabin on the first floor. Moments later she was listening like a cleaning lady at a keyhole. There was no sound from within. And no light. Her heart around her tonsils, Shelly turned the doorknob and entered the room of her nemesis.

The first thing she realized is that an ankle is just a device for finding coffee tables in the dark. Trying not to whelp with pain, she asked herself how the hell Kit had talked her into this. She couldn't trust herself to stay away from the man. She would have to put out a restraining order on herself. She would have to have herself followed by a private eye to prevent her from doing dumb-ass things like breaking and entering into the bedroom of a—the light flicked on—*psychotic maniac.*

Coco was standing in the center of the room in flamingo-pink underwear, pointing a small handgun directly at Shelly's chest.

"Christ Almighty! What's with the gun? I know it's tourist season, Coco, but I don't think that means you're actually supposed to shoot us!"

"I thought you might be Gaspard. Zis is my contraceptive. My, 'ow you say, 'safe sex.' "

"Give me Kit's passport and tickets and money. Which you stole. Unbelievable! After all he's done for you, it wasn't very nice, was it?" *Very nice?* That Royal Academy Classical Education was standing her in good stead again.

"I am sorry, but zat is not part of ze plan."

"Well, I don't suppose Dominic waiting for me by the pool was part of your plan either. But if I'm not back in five minutes, he's getting the manager."

"Dominic? You think 'e is waiting for *you?*" Coco eyed Shelly's thong and fishnet tights. "You are making me laugh! Why don't you take your sunglasses off, so zat you can see 'ow very ridiculous you look."

Shelly snatched off the shades, which she'd forgotten she was wearing. "For your information, Dominic finds me very attractive."

"Yes, well, alcohol will do zat to men."

A great rage welled up in Shelly. She lunged at Coco's hair, yanking with all her might at those famous black tendrils.

Shelly didn't see Coco's foot coming, just the wall which she was suddenly hurling, alarmingly, towards. As she lay splattered and dazed on the floor, she realized, groggily, that her blood seemed to be on the wrong side of her skin. And that that couldn't be good.

The sight of a gun-toting Amazon bearing down on a not particularly courageous classical female guitarist had the predictable effect. Shelly screamed, for all her worth.

Coco clamped her hand over Shelly's mouth. Shelly sunk her teeth into the singer's hand, forcing her to drop her gun. Shelly lunged for it, but Coco stepped on her arm, nailing her to the floor like a butterfly specimen on a display board. Coco muttered something which Shelly presumed was French for "say good-bye to your ovaries, darling." Frantic, she groped for whatever she could grasp. A can of underarm deodorant, it turned out, with which she maced Coco's eyes. The woman fell to the floor and writhed, head in hands. Shelly would have offered to see if there was a homeopath in the house, but there was nothing hippy trippy about Coco now. The woman was more like Boadicea with PMT.

Shelly used Coco's distress to grab the gun, and then to retrieve Kit's passport, wallet and tickets from the Prada bag by Coco's bed. There was the sound of footsteps in the corridor outside and the hall lights snapped on. Coco, her eyes streaming, disengaged and bounded, Bolshoi Ballet-esquely, right out of the first-floor window.

Shelly had no choice but to follow suit—but with less gazelle-like grace. Even though she knew the real achievement would be not shooting herself in the foot, *literally*, she stowed the gun and the documents down her fishnet tights, gingerly lowered her legs over the window ledge, then sort of avalanched down the side of the building, clawing at awnings and tree branches and finally thudding into a rain puddle, ten feet below, in a jumbled heap.

From her horizontal position, the lopsided moon looked drunk and jaundiced in the cloudy sky, but gave just enough light for her to discern Coco's lithe figure, darting through the shadows towards the beach in her luminous underwear. When Shelly, wincing and winded from her fall, finally made it to the inky water's edge, the gale shuddered against her face so forcefully it made further pursuit impossible. All she could see through the deluge were the lozenges of light from a large sailing vessel. The clipper, brought in for the colonization re-enactment ceremony, was yanking at its chain in the big sea, banging against the Blue Safari 800, a tourist mini sub gifted by the French government for the auspicious occasion.

Shelly limped back towards the pool hammock, but Dominic and Gaby's camera crew had retreated indoors. She paused beneath the cabana lights to examine the bounty for which she'd risked her life. She flicked open the passport. There was a picture of Kit, looking piratical. (Christ, even his passport photo was attractive, she sighed, whereas *hers* looked like she'd just been arrested for bludgeoning badgers.) And beneath? When Shelly dropped her eyes to the bottom of the page, she exhaled a breath which sounded like a tire going flat.

Beneath Kit's photo, in tight black text, was printed somebody else's name.

Shelly felt the flicker of a migraine forming in her left temple. To Kit Kinkade, truth was not just stranger than fiction, it was a total stranger.

She stood there in the wind and the rain, dumbfounded by his latest deceit, completely lost in thought—which, Shelly had to admit, was proving to be totally unfamiliar territory of late. She scanned Kit's photogenic features. You're supposed to be able to read Americans like a book, but her Yankee husband was proving positively hieroglyphic. Why was he always so secretive? Like a spy. She didn't know who Kit was working for, but she had a pretty strong suspicion it was the enemy.

The Differences
Between the Sexes:
Positions

Men think that "Mutual Orgasm" is an insurance company.

Which is why a woman's favorite position in bed is doggy style—he begs like a dog while she rolls over and plays dead.

13 Double Agent

"Rupert Rochester of Ruttington—*Baron*? You're called Rupert Rochester?"—Then, more slowly, "And you're a bloody *baron*?"

"You know, you really shouldn't wander around after dusk wearin' your wallet on your sleeve." These were Kit's first words upon finding her peering at his passport beneath the cabana torch lights, his wallet lying discarded at her feet. Kit picked it up and rummaged through it, relieved to find all the cash accounted for.

"Rupert Rochester?" Shelly repeated, numbly.

"Oh. Ah. Well, yeah," he said casually. "Didn't I mention that I'm travelin' under a false name?"

"Of Ruttington? Baron?"

Her husband seemed to be able to shed identities with snake-like ease. Who was this man? Her spouse wavered in the heat of her scrutiny. The truth about him was proving harder to find than Calista Flockhart's pantry. Like all good con men, Kit knew to both conceal and reveal at the same time. It was psychological sleight of hand.

"Why?"

"'Cause, um, well—that's my married name."

"You're *married*?" The word jolted through her. "To someone besides me? What are you? A *mormon*? I'm pretty sure question number one on the entry form was, '*Are you single*?'!"

"Well, mentally, emotionally and physically I'm single. But technically I *am* married, yeah."

"So you're a"—she tried to rev up her stalled brain and put it back into gear—"a bigamist?" Kit had thrown not a wrench but an entire toolbox into the works.

"Hey, it sounds more excitin' than it is. In reality, it just doubles your chances of havin' to take the garbage out."

A few responses occurred to Shelly simultaneously.

1) Why couldn't she see his lobotomy scar?

2) How the hell did he fit his cloven hooves into those running shoes?

3) Flee!

With option number 3 seeming the most sensible under the Salt-Lake-City-esque circumstances, Shelly spun on her heel and bolted as fast as her jarred ankle would take her, through the driving rain, back into her bungalow, where she deadlocked the door behind her. She'd been in a fog. But the fog was starting to lift. Kit Kinkade had merely been orchestrating her emotions and she had played along, as though responding to some invisible conductor's baton. But this latest revelation had cooled her ardor to the temperature of a polar pond.

Oh, thank you, vagina! she raged at her body organ. Thank you for getting me into this. She thought about disconnecting her sexuality. Yes! That was it. She just wouldn't pay the bills. She would ignore the reminder notes in red ink. She would allow her libido to be cut off. There was a knock at the door. But having renounced sex, she was a free person. She would simply ignore it, then leave first thing in the morning to live in a cave somewhere and study calligraphy.

Kit was still knocking at her door. "I know it looks bad, but really it's not what you think. Let me in, Shelly. Give me a chance to explain."

"Go away, *Rupert!*" Shelly stashed the gun at the back of her underwear drawer, changed out of her ridiculous outfit and, taking a pack of cigarettes from the minibar, ripped it open and lit up. And this was a woman who didn't even smoke.

"Just open the door and let me in out of the goddamn rain. It's a total downpour. I'm gettin' drenched out here!"

"Well, I'm getting bleeps on my psycho-radar in *here*."

"I'll come clean, okay? Please, Shelly, come on. Lemme explain."

"Piss off, Kit. I don't know how else to say it . . . except perhaps with a *stun gun*."

"I *do* have a wife, worst luck. Though you're welcome to refer to her by her real name: Spawn of Satan."

"The picture in the wallet," Shelly deduced. She slumped against the door, placing her ear near the keyhole while puffing frantically on her cigarette. She was pretty sure that was what she'd seen people do in movies whenever they seemed on the brink of stabbing a swizzle stick into a temporal lobe. "Go on. I'm listening."

"Like I told you, I went on hiatus from that crappy soap opera and hit the backpackers' trail: Kathmandu, Goa, Koh Samui, Chiang Mai, Marrakech, Bali, Bondi . . . I met Pandora in Koh Samui. She was a Trustafarian, bummin' around the world. We had some crazy adventures. It brought us together, you know? And, I guess, the attraction of being so opposite too. When goin' travelin' I got inoculated against malaria, typhoid and hepatitis . . . but not against Pandora-itis."

"Look, could we do this in fifty words or less?" Shelly asked frostily through the door. After all, she had a hermit's cave to get to. "So how did she become so toxic? This 'wife' of yours?"

"Okay. The shortened version. Can I come in? I'm still gettin' real wet out here."

"Good!" Shelly shouted through the door. If she had her way, he'd also be whipped raw with a salt-soaked rope, and pegged, twitching, in the sand for the crabs, like the true pirate he was.

"It was a mistake. We married within two measley months. We had to get hitched fast to avoid immigration hassles. Then Pandora's brother was killed in some drug-related incident and she inherited the stately pile—"

"What's *that?* A royal's hemorrhoid?" Shelly puffed cinematically on her cancer stick in a caustic, Lauren Bacall kind of way.

"Ha ha. From that moment on she started to change. No more laughin' at my stupid jokes. She started criticizin' my clothes, my music. She enrolled me in elo-fuckin'-cution classes. She made me give up my buddies and only hang out with her snobbish pals: 'I'll let you play with *my* hyphen if I can play with *yours.*'"

"Oh poor boy, my heart bleeds," taunted Shelly. "Forced to go social climbing when he had no head for heights. Call Amnesty International."

"It may be news to you, Shelly, but when someone you love turns on you, well, it's a kinda out-of-body experience." (Tell me about it, she muttered, incinerated in a cloud of cigarette smoke.)

"'Denial,' I think shrinks call it," Kit elaborated.

"Yeah, yeah," Shelly ho-hummed. "That thing that's not just a river in Egypt."

"I remember feelin' that I wanted to just crawl into an ashtray and die. I'd adored her so much."

Shelly groaned contemptuously. "Just wait while I turn down *The Jerry Springer Show* so that I can hear you better . . . Oh! Wait! It *is* you. If you loved her so much then why didn't you try to save the marriage?"

"I did, goddamn it! I read all the books, saw all the therapists. *She*, meanwhile, was lookin' for a recipe that would best disguise the taste of strychnine. Although, would it really matter? *Now that I'm about to die of pneumonia?*"

Why should she believe him? This was just another case of Nothing but the Truth, the Whole Truth, the *Varnished* Truth.

"So." Shelly put her head into her hands. "You want me to believe that after all the dangers you've survived on your travels—the avalanches, by tumbling with the snow and swimming to keep at the top; the forest fires, by heading into the wind and jumping over the flames; the tornadoes, by staying at right angles to its course; the lightning storms, by lying flat on the ground; the snake bites, the hypothermia, the earthquakes—you couldn't survive one puny little marriage to a pissant trustafarian?"

"Spare me the Third Degree Sarcasm, Shelly. I got enough of that at the goddamn Stately Pile. Look. Bottom line. In marriage you can survive without love, but there's got to be like."

"Go on," Shelly mumbled, snidely, almost inhaling her whole cigarette in one breath. "By now she won't even talk to your *plants* unless it's through her solicitor, right?"

"Right. What I didn't know about the upper-class English," Kit persevered, "is that they don't marry for love. There's always a lifeguard by their gene pool, ya know? Pandora only married me to get back at her dad. She never stopped talkin' about what a rip-off artist he was."

"Ho hum," Shelly yawned. "The old 'family tree full of sap' routine. You'll have to do better than that, Kinkade."

"Oh, believe me, I wanna do just that. That's why I left. Anyway, when her corrupt old man dies of a heart attack—shock, Pandora reckons, after her big brother OD'd—Pandora takes over his company."

"And?"

"Let's just say that she's now followin' in her father's fingerprints."

"You can talk, *Rupert*. None of this explains your false name."

"Oh that. Well, at the time Pandora was worried about my drug conviction in the States, and . . . "

"*Drug conviction*? A bigamist fraudster who is also a wanted felon with a drug conviction?" Shelly sucked so hard on the ciggie she nearly swallowed it. "Oh, this just gets better and better."

"Only for Ecstasy."

"Well, *that's* a relief," she said, her voice dripping in disdain.

"Pandora thought my drug conviction would hinder her world travels, so she got me a false passport. When I married her in Thailand, it was under the name she'd chosen—Rupert Rochester. She added the Baron bit to impress her chinless pals. But Kit Kinkade's my real name. Anyway, what I'm tryin' to say, Shelly, is that I made a dumb-ass mistake. I wanna start over. It was only because I was broke and desperate that . . ."

"You thought you could parlay a spontaneous wedding and tropical honeymoon into an all-expenses-paid escape route from England," Shelly clarified, huffily.

"Well, yeah, basically."

"Which is why you were wearin' that blonde wig when we got married?"

"Well, um, yeah. I've always found the best way to deal with any crisis is to stand firm, face your fears, *then lie your goddamn head off.*"

Shelly cross-examined him further. "What about Gaby's film footage? You're not in disguise now. If you're on the run, won't a prime-time slot on T.V. slightly blow your cover?"

"By the time her shitty show's screened in England, I'll be safely in Madagascar where no one can find me. But I can't get gone until we get the rest of our cash from Gaby tomorrow."

"So what you're telling me is that basically you've just been using me! This whole bloody time!"

"Well, initially yeah. I confess. I was desperate! I had no choice but to pull somethin' out of a hat and see if it'd hop. But then, well, I . . . I got feelin's for you."

"And I got a nervous breakdown!" Husbands are Novocaine for the soul, Shelly thought, igniting another cigarette from the butt of the last. "Why should I believe anything you tell me?"

"Occasionally a husband makes the transition to person, you know. I could make you really happy, Shelly."

"Why? Are you leaving?"

"Yeah, with you. To Madagascar. Just as soon as you give me those tickets."

"Me? With you? To Madagascar! No way. I'm never going anywhere with any man ever again."

"Yeah, yeah, I know. Your mom was right all along—all men are bastards and all women are wonderful."

"Listen, Kinkade, I'm not angry because I'm a woman, I'm angry because you are a prick!"

"You accused *me* of actin' like a woman, right? Well, *you're* actin' like a guy. Here I am, pledgin' myself to you. Only to discover that you're too scared of commitment. You are just a sex-change waitin' to happen, j'know that?!"

"I do *not* have trouble with commitment! Commitment is what got me into trouble in the first place! Commit. Commit. My only commitment will be to an institution for the criminally insane for ever allowing myself to marry *you*."

"Okay, your old man let you down. And you got hurt. So now to prevent bein' let down by a man ever again, you must sabotage our romance, by tellin' yourself you don't love me anymore."

"That's not true!" Shelly paused for dramatic effect. "I never loved you in the first place."

"Open the door and say that to my face."

She opened the door. And said it to his face.

And he said, "Can I kiss you?"

"Only if I can leave my cigarette in my mouth."

He manacled her wrists and pushed her back against the door-jamb, grinding his hard body against her hips. He tore the cigarette out of her mouth and kissed her so long and so lusciously that when he finally pulled away, she had to check she still had her pants on.

"What would you say if I took you to bed?" he said, his eyes sparkling with dark desires and wicked notions.

"I'd say I can't talk and laugh at the same time," she replied, pushing him away. She could control her lust. She must. What was she otherwise? Just an organism. A blind, brainless sea cucumber like the ones she'd seen on the ocean floor.

"Is that right? Here's the moolah you lent me, by the way." He pressed the money into her hand, but didn't let go. "Oh—look at those bumps and bruises! Oh honey. Did you get those on my behalf?" Kit ran a long, cool finger delicately up her arm. "I diagnose complete bed rest for at least a week. Doctor's orders."

"Oh right, *doctor*. Another lie. You know, I'd rather have a lethal injection of Ozzy Osbourne's bathwater than go to bed with you," Shelly said, but she didn't squirm free.

"You can't deny yourself affection, Shelly. How can you? It's like denyin' yourself oxygen. The mortality rate of women who have a lot of sex is less than half of gals who don't. Sex also gives a woman better resistance to stress, clearer skin, increased tolerance to pain, improved circulation, stronger bones, memory enhancement, less chance of heart disease and healthier breasts."

"How the hell do *you* know?"

"The doctor I played in that soap was a gynecologist." Kit smiled, breezily. "I know your mom taught you to resist males, but I could teach you a different sort of Male Resistance trainin' altogether . . . the contraction of the vaginal muscles durin' orgasm."

"Oh." There was that Oh again. Her heart was skipping beats like a boxer in training. "So, what . . . what would a doctor prescribe for these abrasions of mine, do you think?"

"Full stomach-to-stomach resuscitation," he said, as he tenderly kissed each scratch on her arms. Her body gave in straightaway. Traitor! she said to her crotch as it moistened insubordinately. Kit scooped her up in his arms and carried her to the bed. His body was solidified light—all pure energy and heat. What chance did a woman stand? The man was the Sperminator—melting all logic and self-restraint in his sensuous wake. As soon as he had placed her upon the pillows he was licking and sucking her with the sort of sibilant exuberance men usually reserve for a plate of oysters. If she'd been able to talk, she would have quipped that she was oysters on the half Shell-y. When he laid his body on hers, feelings exploded in her like champagne. As Shelly Green finally, breathlessly, moved towards the consummation of her marriage, a long, low sigh escaped from her parted lips—as though she'd just reached the next level of Ashtanga yoga meditation.

It looked for one storm-tossed moment as though their leaky marriage might just make it to shore. Nothing could stop them now . . .

WE INTERRUPT THIS SEDUCTION TO BRING YOU A NEWS BULLETIN.

The sound was deafening and terrifying—the unmistakable, dull thud of a bomb. Kit sprang to the window, half-naked. "The re-enactment ship! It's on fire. Must be the Liberation Front."

With cunnilingus on offer, Shelly found herself curiously indifferent to political reform. She called him back to bed. She was primed now for some meaty lovemaking, festive and zealous. She would have an aphrodisiacal, paradisiacal consummation and she would have it *now*, terrorist attack or no terrorist attack, goddamn it!

But Kit didn't return. Reluctantly she threaded her arms into his shirt and joined him on the balcony. The dock was alight also, great tongues of flame licking skywards. The heat ignited the fireworks, which had been set up for the re-enactment celebration but postponed because of the winds. The stormy sky was suddenly a phantasmagoria of fizzing lights.

The manager was scurrying around on the beach below Shelly's bungalow, alerting nobody in particular that the mini sub was being stolen. "*Le sub! Le sub!*" The distant whah-whah screech of sirens heralded the arrival of the ambulances and police cars. There was pandemonium below as guests from the fancy-dress party at La Caravelle ran towards the beach to check what had happened. Shelly watched as four Abba-lookalikes collided on the path beneath her balcony and crumpled on top of each other. They were immediately pinned down by a giant armadillo who'd tripped over them and was now trying not to be disconcerted by the fact that his nose was slotted up President Bush's bottom.

"I gotta go back to my room," Kit announced, abruptly.

"What! *Now*? Why?" Shelly followed him back inside.

"Have you got the passport and tickets?"

"Yes, but . . ." She looked at Kit, bewildered. "I don't know if you're aware of this, but your husband is not supposed to lose interest in you sexually until *after* you've consummated your bloody marriage!"

"I am *not* losin' interest in you sexually. How can you say that?" He licked his lips, pointedly.

"Gee, I dunno. Maybe it has something to do with the fact that during sex I looked up to notice that my husband *was in another bungalow!*"

"Sorry. It's an emergency, Shelly. I've gotta go." With brusque urgency, he ripped his shirt off her body, and stabbed his arms into the sleeves.

"I'll go with you, then." Shelly reached for a pair of jeans.

"No."

She froze. The mechanically chilled air of the hotel room went clammy. "*No*?"

He looked at the floor, caught up in some private darkness.

"Why? What are you hiding *this* time?" Under the surface of his daily life was a whole other life that Kit lived, as if underwater. "Tell me. Explain yourself."

Kit was guiltily cracking his knuckles as though to punish his hand. "What would you like for dinner, Shelly? A can of worms? 'Cause that's what you're gonna get if you keep interrogatin' me like this."

"Fine. Let's ring room service then, shall we? . . . Waiter!" she shouted into the phone. "One can-of-worms-opener please!"

"Whereja put my passports and stuff?" He started ransacking her room.

"You are not leaving until you tell me what the hell's going on." Shelly barred the door.

Kit ran an agitated hand through his hair. "You'll just have to trust me."

The "T" word again. Hmmm. Truth and trust—weren't they the first casualties *in a time of war*? It seemed Shelly's only option was to undertake her own undercover work. She meekly handed over his hidden documents and let him out. She dressed quickly and then silently left the bungalow, shadowing him. Together they dodged police, firefighters, hysterical guests and falling coconuts from the storm-tattered trees, but he remained oblivious to his stalker. Eventually they reached his bungalow on the other side of the resort. Outside his door there were room-service plates and she noted, with rising panic, that they were meals for two.

The moment he turned the key in the lock, she was beside him, seizing his elbow. "Who the hell are you hiding in there? Coco? Your mysterious standby traveling companion? Elvis Presley? Osama Bin Bloody Laden?"

Before he could stop her, Shelly Green pushed past him and burst into the room. She stood, transfixed with surprise, dripping rainwater on the carpet. The TV was on; a *Simpsons* rerun. A Creole woman had risen in alarm at Shelly's abrupt entrance. But this was not what skewered Shelly with amazement. Sitting on the floor in front of the TV, chewing crisps in open-mouthed absorption, was a little girl, aged about eight.

Shelly reeled around to face Kit, who was hard on her heels.

He paused, not knowing what to say, then shrugged, fatalistically. "Shelly, meet my daughter, Matilda."

"You're a . . . a father?" she asked, flabbergasted. The revelation cleaved her cranium like an ax.

"Yep."

Shelly shook her head vigorously as though trying to dislodge swimming water from her ear.

"So, not only am I a wife but a *stepmother*?" She had a coughing fit worthy of Keats before collapsing onto the bed. "Jesus Christ. I teach children all day. I'm allergic to children. On certain days I absolutely hate them."

Matilda eyed her suspiciously, rose from the floor, approached Shelly and kicked her hard on the shin.

It was obviously the start of a beautiful friendship.

The Differences Between the Sexes: Admitting You're Wrong

Men can never admit they are wrong.

Women can admit they are wrong . . . starting with having chosen a guy who can't.

14 Classified Information

"Matty, this is a friend of mine—Shelly. I know it may look as though we don't get on—"

"But deep down, we loathe each other!" The muscles in Shelly's throat had knotted and her voice came out half-strangled. "Why didn't you tell me you have a child?"

"'Cause you're always sayin' you don't like kids. Somethin' to do with their unpredictable defecatory habits, wasn't it?" Kit scooped Matilda up into his arms and kissed her devotedly. She was a rangy kid, all limbs and flying hair. He ruffled her curls, which were the color of lemon sorbet. "I heard you tell Gaby that children are just the things that stand between adults and the DVD movie they're watchin'."

Kit's child turned a furtive, intelligent face in Shelly's direction and assessed her, coolly. She had caramel freckles and green eyes, just like her dad.

Shelly rubbed her shin where the kid had kicked her. "Silly of me, huh, not to understand the craze for parenthood! Listen, *Kit* or *Rupert* or whoever the *hell* you are." She wrenched Kit's shirtsleeve. "You've f—" she glanced at Matilda before censoring herself. "You've f-u-c-k-e-d me around quite enough. I want the truth. And I want it now. You owe me that much."

"Daddy, why is that lady s-p-e-l-l-i-n-g stuff?" was Matilda's wry response.

Kit looked at Shelly, slack-faced, dead-eyed, with all the fight gone out of him. "Okay." Kit thanked the baby-sitter, paid her some money and let her out. He gave his daughter a blanketing embrace before cozily tucking her beneath the bedcovers in her room and turning off the TV. "Night, night," he said, tenderly.

And so, finally, with the wind howling, the sirens wailing, the police shouting and the fireworks detonating, Kit Kinkade stopped lying. On the balcony, closing the door to ensure they were beyond earshot of Matty, he sat Shelly down on a sun-lounger and began his confession. Shelly watched and listened, steeling herself for a body blow.

"The woman lookin' after Matty is the mom of Coco's boyfriend. The one who was killed. A year ago. When I arrived here ahead of you and the crew with the kid, I knew I'd have to confide in someone. I also needed a baby-sitter, so Coco helped me out. That's why she had the key to my room. I gave her some money—to keep her sweet. That's where most of my prize money's gone—into payoffs and bribes. You can understand now why I had to get Coco bailed out. I didn't want her tellin' Gaspard that I was hidin' a kid. You can never really trust a revolutionary. To save her ass, she might have told the cops. And I couldn't put Matty in danger." He sighed resignedly. "I've looked after my daughter since she was born. Nursed her through teethin', chicken pox, measles, the works . . . But the more I loved Matty, the more Pandora hated me."

In the distance, thunder rumbled—as though indignant on Kit's behalf. Shelly looked at him, confounded. God, how many more layers were there to this man? What was he? An *artichoke*?

"Anyways, about a month ago, Pandora gave me this ultimatum. She said that our Jagger 'n' Jerry–type Hindu weddin' in Thailand wasn't legally bindin'. If I agreed to take £100,000 for full and final settlement and go back to the States, she would 'probably' allow me to see Matty once a year. She said there'd be no more money 'cause I hadn't 'earned my way into her life.' Even when she talks about emotions, she does so in money terms." Anxiety zigzagged across his flawless forehead, creasing it with worry lines. "I didn't want her lousy cash. But I knew I'd die without my kid! Pandora might as well have just cut my dick off."

"Gives a whole new meaning to severance pay," Shelly said, disdainfully. Why the hell should she believe him this time?

"I told her I'd never give up Matty. I told her I'd get custody." He was pacing back and forth across the tiny balcony. "Well, she just laughed in my face. She said I'd never get custody 'cause she would say that I was an unfit father. She threatened to tell the courts about my drug conviction." The sky opened up, as if in the throes of sorrow. "And then there was the group sex thing in Phuket."

"An orgy. But of course!" Shelly groaned. Fretful rhythms of rain on the bungalow roof reflected her own agitation.

"I reminded her that she was in that orgy too. 'Yes,' she then said to me, 'but I wasn't stoned enough to allow anyone like me to take photos.' . . . We were a couple of kids havin' fun. But she can twist everythin' to make me look evil. She said she'd lie and they'd believe her, 'cause she's establishment. All her uncles are judges. She told me if I didn't do as she asked and get the hell out of her life, she'd make sure I never ever saw Matty again. Then she told me she was leavin' the country on business for a month and for me to think over her 'kind offer' while she was gone."

Shelly studied her chameleon husband in the half-light. He was a chaos of contradictions: one minute all bad-boy bravado—and now doting dad? But she'd fallen for enough of his tall tales. "Then what happened?" she asked suspiciously.

"To add to her charmin' ways, she then left the country, closed all the accounts, stopped payin' the bills. Suddenly I couldn't get gas for the car. I couldn't even buy food. There I was, marooned in Sainsbury's, my credit card rejected at the counter. I was forced to try to arrange financin' on a few lamb chops at ten percent," he said, making a halfhearted stab at jocularity. "I took to hauntin' the Harrods food hall just to see what protein looked like. The Tooth Fairy was takin' IOU's . . . "

But Shelly's mood was as gloomy as the sky. She shivered, gathering her clothes more tightly around her. "Go on."

"When Pandora rang to see if I'd become desperate enough to accept her terms, I swore I'd just tell the courts about how tight-fisted she was bein'. She told me *she* would tell the court that she *did* give me money for Matty but that I'd spent it on drugs and women 'cause I was not a proper, responsible father. That I couldn't clothe or feed or care for our child properly 'cause I was, to use her exact words, a sponger, a gambler, a drinker and a wastrel."

"Why didn't you just get a job?"

"'Cause she threatened to reveal my criminal record. She also threatened to rat me out to the immigration authorities for travelin' on a false passport. Gettin' deported—now *there's* a great way to win custody. That was her plan—to give me a fiscal enema so I'd have to accept her offer and get the hell out of her life."

"Well, you do have enough skeletons rattling around in your closet to fill a cemetery," Shelly curtly contributed.

The light that had been streaming onto the balcony from a neighboring bungalow was extinguished. The moon was now gone too. Shelly sat there in the blackness, staring up at—nothing.

"Hey, I'm far from perfect, doan' I know it. But I would never, ever leave my daughter. But I didn't even have the money for a lawyer. Anyways, lawyers would just charge an arm and a leg to tell me what I already knew—except they would tell it to me in Latin. That dead lingo you love so much. Divorcicularus You-Are-Screwed-Maximus." Kit braved a smile, but it clung to his lips like cookie crumbs. "Courts are on the mom's side, even though Pandora has never done one friggin' thing for Matilda."

"And that's when you decided to run away with her?" A disquieting loneliness crept over Shelly.

"Yeah. That was when I rang Alec, an old backpackin' pal. Turns out he was workin' on *Desperate and Dateless* . . . Well, you know the rest. Shelly, I'm sorry I lied but all I want is to escape to a new life with my darlin' girl. Like the Creoles of Réunion, all I want is freedom and independence!" He made a mock revolutionary salute.

"But you're traveling with an illegal four-foot substance!" A wire tripped and Shelly's temper detonated. "You've got undeclared kiddie contraband. You are child-laundering! Have you possibly heard of The Hague Convention? Any parent arrested with a stolen child goes to prison."

"Of course I've heard of it! But that's why my plan is to get to Madagascar—reasonable food, not too uncivilized, a CNN feed. Matty can't be extradited from there—they haven't signed The Hague Convention treaty. Me and Alec, we found it out on the Net."

"But what if you get caught before that? Christ." Reality knifed into Shelly's abdomen. "That makes *me* some kind of accomplice!" She had a sudden vision of herself in a film like *Midnight Express*, biting tongues out of guards' heads and being anally ravaged.

"No, it don't. We also looked up the Children's Act. I can take my own kid out of the country for up to four weeks, so I ain't actually committin' any offense. Well, not yet."

"Oh no . . . except bigamy, fraud and abduction!"

"Look. Hundreds of thousands of people go missin' in Britain every year. There'll be a grainy photo of us taken in happier times with a poster readin' 'MISSING.' Pandora will say she's anxious for news and concerned for our safety. In seven years she can have us legally declared dead, gain access to Matilda's trust fund and live happily ever after. That's what she's really worried about—someone else gettin' their grubby paws on her kid's cash."

"Missing . . ." Shelly repeated, looking at Kit with searching earnestness. "The word 'missing' will describe Matilda's mother's feelings when she finds out you've stolen her darling daughter?!"

"Feelin's? Matilda's mother *has* no feelin's. She's a cruel, heartless, ruthless bitch. Hey, but I wish her only well," he said sardonically.

Shelly thought of her own mother's beautiful and blind devotions. "It isn't easy being a mother, you know, otherwise dads would do it!" she snapped.

"I *do* do it! I know Matilda off by heart!" he thundered. "I'm the one who knows exactly how many of her library books are overdue. I'm the one who knows exactly how many donuts she's sneaked before dinner. Her favorite food, her secret fears. Pandora doesn't love her! She never has! She only wants to keep her to hurt me."

Shelly felt a tug of compassion but, used to Kit's adroit

intellectual sophistry, ignored it. "Children belong with their mothers, Kit."

"Christ! You can't really believe that men are somehow less equipped emotionally to look after their kids. That notion belongs in the same goddamn historical trash can as the idea that women are too feeble to vote, or I dunno, fly planes or to take up medicine, for Chrissakes," he railed, pacing faster. "The art of motherin' ain't necessarily instinctive, you know. Men can care for their kids every bit as well as women."

"How sweet. You want to spend more time with your daughter . . . You mean *do* more time with, because you'll both be in bloody prison!"

"Parenthood ain't a hobby. You don't just give up. I was raised without a dad. So were you. And it left a hole. In both of us. I ain't gonna do that to my kid! I know you and your mom had a unique and powerful bond. And I'm happy to admit that most women make great moms . . . but what they can't do is make great dads. And this little kid definitely does not have a great mom. The first thing Pandora would do is put her in boarding school, for fuck's sake."

"Boarding school? Well, it's not exactly Dickensian on the cruelty list."

Kit sat down beside Shelly and spoke quietly, a desolate sadness in his voice. "I knew Pandora took sleepin' tablets, but I didn't realize she was addicted or that Temazepam could make you so aggro, 'specially if taken with booze. But on the few occasions Pandora did look after our daughter, I'd always come home to find Matty dopey and dozy and then one day I found out why. Pandora fed her sleepin' pills to keep her quiet. And when she wasn't quiet she slapped her."

Sympathy and skepticism tug-of-warred in Shelly.

"Pandora should never have had a kid. She should have just got a cat, so that when she got bored, she could have it put to sleep."

"How can you say that about any mother?" demanded Shelly. "You're sick—sick in the head to say such a thing! When you *do* get nabbed, you can always plead mentally unfit to stand trial."

"Yeah, because who'd want to go to court where a judge who hasn't *seen* a kid since 1925 rules that all children prefer their moms? Judges always think that women have Advanced Parenthood Proficiency Certificates 'cause they like the 1950s *Leave It to Beaver* fantasy of Mom and kiddies at home cookin' apple pie, with Daddy bringin' home the bacon. I will not lose my daughter," he said, with combative devotion. "If I leave Matty with That Woman, the poor kid'll be out exchangin' her allowance for drugs in about a week. Nothin' and nobody is gonna stop us from gettin' to Madagascar tomorrow."

"So, just to recap, basically you were so skint you only got married for the rice," Shelly said coldly.

"Hey, I like to eat. It's a bad habit I picked up as a kid."

"And on the honeymoon all you wanted to do was sit in the moonlight and run your fingers through our cash."

"I was just usin' you, yes. But, Christ, then you fell for me and—"

"I didn't fall! I was pushed! By you!"

"That ain't true. I tried to put you off me. The day we were hitched. By actin' all cool and offhand. I tried to put you off by leavin' London early. I tried to put you off by takin' separate rooms, by pretendin' to be hot for Coco, by not bein' around . . . "

Every word burnt her. "Oh, don't try to spare my feelings." Shelly gave a bewildered sob. She couldn't bear to hear any more nimble rationalizations. "I knew you were using me at first. But tonight? You mean you just came on to me tonight to get back those tickets? One of which you pretended was for *me*?" Shelly felt a hot prickling behind her eyes as she remembered his tender mouth on her.

"Don't tell me a woman has never used sex to get what she wants."

"Sex *is* what I want!" Shelly lamented. "Sex is what I've wanted ever since I got into that bloody limo!"

"I like you, Shelly, I do. Much as I fought it, you got under my skin somehow. You're funny. You're sexy. You're smart."

"Yeah, well, opposites attract."

"And with some sun on your face"—he leaned forward and traced the constellation of freckles on her cheeks—"and salt spikin' your hair, you just look better an' better. Every time I see you a smoke alarm goes off in my boxer shorts. So, God knows I don't wanna hurt you. But Matty comes first."

"Running is not the answer, Kit."

"Says who? You ran from your fear of performin'."

Shelly winced. A direct hit.

"You'd be welcome to come with us, though. I've bought a little beach hut there."

He put his hand out to her.

"Let me think about that . . . Travel to Madagascar with a bigamist child-napper with a false identity and a criminal record for drugs, who is on the run from the police . . . Hmm, you know what? I just don't feel all that aroused anymore. It's been nice knowing you, Kit, but before we divorce, are there any other felonies you'd like to commit? Arson perhaps? *That*'d be a new one for you." If Shelly had been a nuclear reactor, she would have been in meltdown by now. It had all just been too, too much. "Or perhaps there's some other little thing you'd like to tell me? You know, that you're a spy or a transvestite? Or beamed down from some Mother Ship? You're not *missing*, Kit. You are lost."

"Lost? I know exactly where I am."

"You know where you are, but not who," she said sadly.

"I'm a father. That's who I am. I know you don't want kids, but if you had a child of your own, you'd understand."

Shelly felt as gutted as a fish. "It's not that I don't want a baby of my own. I just don't want to go *through* it on my own. Like my poor bloody mum did. Because men always leave."

"I would never leave my child."

"Yes, but *taking* is even worse."

"You're not gonna rat us out, are you?" His face took on a cloudy cast. "We'll be gone tomorrow. We'll be safe."

"No," she said, dispiritedly. She closed her eyes, the way a high diver does just before leaping off a bridge. "I just never, ever want to see you again."

"Fine."

"Fine." She wriggled the wedding ring off her finger and placed it meticulously on the table.

"Could you at least *try* to see it from my point of view?" He made one last attempt.

"I'd like to, I really would." She turned away so that he couldn't see what she was feeling for him. "But I just can't stick my head that far up my own rectum." She wanted to sound savage, but tears were stinging her eyes and straining her voice. Never to kiss his soft mouth or look into his dancing eyes. But the duplicity, the deceit—a woman would have to be emotionally Teflon-coated not to be distraught and adrift. It was as if she'd been thrown, headfirst, into the icy embrace of the Atlantic.

As she trudged through the teeming rain back to her own bungalow, puddles shimmying in the wind, Shelly felt furious that she'd ever allowed herself to trust a man. Surrendering to another wounded sob, Shelly concluded that when it came to learning Life's lessons she was a straight D student. Why? Why had she persevered against all her instincts? Because the bloke could charm the knickers off a nun, that was why. She found herself wishing that she'd kissed him one last time, kissed him with everything she felt, then reprimanded herself for the thought. Lust, she decided, should be classified as a Class A addiction. But she was now in Romance Rehab.

The Differences Between the Sexes: Devotion

When the right man comes along, women have the strength of character to say, "No, thank you—I'm already married."

Men, on the other hand, go straight from puberty to adultery.

15 Coochi Coochi Coup

At first Shelly's tears drowned out the rain, but as her sobs subsided she noticed that the constant thrumming on her bedroom roof was definitely getting louder, as if every garage drummer in the world had converged to stage a convention. Gothic, witchy fingers of tree branches scratched at her windowpanes. The cymbal crash of thunder percussed in time with her headache. Shelly was just about to ring the local mental institution to get a list of the interesting craft and leisure activities available for her imminent arrival—when her bungalow door was shouldered open and her tormentor strode in, sleepy child in arms.

For one ludicrous moment, she presumed he'd come to apologize, but dismissed this hope when she noticed that Matilda was not his only luggage. Two knapsacks were tossed into a corner, followed by a menagerie of stuffed animals.

"Let me guess. You're here because your High Command on Planet Neptune told you it was time to start Phase Two?"

"Strangely, no." Matilda's pink, pajamaed legs straddled her father's hips. They curved around him like fleshy parentheses.

"Well then, who said you could come into my room?" Shelly pulled on the terry-toweling hotel bathrobe over her cotton nightdress.

"Our bungalow got requisitioned as a hospital for the poor bastards injured by the bomb."

Shelly noticed that while Matty was shielded by Kit's denim jacket, her dad was wringing wet. It was now raining raucously, cacophonously, end-of-the-worldly.

"In London, even the rain is polite," Kit told Matilda, who was yawning herself awake. He put her down. "It just goes, rain, rain, pitter patter. But in the tropics it goes *rainnn!!! Rainnnnnn!!!*" While Matilda giggled, he turned a somber countenance towards Shelly. "It really is gettin' biblical out there—Noah-time even."

"Daddy, you know what I keep wondering?"

"What, darlin'?" Kit asked tenderly, kissing the crown of her golden head.

"Why didn't Noah just, like, swat those two wasps?"

Matilda made her father laugh with pleasure and surprise. He laughed with his eyes this time, too, Shelly noticed.

But Shelly remained immune to cute. "You can't stay here!" She was waving her arms as though shooing away those very wasps Matilda had mentioned. If the little girl hadn't been present, Shelly could very easily have given vent to an emotional storm to rival Mother Nature's. She knew people always said that marriage was something you had to "weather." But she just wasn't equipped with the right emotional anorak.

Matty slid out of her father's arms, and, hands on hips, strode towards Shelly like a bonsai gladiator. "Don't be mean to my daddy. My dad's the bestest!"

And her dad repaid her with a look of unremitting adoration. "Out of the mouths of babes," he smirked. "Come on, Shelly. You can't turn us out. Not with the cyclone comin'."

"Cyclone? Did you actually hear that on a weather report? There's a *cyclone* coming?" Shelly lunged hysterically to the window. Clouds wrestled across the black sea. Lightning ripped open the sky. "Oh, what a honeymoon! Take a bullet and put it through my brain. I have just lost the will to live."

On cue, a great gunshot of thunder shuddered through the night. Matilda's eyes widened and a sob choked out of her.

"Oh, weather reports," backtracked Kit, cosseting his daughter once more. "The only thing we can rely on about weather reports is how unreliable they are, ain't that right, Shelly?" He gave her a pleading look.

"What?" She looked down at the tearful little girl. "Oh yes. Nobody takes a weatherman seriously. Not even other weathermen. That's why they started calling themselves 'meteorologists.' In a hopeless attempt to look more scientific."

Kit smiled his gratitude as Matilda stopped wailing. "Basically, these are guys who look out the freakin' window for a livin'," he told his daughter soothingly, placing her on Shelly's bed and tickling her till she was squirming with pleasure.

His daughter broke into a wet-lunged laugh, a squall of giggly joy. She slithered free of her father's fingers and became a whirlpool of activity, trampolining, somersaulting, moonwalking and talking, talking, talking. Within minutes, she seemed to have left a bathtub ring of objects wherever she'd been, Beanie Babies, decapitated Barbies, Harry Potter models, PollyPockets, socks, a half-eaten banana and the soggy bottom of her teeny-weeny bikini. Shelly ran along behind, trying to control the chaos.

"Hey." Kit caught his daughter as she ricocheted past and hugged her close. "More good news."

Shelly, who'd just accidentally trodden a soggy banana into the carpet, shot him a scathing look. "If it's anything like the last news you gave us, just call the paramedics now, would you?"

"I've got Maltesers!"

"Oh goodie," exclaimed Matilda. "I'm a hoc-o-cholic," she told Shelly somberly, before hunkering down on the bed for a feast. "Who sleeps here?"

Shelly replied, flatly. "Only me."

"Well, what do you do with the other side of the bed?" the hoc-o-cholic wanted to know.

"Not much," was Shelly's reply, looking pointedly at her husband.

Matilda flicked on the TV remote—only to find a blizzard of interference and a hiss of disturbance on every channel.

"They can't just take over your room! I'm ringing reception to sort something out," Shelly said, Miss Efficient. "What's French for, 'I don't want to sound like a heartless bitch by throwing father and daughter out into the jungle where wolverines are no doubt devouring their young as we speak, but this maniac of a man has actually screwed me around enough already'?"

"Um, I dunno. But anyways, there's no staff and the line's dead."

Shelly snatched the phone from its cradle. No dial tone. She glowered at Kit. The claps of thunder became louder and more frequent. It was almost like applause, they were coming so regularly. The hail on the roof now sounded like a hundred panel-beaters.

Kit caught Shelly's eye and raised a concerned brow. He also shed his wet shirt. The sight of his tanned, toned torso created an electrically charged atmosphere to rival the storm. She tried not to watch as he reclined on the bed to fiddle with the radio dial with his legs forked, because the pose was one for lovemaking. How could she still find him attractive, she scolded herself, after all he'd done? Obviously a career in astrophysics did not beckon.

"The forecast reckoned the cyclone would skirt the island," he reassured them. But on the local station, a military band was playing Frank Sinatra's greatest hits, interspersed with urgent appeals in French: *"Restez calme! Gardez l'ordre!"* with the occasional translation, an astounding concession to English-speaking tourists, begging them to keep calm, to keep indoors, to keep trusting the *gendarmes mobiles.*

"*Les mobiles!* Christ. That's not thunder we can hear," Kit whispered to Shelly, intensely. "They're gunshots!"

"What?"

"*Emeutes, des blocus, militants.*" Kit repeated phrases from the radio. "Shelly," he said with repressed urgency, "I may not speak Frog, but that sounds as though we're in the middle of a goddamn revolution."

Shelly looked at him for a beat before placing her hands over her ears. "I'm sorry, but my brain is in overload now. You'll have to excuse me, but I am not accepting that information. Or, for that matter, any more information about anything."

Shelly lay on the bed beside Matilda, who was now snuggled up beneath the hibiscus-patterned quilt, fighting off sleep. She frantically flicked back through her Lonely Planet guidebook. She was pretty sure that "cyclones" and "coup d'état" had not been mentioned. But then she glimpsed the author photo, revealing a washed-out New Ager. "When he's not on the road," read the scribe's bio, "Olaf can be found tending veggies and watching wallabies in the yurt he shares with partner Gert." Who would *ever* go on holidays with these people? No wonder she was in such trouble. Dejected, Shelly placed the pillow over her head, which is why she didn't hear the door open until Coco was in the room. Coco's hair, soaked through from the rain, now resembled a nest of torpid worms. Gone were the "I'm-just-off-to-tone-my-aura" beaded sarong and love beads. In their place camouflage pants, combat boots, bomber jacket.

Shelly greeted her with all the enthusiasm with which she'd welcome a yeast infection.

"Whassup?" Kit demanded. "Gunshots. Blown-up boats. Hijacked subs . . . *coup d'état*. Am I right?"

"Ze Town 'All, eet 'as been attacked." She was out of breath, bent double, winded. "Some officials 'ave been wounded. Ze police, zey are saying law and order 'as broken down and zere is mob violence. Zis is bullshit! Zey just want to declare an emergency so ze flics can detain without trial. Ze uprising, it eez being crushed."

Kit looked alarmed. But Shelly was more surprised by the fact that Coco had just used several words containing more than two syllables and more or less in the right order.

"And zat is why you please 'ave to 'ide me."

"We do not *have* to do anything!" Shelly protested, leaping to her feet. "Except perhaps perform a citizen's arrest!"

"Yeah, 'specially after you tried to rip me off, Coco," Kit added, bitterly.

Coco shrugged. "The revolution, eet eez more important than you. We needed ze money—ze tickets I would have cashed and bought bandages and bullets. My accomplices, zey are taken prisoner. So, now you must 'ide me. Because you have somezing to 'ide also, no? And zere she is." Coco pointed her painted talon at Matilda, curled into the fetal position beneath the sheets. "I won't tell about *l'enfant* if you don't tell about me."

"Okay. We'll hide you," Kit said without hesitation.

"We will *not*."

"Shelly, we have no choice."

"*You* may not have a choice, but *I* do." Shelly suspected she'd need a couple of bottles of whisky before she thought that running foul of Super Flic might be a good idea.

The storm intensified. Hail now battered the windows like fists.

"Gaspard, 'e is going door-to-door. You say you 'ave not seen me. Now take your clothes off and do the 'appy married thing. And then you are so angry when someone comes in and stops you 'aving sex on your 'oneymoon."

"Having sex?" Shelly burrowed into her terry-toweling robe. "I'd rather reuse Towtruck's dental floss."

"Don't hold me in contempt, Shelly. Just hold me," Kit smooth-talked, opening his arms to her. For a heartbeat she teetered like a tightrope walker. But then she determined not to lose her balance this time.

"Contempt of court more like. *Divorce* court."

"You are divorcing 'im?" Coco asked.

"Yes. I want someone with less experience!"

"Come on, honey." Kit tried to shake the robe from her shoulders. "We've gotta stay married. I mean, look how well we argue! But not in front of the kids, okay?" he whispered, pointing to his slumbering daughter.

Shelly flicked his arm away as though it were a viper. "Listen, pal. You may be on the run from the police, but to me you're the star of a program called *America's **Least** Wanted*. I will *not* get into this bed with you."

"Stop zis madness now!" Coco spat, furiously. "You get into ze bed and you lerve each other. I hide in ze *salle de bain*." Coco moved backwards towards the bathroom, mopping her wet footprints from the floor tiles as she progressed.

"But what does Gaspard want you for? What have you done?" Shelly cross-examined.

"I agree with my boyfriend. Like the Corsican resistance, we will destroy tourism to attract international attention to ze way ze French government is breaching Réunion's right to self-determination."

Shelly reeled. "*You're a terrorist!*" she shouted at a decibel level that probably set off car alarms in New York City. Matty jumped in her sleep as though electrocuted.

"Shhhh!" Kit put a finger to his lips. "Let's just keep it between you, me and the French Secret Police, okay?"

"I am part of ze Réunion Liberation Front. We are supported by the Aboriginals, Maori and Kanack indigenous rights movements. My new lover, Gaston, 'e is zee leader."

"Oh God, the boat. Did you blow up the re-enactment boat?" Shelly was practically hyperventilating.

"Why do you sink I 'ave been working 'ere in this hellhole all zis time? Gaston needed someone to plant ze explosives."

"And who would suspect a New Age bimbo singer?" Shelly supplied. Who would have thought that this airhead would turn out to be a woman of mass destruction, the type prepared to die for her beliefs . . . *and take you and every tourist in the same boat with her?* She looked at the interloper, aghast. "Do you have any idea of the punishment for acts of terrorism?"

Coco shrugged. "No one was killed. The *Glorieuse* eez not ze *Rainbow Warrior*. Eet eez only a minor incident."

"*Minor?* There's no such thing as a civil war, Coco, you know.

Only uncivil. How are the Réunion Liberation Front financed?" Shelly persisted.

"The Gaddafi Charitable Fund 'elps, and our military wing, eet is planning to kidnap businessmen and hold zem to ransom."

Kit took over the explanation. "Coco's boyfriend, the head of the revolutionary group, is either a genial Jesuit or a Mauritian Marxist, dependin' on which newspaper you read," he expounded.

"Oh great. Leftward ho!" Shelly slammed her head onto the palm of her hand.

"What else can we do, huh? Ze French have denied indigenous rights to all ze land. Zey are transmigrating—offering civil servants from Paris double zeir pensions to retire 'ere, to boost ze white population. But People's Power is emerging!" Coco soapboxed with indomitable resolution. "In fact, 'alf ze 'otel workers are secretly members of ze Liberation Front."

"Shhh!" Kit insisted. They cocked their heads, as one, towards the sound of male voices. They could hear fists rapping on wood and a muffled exchange of voices close by.

"It's Gaspard," Coco said. "You must 'ide me."

Shelly blocked Coco's path to the bathroom. "But this will incriminate us. This will make us accessories to your crime. *'I'm sorry but Coco can't come to the door right now. She's busy plotting the destruction of the world as we know it.'*"

"Still waitin' for that spine donor, huh, Shelly?" Kit asked, kicking his daughter's detritus beneath the bed. "No wonder you froze on that stage at the Wigmore Hall."

Shelly pretended his words hadn't cut her.

"Life ain't some game show with prizes behind each door, Shelly. You have to fight for what you want in life."

"I can't lie. I'm not a liar! Unlike *you*."

"It's the old dilemma of whether you do a little bit of bad in order to do a great deal more good," Kit said in a piercing whisper. "Like me lyin' to get on the show to escape with Matty. I'm beggin' you, Shelly." He took her by the shoulders. "Losin' her would be unendurable!"

They all jumped when the knock came rat-a-tatting brusquely on the wood. Coco scooped Matilda's sleeping body up off the bed and evaporated into the bathroom. Kit looked at Shelly, pleadingly.

Shelly knew that marriage wasn't meant to be easy, but coups, psychotic police chiefs, cyclones, false passports, militants hiding in bathrooms, deranged ex-wives . . . Shelly had been in car accidents less dangerous than this marriage. Once more she could envisage herself in that hideously unflattering prison uniform. At least the stripes were vertical, which would be vaguely slimming. Shelly handed Kit her bathrobe and nightie with a look of martyrdom. "A girl needs combat pay to be married to you, Kinkade!"

Kit slipped Shelly's wedding ring back on to her finger, ripped off his own clothes, knotted a towel around his waist, mussed up his hair and, just as Shelly had positioned herself provocatively among the pillows, opened the door to Gaspard. A howl of wind and the fungal reek of wet shoes blew into the room with him. His heavy face seemed carved from granite.

"Do you know why I am 'ere?" The police commandant was still doing his best impersonation of a gargoyle.

"Um," said Kit, lying back on the bed. "To discuss the fact that existentialism has no future?" The air was freighted with tension. Kit casually draped his arm around his "wife."

"Terrorists put explosives on ze ship and zen stole ze submarine." Gaspard stood over them, his wet cloak splattering them in icy drips. He leaned into their faces. "I will destroy every tree in zat jungle to find ze rebels who 'ave done zis. Zat is why it is called guerrilla warfare—because they are all apes," he said, arrogantly, blasting them with garlicky breath so bubonic he was no doubt planning to use it for deforestation.

"I thought you French were famous for your revolutions? What about all that rock-throwin' you guys did back in 1789 and 1968?" Kit said gamely.

Gaspard's face twisted into a tetanic rictus. "Free speech, like most things that are free, is not worth 'aving—unless you 'ave something intelligent to say. Which you don't. So shut your mouth." And he slapped Kit's face.

Kit rubbed his jaw. "If this is free speech, then let me live in Algeria," he scoffed.

Gaspard regarded the honeymooning couple like a naturalist casually observing the routines of an insignificant species. "Your director. She said zat you are divorcing," he interrogated, suspiciously.

Kit slid his hand beneath the sheet and patted Shelly's flank, affectionately. "Who could leave a babe with a body like this, huh?"

Shelly, who was trying to win gold in the Fixed Smile Event, pinched her "husband's" hand hard.

Kit let out a small yelp, which he tried to camouflage as a cough.

Gaspard was snuffling around the room like a bloodhound. Shelly noted the telltale armpit bulge of his gun. "Did you see anything, 'ear anything? 'Ave you seen Coco?" Gaspard trilled his fingers on the top of the television, as his eyes ransacked the room. "La Tigresse is Gaston Flock's lover. He 'as been using 'er for money, for *chantage*—blackmail. Do you know what we call a Creole man without a girlfriend? 'Omeless. We 'ave now discovered that he 'as also been using a little beach hut she rents as an arms cache. So now we 'ave a warrant to re-arrest 'er. When we intercepted 'er comrades she was seen running back 'ere to ze hotel."

Shelly risked a glance at Kit. A muscle flickered at the corner of his mouth but he controlled himself. "The only thing I've heard, pal, are the moans of my beautiful bride. The only thing I've seen, her exquisitely pert breasts," said Kit serenely, as he ran his hands proprietorily over Shelly's body. "Ain't that so, honey?" Kit shot her an imploring glance.

"Uh-huh." Shelly tried to neutralize her inflection, while nodding wanly. She also surreptitiously dug her nails into Kit's hand. The squeak he made was quickly elongated into a sigh of anticipatory pleasure. Shelly just hoped she'd drawn blood.

Gaspard was moving towards the bathroom, wielding his torch like a machete. Kit rolled over on top of Shelly, pinning her down with his body and parting her legs with his knee. "And now if you don't mind, commandant. This *is* our honeymoon after all . . . " Kit writhed on top of Shelly, nibbling her neck and biting his way towards her breasts. "I know the urgency of sexual passion is probably hard for you to grasp at your age. It probably takes you two weeks to get a soft-on, right?"

The other policemen on the threshold chuckled and nudged each other, guns half-cocked. The gendarmes' snickers were silenced by their commanding officer's withering scowl. Behind them, the rain fell in sheets and the wind howled. Gaspard narrowed his eyes and took a step closer to the bed. Kit kissed Shelly deeply, flicking his tongue into her mouth and moaning.

Gaspard moved, reluctantly, towards the door. "I will be watching you," he threatened sourly.

"In that case, you naughty boy, I'll have to charge," Kit admonished.

Shelly squeezed her eyes closed, terrified of the police chief's response.

"Commandant! Really!" she heard Kit say. "I'm sure they didn't teach you that hand gesture at the Police Academy!"

When the door slammed shut behind him, Shelly bit Kit's earlobe. "Get off me, you deranged bastard!" she hissed hotly into his ear.

Kit cursed under his breath and dismounted abruptly. Recovering, he patted her bottom. "By the way, nice ass," he said breezily. "Nearly as lovely as your tits."

"You have set a standard for marital hostilities which can never be equaled," Shelly spat scathingly.

"Come on. Don't tell me you didn't enjoy that. You were hyperventilatin' with horniness."

"I was just trying to stop myself from throwing up."

Kit pulled her into an embrace. "Come here, and let me thank you properly."

Shelly leapt out of bed. "I'd rather give mouth-to-mouth to a dead squid. The only time you'll be having sex again is on a conjugal visit, because you will shortly be going to prison!"

Kit disappeared into the bathroom to retrieve the sleeping Matilda, whom Coco was cradling in the tub, hidden by the shower curtain. Shelly watched Kit gently lay the back of his hand against Matilda's cheek. A smile flickered across his face, as soft as a dream. The piquancy of Kit's devotion to his daughter shocked Shelly and gave her an unexpected pang—a pang that evaporated just as quickly as it had arrived when Kit said:

"I'll take the left side of the bed and you take the right. With Matilda in the middle." Kit laid his daughter down delicately, pulled up the covers and kissed her forehead, adoringly.

"Actually, you know, I have no plans to *speak* to you for the rest of my life, let alone *share a bed!* I've done my bit, so just go now and never darken my sheets again!" She hardened her heart. "Matilda can stay but not you!"

"Night," said Kit, shucking off his towel and crawling into bed.

Shelly tugged at his foot. "I was hoping to conclude our honeymoon with a minimum of broken bones, Kinkade, but that is starting to look highly unlikely."

"Now, please, I come with you too, okay?" Coco added, bouncing onto the bed.

"I'm sorry, madam," Shelly said in a fake air hostess voice, "but this bungalow is limited to only two carry-on explosives. *And they're in my bed already.*"

"I am sorry I 'it you in my cabin. But it's a bitch-eat-bitch world. No?" Coco said, sprawling across the foot of the bed. "I just need to, 'ow you say, lie low till dawn."

"Kit! Kit! Get up." Shelly prodded him, but he showed no cognitive response. "I know you're not asleep." He snored loudly. "Get up," she ordered. "Otherwise one of us is going to make the news headlines for doing something violent. And it won't be you. Kit? . . . Kit?" But he just snorted and rolled over.

Shelly stood there looking down at her bed, strewn with the sleeping bodies of people she, right at this moment, abhorred. This, she realized, is what holidays gave you—*hatred towards your fellow humans.*

And so it came to pass that Shelly Green finally had her man in her bed. The woman could have jumped for joy.

Right off the nearest cliff.

The Differences
Between the Sexes:
Weather

Men say that women are like cyclones: they're wet when they come and take the house when they go.

Women know better: it's men who are like cyclones: you never know when they're coming, how long they'll stay . . . or how many inches you're gonna get.

16 The Firing Squad

"Ningland" was the first word Shelly heard as she stirred from a sulphurous sleep.

"Huh?" She seemed to have a squashed Malteser in her ear.

"Ja live Ningland?"

Shelly prised open one eye to see a green-eyed girl gazing serenely back at her. They were sharing a pillow. And then she remembered. It was her stepdaughter.

"Do I live in England? Ah—yes."

Outside, the storm was still lashing. Rain beat horizontally against the windowpanes. She noted with relief that Coco had vanished. She tried to concentrate on what the little girl was saying. "Sorry?"

"Why don'tcha wanna be my new mum?" Her expression was guileless, unguarded. She had her father's good looks, only softened, sandpapered down.

"How can I be your new mum when you already have one?"

"She's shellfish."

"I'm sorry. Your mother is an edible mollusk?"

"She just thinks of herself," Matilda elaborated.

"Don't you miss her, Matty?" Shelly said, digging Malteser residue out of her inner ear.

"My dad is the bestest. And my mum is the worstest. I like her . . . It's just that I've started to outgrow her," she explained, somberly, licking a Malteser smear off her pajama sleeve.

"But she loves you, surely . . . "

Matilda shook her pale head and clutched her Hissy the Snake Beanie Baby to her heart. "But Daddy loves me. So we left. And now she'll just have to suffocate the consequences."

"Oh, will she now?" Shelly couldn't suppress a smile.

"Does your mummy love you?" the kid asked.

"She did. A lot. But she's in heaven now with God."

Her sea-green eyes widened with enthusiasm. "God is nocturnal, you know."

"You mean eternal."

"That's what I said, silly. Does your daddy take care of you now?"

"Um . . . No. Not really."

"Oh, well, *my* daddy will take care of you, too. One grown-up is enough, you know."

"Yes, but *which one*?" Shelly said, shooting a meaningful glare at Kit who had just levered open one eyelid.

Kit gave a devilish smile. "Oh, Shelly—wakin' up with you like this reminds me of the time we were happy!"

"Oh really?" Shelly said coldly. "I must have been asleep that day. *You*, Kit Kinkade, are the place that good times go to die."

Kit gave a laugh, which was full of his old punchy charm and brio, the respite of not having to lie anymore, she supposed, and the joy of his imminent escape.

"I'm glad you find it funny. I'll probably see the funny side too—*in a decade or two.*"

When the pounding on the door began, Shelly presumed it was Gaspard and galvanized into action, secreting Matilda beneath the bedclothes. "Christ! He's found out we hid Coco. We're all going to prison! For *assisted* suicides!"

Kit was less convinced. "That man couldn't find his own cock without a search warrant," he said quietly, out of earshot of Matty.

Shelly's cheer at discovering it was Dominic at the door was short-lived. Yesterday, what they thought were claps of thunder had turned out to be gunshots. Today, what they thought were gunshots turned out to be claps of thunder. Very loud claps. Accompanied by blasts of wind strong enough to make the bungalow shudder as if in its death throes. The cyclone was coming, intolerant and ruthless—Mother Nature's PMT.

"Ze bungalows closest to ze sea 'ave 'ad a wash through," Dominic said, panting. "Zis is when waves from two different directions gush through ze buildings. And eet eez going to get worse. You must go to ze cyclone shelter, *chérie*," he insisted, eyeing Kit with hostility.

"You go, Shelly. I can't." Kit ran his hands through his tangled hair. "I mean, I need the bucks from Gaby, but Christ! I doan' wanna blow Matty's cover," he whispered, his brow pinstriped with worry lines.

"Hey," said Shelly, rallying. "Don't turn into an alien from Planet Doom. That's *my* job."

"Gaby?" eavesdropped Dominic. "What a heroine! She and her crew are out zere somewhere now, filming ze cyclone."

"It's too risky," Kit procrastinated, his voice jagged with alarm.

"Look, Kinkade." Shelly took Kit to one side. "I'm looking forward to spending more time with you about as much as I'm looking forward to my own execution. But Matilda's not safe here. Besides, there'll be so many people in the shelter she could be anybody's daughter. We'll maintain she's the rock star's kid. I know he says he has no offspring, but I bet his accountant knows otherwise."

"*Dépêche-toi!!*" urged Dominic, showing little interest in the eight-year-old girl Kit had apparently conjured out of a hat and was clutching to his chest.

By the time they reached the bedroom door, Matty's nightie was billowing around her like a kite. Outside, it was much, much worse. The sky seemed to be hemorrhaging. The air was menthol-cold. Shelly fired her collapsible umbrella at the deluge but it flapped inside out then flew out of her hand. She was soaked through the second they left the shelter of the bungalow. The wind was ravenous, eating all in its path. Trees waved drunkenly, their heads bent at crazy angles, their once lush foliage now twisted and twined like a gorgon's hair.

The sea was black and nasty. Waves white as fangs bit into the shore. Out at sea, massive walls of water avalanched, spewing vertically when they hit the coral cliffs. Salt water slapped against the broken trees with a hiss. Just then, a massive wave, like a huge malicious grin, loomed up from the horizon. It burst upon the resort, foam groping at buildings with greedy fingers. It became impossible even to see the ocean, so thick was the air with spray. The four huddled in the grove to catch their breath before attempting the final dash through open ground to the bunker. The immensity of the weather roared at them. The palm tree trunks, stripped bare of foliage, stuck up like exclamation marks. And they had a lot to be alarmed about, Shelly commiserated.

"Do not worry, *chérie*," Dominic yelled above the howl of the wind, placing his steadying arm protectively around her waist. "I will never leave your side."

"Oh really?" Kit burrowed Matilda's head into his demin jacket. "I would have thought you'd only ever had one long-term lover—your right hand. Okay. Let's go."

Heads down, they leaned into the wind like cartoon characters, traveling one inch per hour through the incontinent rain across the sodden lawn. They burst into the cyclone shelter, a mildewed cement bunker burrowed back beneath the main reception of the hotel. With only one netted skylight, a few small storm windows looking out onto the lawn and two tiny toilet cubicles, the place had the ambience of a public lavatory, only not as spacious. Not even a sardine would feel at home. Obviously there would need to be some kind of roster drawn up, determining whose turn it was to breathe, Shelly thought dismally.

"We seem to have checked into a roach motel," Shelly said wanly, to her sodden and shivering companions.

Kit glanced at the cluster of crumpled threadbare cushions scattered against the far wall. "What? No pillow mint? What kind of a luxury resort do you call this? Do you think there'll be bunker service?"

But the only food on offer was an abundant supply of war–issued jam sandwiches . . . issued about 1945, that is.

The human menu was more diverse. In the next hour about forty of the resort's guests found themselves crammed, haunch to haunch, into this cement box. The coke-hooverers, the upper-class riffraff, the crooked South African accountants, an Aussie beer baron, a famous French pornographer, former talk-show hosts and other micro celebs delivered a general gnashing of cosmetic orthodontia. They were in a froth of indignation. These people had tanning salon beds to get to! And bikini waxing to be done! In their beet-faced umbrage, they remained totally unaware of the severity of the situation. Shelly could see the headline now: ATROCITY IN THE TROPICS. MODEL DENIED ACCESS TO ANKLE REHYDRATION CLASSES.

The Fading Rock Star crashed into the bunker in a pharmaceutical haze. Instinctively he pushed one of the more famous groins of the 1960s towards the center of the crowd and made camp next to a contributing editor of *Vanity Fair* in lemon cashmere. The editor started muttering to some baron or other, the kind of man who thought of "new money" as just "old money" that had momentarily escaped. The baron, who had never got over the social embarrassment of having once seated the younger son of a Marquis below a Lord Justice of Appeal, now found himself rubbing thighs with an It Girl who seemed determined to show him her labia piercings, which, she informed the startled peer, she called her "curtain rings."

The manager, notwithstanding his recent course on how to scale the cliff face of Hotel Management Strategy, was ill-equipped for crisis and passed the organizational baton to Dominic, who promptly rehearsed his aquaerobic ladies in a spirit-lifting version of "Camptown Races" and "Kum Ba Yah," with their disgruntled husbands raggedly harmonizing. Shelly looked around, but the only other activity on offer was to join the specimens of drooly-mouthed French senescences as they tried to remember English words for Scrabble—an activity that made Albanian daytime television look riveting.

Still determined not to speak to her "husband," Shelly soon found herself in a deep discussion with the hotel tennis coach about the island's edible fungi.

Kit, meanwhile, was exhausting conversational possibilities with the hotel masseuse, whose psychic channel to Ramtha, a

30,000-year-old warrior queen, was being blocked by some rival psychic from Sante Fe.

By evening, if they wanted to avoid DIY lobotomies, Shelly and Kit had absolutely no choice but to talk to each other.

"This is the sort of time most married couples would pull together and draw strength from each other. What shall *we* do?" Kit asked, humorously.

"Could you please not sit near me? I don't want people to think we're together or anything," Shelly replied.

"Let alone *married*," Kit added facetiously. "Dinner?" He offered her a cellophane-wrapped package from a passing tray. "J'know what I love most about these tropical island holidays?" he asked her, making a stab at camaraderie. "The salt, the sand, the exotic insects—and that's just in the sandwiches!"

"A toast to you, Kinkade," Shelly replied, swigging back her warm bottled water. "Without whom malaria, sunburn, infected mosquito bites, foot fungal rot and premature death would only have been a dream."

"I need to talk to the manager about gettin' to Madagascar when the airport reopens after the cyclone. I also need to find Gaby to get the rest of my prize money. And all without anyone gettin' wind of Matty."

"Gaby's still out filming, poor cow. But what does it matter if she does find out? The next installment of her show—*The Honeymoon from Hell*—won't go on air till next month."

"TV people are like hunters. They set baited traps, then lure unsuspecting prey . . . you can never trust them,"

"No, not like I can trust *you*," Shelly said glibly. "Anyway, you're wrong about her, Kit. She's been a good friend to me, actually."

"Friend? Shelly, female television hackettes think that the only women who need girlfriends are lesbians."

"Okay, she's driven, I admit that. But do you have any idea how hard it is for women to get jobs as directors in that macho industry?"

"Yeah and she'd sell slides of her cervical smear examination if the goddamn ratin's were right."

Kit smiled down on Matilda, who was placing her Beanie Babies in and out of a Barbie boat in some intense and intricate game. "Anyway, I need someone to watch over Matty for me while I talk to the manager. And in the absence of a responsible adult, I guess it's gonna have to be you."

"Responsible! You're the irresponsible one. *I* didn't marry outside of marriage. I am profoundly capable of looking after a little girl. Most women are," she added pointedly.

But as soon as Dad disappeared, Matilda immediately tried to exercise her rights under the Beijing Convention on the Rights of the Child to stay up past eight o'clock in the evening and eat sweets for supper. Shelly's suggestion that actually salad vegetables were a preferable dinner choice, health-wise, than licorice, was met with a facial response more readily associated with the accidental eating of a slug.

"I'm electric to vegetables." Matty gagged.

"Allergic?" Shelly suggested.

"That's what I said, silly. Also, I have a headache in my leg."

"Oh, well, what does Daddy normally do when you have a headache in your leg?"

"He gives me one of these pills. Half of one." She rummaged in her Beanie Baby Club satchel for a bottle of children's Tylenol.

"Here, let me open it for you. It's got a childproof cap."

"But, how does it know I'm a child?" she asked, wide-eyed.

"Good point." Shelly smiled. "Shouldn't you be taking that liquid stuff?"

"The grape drops?" Matilda shot her a scathingly aloof look. "That was, like, when I was *totally* young."

"Oh right." Shelly laughed. "Not like now."

Matilda passed the rest of the time by asking questions. "What is bigger? A trillion, billion, squillion, gazillion or Infinity?"

"Um . . . "

"Why do I have two arms, two nostrils, two legs and only one mouth?"

"Um . . . "

"What do you call a male ladybird? Does the Queen have a passport? . . . If moths like light so much, why don't they come out in the day?"

"Um . . . um . . . um . . . "

It took just under half an hour for Shelly to crack. "I don't *know*, okay? I don't know why the Egyptians wrapped up their dead in bandages even though it was too late to make them better. I don't *know* why Adam has a belly button when God invented him. I don't know how a cat can lick itself dry. And I don't *know* why floorboards only creak when it's dark. Maybe your dad knows. Let's go and ask him, shall we?"

When they'd located Kit, ensconced in earnest conversation with the manager, Matty stamped Shelly's wrist with a Banana In Pajamas sticker. "That's for being a good Beginner Mum." She grinned.

Shelly snatched her hand back. "Me? Oh no. I don't think so," she panicked. "Why don't you take your little girl back to the manufacturer, Kinkade, and get a new kid. I mean, *this* one's obviously faulty."

"She's only sayin' that, Matty, 'cause she's momentarily fallen out of love with me."

"I'm sorry, Matty. But I can't fall *out* of love with your daddy, because I never fell in!"

On cue, Dominic, finally free from "Kum Ba Yah"/hokeypokey duties, rapturously seized Shelly's hand and cannibalistically kissed his way up her arm to her mouth.

"I think your toy boy seems to be under the misconception that he is hostin' a TV talk show," Kit commented, snarkily.

"Dominic always kisses everyone hello. The French are very civilized that way," she pointed out.

"That wasn't a kiss. That was mouth-to-mouth resuscitation."

"He's a trained life-saver. He can't help it."

"He's a trained picker-upper of sad, gullible women in wine bars. Oh, your mom would be so proud."

"For your information, Dominic is only working here until he makes a name for himself as an actor."

Kit guffawed, then groaned. "Oh, and the world *so* needs another one."

"You, *ma chérie*, are too sensitive for this *con*. Too sensual. You need a man who will let you shine. You are too bright to stand in 'is shadow." The snake-hipped entertainment officer with the artfully tousled blond hair worked his way up Shelly's neck this time, with soft, gentle kisses.

"You see what an agreeable person he is?" Shelly purred.

"Yeah—he just agrees with everythin' you say. Come on, Shelly. The obsequious maggot's only comin' on to you so that Gaby will feature him in her god-awful reality series. If you can't see that, then obviously your mother must have drunk during pregnancy."

"No. It's just that I left all my major brain lobes as a deposit, back when I married *you*!"

Towtruck squelched towards them, with Silent Mike in inevitable tow. "Christ!" he roared, shedding layers of rain-sodden garments. "It's fuckin' awful out there! I'm as wet as an

Arab's fart." Silent Mike chuckled with dutiful sycophancy.

"Admit it," Kit teased the cameraman. "You've been plagiarisin' Shakespeare again! What a class act. Vampirically leechin' on to other people's lives for your pathetic television exploitations."

"Hey, you didn't feel all that bloody exploited when you got paid that twenty-five thousand quid, I noticed, you hypocritical pig." Gaby, her hair bedraggled and glasses fogged, panted up behind her crew. Shucking off her waterproofs, she motioned for Towtruck to begin filming Kit. "Turn over," she ordered, flaunting her mastery of TV parlance.

Towtruck, who was soaked, shivering and thoroughly disenchanted with his lot, belligerently obeyed, placing his eye to the camera, turning it on and grumbling, "Speed."

"Yeah, well, I feel exploited by your show now," Kit seethed. "Reality TV is like *This Is Your Life* hosted by *Satan*. And speakin' of money, you owe me another twenty-five thou, you know. Due today. Shelly and me, we've officially been married one whole week."

"What show? I have no show! The bride's diaphragm is growing lichen. She's living in the shadow of Mount Divorce! My series would be totally down the toilet if it weren't for the cyclone! I've got such amazing footage. It's total devastation out there," Gaby enthused. "Homes uprooted! Trees flying through the air like javelins! I got a message from the nearest CNN office in Mauritius—who want footage. If somebody dies, I could go global! We're talkin' serious spin-off profit. I must get some bunker footage, come to think of it . . . Mike, did you get sound with that?"

Kit seemed all of a sudden to be in a different time-space continuum. "CNN?" he muttered. "Global?" They were no longer just forty people trapped in a room, they were a themed attraction.

Towtruck came in for a close-up of Matilda, who was bent earnestly over her dinner plate, picking through her sandwich with the absorption of a forensic scientist, removing any offending item—like a salad vegetable or a bit of protein—and laying them out in an accusatory line on her paper napkin. "You are *not* gonna film me again, or anyone else for that matter." Kit stood between Matilda and the camera. "Is that clear?"

"Then give me back the dosh. And the plane ticket. You can walk home for all I bleedin' care." Gaby's eyes were magnified by her glasses.

"I ain't got the money. I've spent it."

"Bullshit. The company have paid for everything. You've had nothing to spend it on. If you don't agree to be filmed right to the end of this honeymoon week, then you'll be in breach of your contract, Kinkade, and you'll get fuck all!"

"Well, tough titty. 'Cause I'm outta here. Go tell *that* to CNN, just as soon as surgeons remove this camera from your sidekick's colon, which is where I'm gonna shove it if he dares to film me one more goddamn time!"

As Kit elbowed his way to the other end of the cyclone shelter, Shelly subtly indicated to Matilda to follow her father. When the child was out of earshot, she implored Gaby to give her husband his next paycheck.

"Why the hell should I?"

"He has every reason not to want to be filmed anymore. Not now that you're shooting footage for international news programs. That wasn't in his contract."

"Why should he care, for God's sake?"

"He's got a lot on his mind, if you'll pardon the exaggeration."

Gaby's feral nose twitched. "Something's going on, isn't it?"

Shelly shrugged. "Mmmm."

"Don't make me read between your mmmms, Green. Come on, we girls have got to stick together. Haven't I always fought your corner? Didn't I stop Towtruck from taking unflattering footage of you all hungover? Didn't I protect you from his sexual advances? Old mistakes do come back to haunt you, you know, Shelly—*especially on video . . .* "

"What do you mean?"

"If you don't tell me what's going on, I may be tempted to run all the footage Towtruck *did* take of you vomiting, drowning and, dear God, dancing."

Fear, exhaustion and disappointment had affected Shelly's critical faculties to the point where she not only thought Gaby was joking, but that honesty would be a good idea. "You have to promise not to tell anyone, or say anything . . . "

"Okay, I promise." Gaby was continually readjusting her glasses on the bridge of her long thin nose in agitation.

"I shouldn't tell you, but by the time your honeymoon documentary goes on air it won't matter anyway. You see that little girl? The one shadowing Kit? She's his daughter."

"*What?*"

"He's just trying to protect her. That's why he stole her from her mother. And that's why you can't film him anymore. He's on the run from his wife." Shelly pieced together the torn pieces of the Polaroid of Pandora she'd kept in her purse. "That's his main spouse—I'm just his small, auxiliary one," she added sadly.

"Christ. You're telling me your husband has one wife too many?" Gaby took off her glasses and polished them maniacally. "That's called bigamy, isn't it?"

"I think *he*'d call that monogamy," sighed Shelly.

"Let me get this straight. Your hubby is a bigamist?" Gaby reiterated, uncomprehendingly. "And a kidnapper?"

"Literally." Both women looked towards the kid in question. "I'm not condoning what he's done, Gaby, but it's impossible to imagine the sheer misery and desperation of a dad denied all contact with his child." (Although it didn't seem to have affected *her* father all that much, she thought sourly.) "I'm not sure how legit the marriage is. I think it was probably a Jerry 'n' Jagger-type knotting of nuptials. But he still has paternal rights. When we get out of here, I'll convince him to have faith in the British legal system. He can use the prize money to fight for custody in the courts."

"Hmmmmm," said Gaby. "Hmmmmm."

But Shelly was way too tired to read between her hmmms.

The cyclone was a malevolent presence hovering just off the island. They waited and waited for the worst winds to hit. The night wore on, weather battering the bunker. Shelly whiled away the hours watching mosquitoes dive-bombing sleeping victims, and geckos scuttling across the walls chasing moths, and listening to the contributing editor saying over and over to the beer baron, "How Extraordinary" and "How Interesting," in a terminally bored voice as he gloatingly reread his latest article in *Vanity Fair*.

And all the time, Kit cradled Matilda, a look of rapturous, paternal love stealing across his face when he thought nobody was looking. He watched over her, hour after hour, a wistfully sad smile on his lips. Now, seeing him lull and stroke and cherish his little child, Shelly felt an ache within—a poignant ache, which made her coil, fetally, around her cushion.

When Shelly woke, sour-mouthed and creak-jointed, she ran a mossy tongue over her teeth. Matilda had crawled into her lap in the night and lay there, a hot, sweet bundle, her fingers gripping Shelly's hand.

Through the one double-glazed, meshed skylight, Shelly watched as a limpid, watery dawn broke. The wind seemed less asthmatic and the rain less theatrical. She felt elated with relief. The worst of the storm was over.

The bunker had an unwashed jockstrap smell. The air was thick with snores and redolent with stewed tea, sweet biscuits and stale cigarette smoke.

"Is it tomorrow, today, or still yesterday?" Matty asked in a sleepy voice. "Is the storm over?"

"Yes. I can't hear the sea moaning anymore, can you?"

"The tide's going out—'cause all the sponges soak it up."

"Oh, is that right?" Shelly smiled.

"My dad taught me that. He teaches me loads of stuff."

"Like what?"

"Like never trusting a dog to watch your food for you while you go to the bathroom. And that my mum loves me underneath. She just doesn't know how to show it. That kind of stuff. Grown-ups are always saying that us kids should grow up more, but I think grown-ups need to grow down. You worry too much and use your angry voice."

"Do you think so?"

"Uh-huh," smiled Matilda's father, stirring by their side. "You sure do."

But Matilda didn't know just how much Shelly had to worry and feel angry about. Nor did she know that Shelly's worries were about to get a whole lot bigger.

When the manager roused himself and checked the weather, he gave the all clear. Guests rallied and stretched, already planning the anecdotes with which they'd regale their dinner party companions when they got back to civilization. Forty people then picked their way over the tangle of each other's toes and legs and confusion of clutter in a scramble for the door. A palpable relief had flooded the room—until, that is, the manager drew the bar back across the storm door. He pushed on the cyclone-proof door with all his might. Other men joined him. They put their shoulders to it, grunting.

"It seems to be jammed," the manager panted, waggling his preposterous, Groucho Marx eyebrows.

"Or perhaps locked," corrected the contributing editor in lemon cashmere as he peered up at the skylight and, through it, straight into the barrel of an Uzi.

The skylight was ringed by men in jungle fatigues, pointing rifles. There was a shattering of glass as a rifle butt snapped through the skylight and a machete sliced open the storm netting.

Shelly had agreed to take part in a little reality television dating program about love and marriage. Not an NC-17–rated horror film.

"Nobody to move," said a young man in a lilting Creole accent. "Vis is a hostage situation."

Shelly had known they were up Merde Creek. But what she hadn't realized was that they had no paddles.

The Differences Between the Sexes: Animal Magnetism

Men refer to women as cows or silly moos.

Women say there's a very good reason why men can't get Mad Cow Disease . . . Because they're pigs.

17 Booby Trap

The dying process begins the moment we come into the world—but it sure speeds up after marriage. "Till Death Do Us Part" had just taken on a whole new meaning. Packing for her honeymoon, Shelly Green had somehow overlooked the Uzi machine gun and small hand grenades that seem *de rigueur* these days on a tropical holiday.

The cellar door fell open and a handful of rebels chuted into the bunker. The leader of the rebel group, a kid of about nineteen, explained to them in fractured English that they, the Liberation Front, were on the run from the police who had chased them here from the Town Hall. They needed publicity and money, he said, and these hostage situations were, apparently, lucrative and promotional. "Christiane Amanpour, she is coming!" he enthused.

Kit paled, no doubt realizing that late-night pundits in Paris, Washington and London would soon be chewing the ends of their spectacles as they scrutinized this very bunker. He cradled Matty

257

as though it was arctic outside, instead of the regulation 90 degrees Fahrenheit.

Shelly's teeth were likewise clacking like castanets despite the tropical temperature. "These . . . these teenagers can't be the rebels who shot the French officials, can they?"

"Well, I think those remnants of bodily organs on their shoes might be a bit of a clue."

"Um, Kit, do you know whether our travel insurance covers *gaping chest wounds*?" Shelly couldn't keep the hysterical edge out of her voice. "Oh yes, this is *definitely* my kind of holiday. *Dear Guests, Do not attempt to use hotel facilities without a portable flame thrower for added protection.*" This is what a girl gets for succumbing to raw desire, she reprimanded herself: a death certificate.

"No need to panic. We can't be taken hostage by someone wearin' a floral shirt and a lai," Kit said lightly, while a slight inclination of his head and a widening of his eyes reminded Shelly of Matilda's impressionable presence. "They're just kids. They've probably taken Viagra eyedrops to make 'em Look Hard. Besides"—Kit lowered his voice—"I have a weapon." A grope through his pockets produced a Swiss army knife. But it was so stiff with disuse that once open, all he could detach was the spoon.

"Oh great. *Spoon* someone to death, why don't you."

"Well, look around," he whispered to Shelly. "There must be somethin' we can use to protect ourselves."

Shelly scavenged the bunker. But all she could find was an industrial-sized staple gun in a box of stored hotel stationery. She handed it to Kit. "At least it's loaded."

"Why don't we just rush them?" the New York Literary Luminary in lemon cashmere suggested, though he stayed, Shelly noticed, safely seated.

"Yes, Kit," Shelly added. "They do seem less well-armed than your average inner-city high school student." The highly protective military combat gear of the six teenage terrorists seemed to consist mainly of Britney Spears T-shirts and tie-dyed beach bandannas which only partially disguised the lower half of their faces.

"And not the most impressive array of firearms in the world either," Kit conceded, cataloguing the arms cache. "Apart from that one Uzi, the rust-riddled pistols seem to be left over from Vietnam and the rifles are battered Winchester lever actions from, like, the Boer War."

"How do you know the names of those guns?"

"From my army days."

"You were in the army?" she asked, amazed.

"I thought I told you. Right before my porn star stint. Joinin' the army was the only way to get out of the boys' home."

"Boys' home? Porn star? Army? Of course. Silly me. I should have guessed." What, Shelly wondered, could ever shock her about him now? The *Sphinx* was less of a riddle than he was. "You know, Kit, you really should get out less."

"Fuck this!" the rock star exploded, scratching his groin in a contagious way. "I have to put the final touches on me remix." He swaggered towards the exit, expecting the usual kow-towing. But the rebels regarded him impassively. "Open the door, you weedy motherfuckers, or I won't give any of yews an autograph," he ordered with huffy ill-humor.

Kit shielded Matty protectively. "Oh, that's smart. I kinda find it best not to insult terrorists—'specially when they're trigger-happy and are holdin' you hostage."

A bullet twanged off the fire extinguisher next to the rock star's heroic head, making Shelly's skull chime. The rock star let out a scream normally associated with childbirth.

Big, tough, testosteroned Towtruck harmonized with the sound of a cat being dissected by a chain saw. The bunker was dank with the smell of anxious armpits as the guests realized the interlopers were more than just slogan-wielding young malcontents. A suffocating silence descended. The hush was finally broken by the It girl, who contributed her opinion in an airless voice.

"They're probably cannibals!"

Shelly rolled her eyes. "Yes, you're right. They'll be toting your earlobes on a necklace in no time."

"Daddy, are we going to be eaten?" Matty asked, wide-eyed.

"No, darlin', course not," Kit soothed her, giving the model a scalding glare. "I gather that fried model, like fried dog, is strictly a rural delicacy."

In a bustle of urgent activity, the militants shooed the hostages to the back of the bunker as though they were chickens. So much for "rushing" the rebels. The hotel guests had immediately adopted the inertia of captives, obeying every order, meek as pets.

The revolutionaries then made a barricade of chairs against the door. Two sentries took up position by the storm windows, peeking over the sills, all anxious eyes and protruding gun barrels. The rest broke tiles and stones from the walls into handy projectiles or filled empty bottles with the kerosene they'd brought to make bombs. The hostages goggled at their uninvited hosts, before looking, en masse, to the manager for leadership. But unfortunately the manager was otherwise engaged in the throes of an oleaginous spasm at the feet of the freedom fighters, begging, one presumed, for his puny life. The guests instinctively turned to Kit.

"What do we do?" Dominic asked in an enervated tone.

"How the hell would I know? Perhaps I should just pop back to my room and pick up my Coup Survival Kit."

"But how long will the fuckers keep us?" Gaby demanded of Kit next.

"Will we survive?" implored the beer baron's wife.

Towtruck ground his prognathous jaw. "Not with no food. I'm that hungry I could eat the crotch of a low-flying duck."

"All we've had are sandwiches, and I'm on the Courtney Cox Wheat-free!" the It Girl sobbed. Shelly looked at the model in amazement. How could she think of food at a time like this? With any luck, starvation would force the bulimics to start eating the anorexics.

"Well, it *is* a hotel. I'm sure we've got a two-week supply of maraschino cocktail cherries somewhere," Kit volunteered, feigning flippancy for Matty's benefit.

Gaby glowered at him. "Be serious! These maniacs are armed. And guns are like men . . . Keep one around for long enough and eventually you're going to want to *shoot* it."

Kit had just started in on Gaby about not shooting off her big mouth for a change when an explosion silenced their whining.

"What in God's name was that?" Shelly asked, anxiously.

"Somehow I don't think it's an early Bastille Day celebration," replied Kit, solemnly.

The electric lights began to spasm intermittently. The fan orbited eccentrically once in its electrical socket before sputtering to a halt. In the bunker's attenuated light, Shelly could still see the tension etched onto the faces of the frightened guests. Her stomach churned and she moved to the small storm window overlooking the lawn to get air. Outside, she saw police in Darth Vader helmets casting tombstone shadows as they sharked in and out of the trees.

Through the broken skylight came the metallic hiss of static from outside. Shelly recognized Gaspard's voice, distorted by a megaphone. "Attention! Zere is nossing to worry about," he assured the hostages—no doubt from within a flameproof, bomb-retardant armored vehicle, thought Shelly, bitterly.

The manager, who had been in earnest conversation with the rebel leader near the barricaded door, returned to address the assembled throng and nervously cleared his throat. His rubbery, overfed, babyish face was farcically solemn. Shelly prepared for another installment from the standard Hotel Management Forked-Tongue I'm-a-Lying-Bastard Phrase Book, first in French and then in English.

"So, I will now speak plainly," he cheeped, which she decoded as, "I'm about to lie."

"In all honesty . . . " which she translated as, "I'm about to really, really lie."

"There is no need, no need at all, to panic." A handy little phrase which Shelly knew meant, "Those with cyanide tablets should take them *now*."

"The police have everything under control. Our friends here with guns have opened radio negotiations. There is talk of an amnesty."

"What did that sweaty man say?" Matty tugged on Shelly's arm. "He's backwards talking."

"I couldn't have put it better myself, Matty." Shelly turned to Kit. "I hope Gaspard will negotiate. What's French for 'don't do anything rash'?"

"From past experience I'd have to say there ain't no such phrase," Kit said seriously.

"Well, what's French for, 'Let's discuss this calmly and come to some compromise with the rebels.'"

"Beatin' the crap out of you is French for diplomacy, Shelly. Remember Rwanda and the Côte d'Ivoire?" While Matilda warbled the "Ning Nang Nong Where the Cows Go Bong" song in a high-pitched tuneless way, Kit cadged a cigarette from the chain-smoking rock star and lit up. It was the first she'd seen him smoke since their limo ride.

"I thought you'd given up?"

"You know, I don't think long-term health effects are a major concern for any of us right now," he said ominously, adding under his breath, "actually, it does take a lot off your mind when your current life expectancy is, oh, *five to ten minutes max.*"

"What do you mean?" Shelly felt the cold hand of dread on her heart.

Kit leaned into her ear. "Gaspard has promised to negotiate. But that's what the French said during that hostage crisis years ago in New Caledonia, just before they stormed in and shot everyone. He's just buyin' time while he gets his marksmen onto the hotel roof. The gendarmes have armored trucks with gun turrets that shoot hundreds of rounds a minute. Gaspard will betray us faster than you can say *Vichy*-ssoises." Kit stubbed out his cigarette and turned towards her, stricken. "How could I have endangered Matty like this? Her mom is right. I am an unfit father." His face imploded with grief. He then swept his little girl into his broad arms. "Matilda." He said her name as if it were a prayer. As he enveloped her with love, Shelly could see that this was one thing he hadn't lied about—his devotion to his daughter.

"You know Jesus Christ," Matty asked Shelly, casually, over her father's shoulder, totally unaware of his anxiety.

"Not personally but . . . "

"Is he true or false? He came down to earth for some strange reason. Was that before I was born?"

"Um, yeah, I . . . "

"Does Father Christmas have God's phone number?"

"Um . . . "

"What is God's phone number?"

"Um . . . "

"Probably 00000000000000 etc., etc., etc. to infinity. Daddy, do baddies have antibodies? Do babies? They must be very small. If I get shot with a bullet will my antibodies be too small to save me?"

Kit made some kind of strangled reply. Shelly had never seen him so vulnerable. He couldn't speak, so strong was the harsh taste of regret in his mouth. She was shocked by the change in him. Shelly felt a dolorous tug at her heartstrings—until she reminded herself how Matty's *mother* must be feeling.

Gaby, one ear pressed to her mobile phone, interrupted Shelly's rueful ruminations by walking towards the marauders, waving a white T-shirt. "Gaby!" Shelly grabbed her elbow. "Where in God's name are you going?"

"I'm going to offer to interview them for CNN. It's just been approved by Atlanta and, anyway, if I give the bastards a platform, an *international* platform, to voice their objections and objectives, they may be appeased and let some of us go."

Kit put Matty down and barred Gaby's way. "These are terrorists, Conran. Not heroic, moustachioed, robbers-of-the-rich-to-give-to-the-poor Batman types with comical sidekicks."

But the *Desperate and Dateless* director sidestepped him contemptuously and strode on, regardless.

"Daddy, who would win a fight? Batman or Superman?" Matty asked. "Or you?" Then she tugged on Shelly's sleeve. "How many more sleeps till we're out of here?"

"No more sleeps, sweetie. We'll be out soon. Here, drink this." She handed Matty a glass of orange juice which tasted like tin.

"How many minutes?"

"Oh, any minute now."

"How many seconds?"

"Any second now." Shelly took a swig of tinny juice and wished it were stronger.

"Are you sure? Are you a million, billion, trillion sure?"

But Shelly wasn't sure about anything . . .

"So, did you ask them if they'd seen any good French movies lately? Probably not. I mean, *neither has anyone*," Kit said when Gaby finally returned from her tête à tête with the rebels.

"What did they say?" Shelly insisted.

"Oh, just the usual claptrap. We have no justice, so our justice is guns and bullets. That they must get back to protect their leader in the mountains, blah blah blah."

"Did you strike a deal?" Kit probed.

It was not a question Gaby seemed to want to answer. Not that she could have anyway, because at that moment the assault Kit had predicted began. The police rushed the bunker, firing salvos of gas grenades, ten at a time. The rebels, in a testament to their bravery or stupidity, were half out of the skylight, raining everything they could find on to the upraised shields of the police, sending paving stones and rocks ricocheting. A tongue of mustard gas smoke reached into the room to taste them. Kit dived on top of Matilda and Shelly, attempting to shield them both with his body. The smoke made their eyes stream and throats seize up. Death, Shelly realized, gasping, really can be a breathtaking experience.

Only after she'd stopped coughing did she realize that the bombardment of the bunker had ceased. As the fug of fumes and dust lifted, she was bewildered to find herself still alive. She patted her body to make sure she had everything she'd started out with. The whole bunker seemed to hold its breath in a tourniqueted silence. The atmosphere was lachrymose with mustard gas haze and gun smoke. The fighting now seemed to be going on outside the cyclone shelter on the lawns close to police lines. Shelly groped her way to the window and, through slits of burning eyes, glimpsed blurred hand-to-hand action outside the shelter, batons whooshing down onto skulls—black police against white police.

One of the adolescent rebels wrapped a scarf around his nose then disappeared outside. When he finally returned, emerging from the fog, blisters from the pepper gas raised on his skin, it was to explain that what Gaspard hadn't taken into account was that over half his force was Creole. And, when it came to the crunch, they'd refused to hurt their black brothers. They had turned their guns on the French, starting with the officer in charge. It was now Gaspard and his fellow Frenchmen who were on the run.

The It Girl began to sob uncontrollably in between shrill utterances of "Do you know who I am?"s.

And minutes later, that was *exactly* what the rebels *did* want to know. Having momentarily escaped imprisonment, they were now reverting to the Recommended Terrorist Escapee Contingency Plan, which involved fleeing to the hills with a human shield—preferably a wealthy one.

Kit responded with counterfeit calm. "Ah, well, you're out of luck, buddy, 'cause, you know, hey, everybody who is *nobody* is here," he joshed.

The eagle-eyed rebels bent over Matilda as though she were a lost kitten.

"A million dollars and you and *zenfant-là* get released—Baron Rupert Rochester," one of the Creoles said as his comrades surrounded Kit like carrion over roadkill.

It was a terrible revelation. Shelly sensed Kit's body stiffen to meet the blow. When the leader pointed his gun at Kit, all Kit cocked was his eyebrow—but Shelly saw the tic rippling under the skin of his smooth cheek.

"Hey, pal," he replied coolly. "I'm sorry but I don't know what the hell you're talkin' about. My name's not Rupert, it's Kit Kinkade."

For that he received a rifle butt in the side of the head. Matilda squealed, heart-wrenchingly, tears plopping off the end of her nose. Kit scooped her into his arms and held her ashen little face close to his chest with a feverish, quivering grip. Blood trickled down his forehead.

"How did you know?" Kit asked quietly, desolation radiating from him in waves.

The rebel leader, still jumpy, tipped his gun in Gaby's direction.

Gaby gave Kit a cold, hungry stare—the stare of a raptor about to seize a rabbit.

Kit turned on Shelly, stunned by her betrayal. "You *told* her?"

Shelly felt a jolt in her abdomen. All she could hear was her own stark, jerky breathing. "I . . . I . . . I was trying to get her to give you the rest of your prize money. I . . . " Her voice trailed away into a miserable whisper as she turned to stare uncomprehendingly at Gaby.

The reality TV director gave a brittle smile before gesturing to her crew to continue filming the errant groom. Towtruck looked to the rebels for permission. They conferred monosyllabically, before a curt nod indicated that filming could recommence.

So *this* was the deal Gaby had struck, Shelly realized, aghast. "I . . . I trusted her."

"Yeah, well, I trusted *you*, Shelly," Kit said, a savage despair in his eyes. Shelly may have married Kit for his looks, but not the one he was giving her now. "What was it? Jealousy that Matty has a father who loves her and you don't? Is that it?"

Shelly was curling in on herself, like the crusts of an old sandwich, as she kept feebly incanting, "I'm sorry, I'm sorry."

"How can you take his side, Shelly?" Gaby nudged Towtruck to train his camera on to Shelly. "*You*, raised by a single mother! Can you imagine what that kid's poor bloody mum is going through?"

Kit kicked out at Gaby's camera. "Turn that fuckin' thing off!"

"Why? Brutality and violence and lying bastard men are part of human nature, so why shouldn't people want to see it on TV?" Gaby said, with the indifferent, calculated practicality of a bank clerk, motioning for her crew to keep filming.

The rebels were gathering up their wounded and motioning with their guns for Kit to follow. Kit seemed to be dragging his limbs against a tide.

"If you'd prefer to avoid the inconvenience of being separated from your scrotum," Gaby said coldly, "then I'd advise you to do as they say . . . Or you can wait for your wife. Your real wife. Did I mention that she's arriving, just as soon as the airport reopens? I took the liberty of calling her. Pandora Vain Temple. I recognized her from the photo. Pantyshield heiress."

Kit looked at Shelly, contempt in his eyes. Shelly felt her colon corkscrew. His voice, when he spoke, was shaking with wrath. "Oh yes, your mom did a real good job on you, didn't she? All that's left of you is a shell; like an insect sucked dry by a spider. You're nuthin' but an empty husk."

Matilda, caught up in other people's darkness, looked up at Shelly, bewildered.

"Matty," Shelly said, arms extended, "let me come with you. Let me take care of her, Kit."

"Like the way you've taken care of us so far? No thanks," he replied bitterly, his face as fatigued as an unmade bed.

And Kit was led away, quickly, Matty in his arms, her eyes quite wide with terror.

The Differences Between the Sexes: Leisure Time

Men think sitting on the toilet is a leisure activity.

In a woman's equivalent "leisure" time she will reorganize the condiment cupboard, wrap the school books in plastic, write the Christmas cards, paste holiday snapshots into photo albums, load the dishwasher, unload the dishwasher, alphabetize the spice rack, make the kids' lunches, press the kids' uniforms, shine the kids' school shoes, sort out the money for the school excursions, finish the kids' homework (which involves reading all of Ulysses in Greek), take the dog for a walk because nobody else will, get masochistically waxed for her man, hand-bake the Swedish muesli because one of the kids has gone vegetarian, call her mother-in-law to let her know how much her son loves her, attempt to master coq au vin for a dinner party for her husband's clients at short notice, finish off her own work from the office, catch the lost guinea pig which has vanished behind the back of the bookshelf and spend half an hour looking for her man—who is still on the toilet.

18 The Ambush

"He only married me for my money, you know. 'Palimony,' from the Latin word meaning to rip out a woman's ovaries through her purse."

"Kit doesn't want your money, Pandora. He only took Matty because he was just so terrified that he might lose her."

Gaspard had returned to the hotel with a troop of French sentries. For a day and a half they'd been outside reception waving cars on or pulling them to the side of the road to interrogate their Creole occupants. Shelly had watched captured teenage rebels being shoved into police vans, their faces a mixture of dread and contempt. Then, finally, she'd seen a sleek, low-slung limousine barracuda its way slowly past the sentries. The door had whooshed open and a shapely, tanned leg had tentacled out. The coiffured woman who followed the leg had given Shelly a long, cool look, during which she summed up Shelly's net worth to the nearest FTSE share.

"And *you* are?" The woman had removed her Armani

sunglasses and stared at Shelly as though she were a microbe under a microscope.

"Shelly Green. A . . . " What the hell *was* she? "A fellow guest" was the best explanation she could come up with, under the eccentric circumstances. "Do you need a drink? I know *I* do," Shelly had volunteered. "And your . . . friends, too," she'd added, a little discombobulated, as two muscular and mean crew-cut men in shades and sharp suits, which couldn't quite camouflage their shoot-to-kill inclinations, emerged from another car behind hers.

"Executive Outcomes—hostage intermediaries." Pandora explained, offhandedly. "They are going to make contact with the rebels and begin negotiations."

The two had given Shelly the once-over with the tricksy eyes of cardsharps. Unnerved, Shelly had quickly led Pandora, who had the deportment of a department store mannequin, towards the wind-battered remains of the poolside pagoda.

Pandora had then folded herself with origami precision into a chair, smoothed the creases from the lap of a designer dress as explicit as a price tag and placed her locked alligator skin valise across her knees—before looking around with disdain at the bullet-nibbled buildings, pockmarked by mortar fire. "A *No*-Star hotel, is it?" she'd asked, in her Princess Anne-ish "loo pepper" accent. "What do you call it? The *Last* Resort."

Shelly had followed Pandora's scornful gaze along the wave-worn shore, where debris from the storm lay banked against the crumpled jetty. Trees were necklaced in seaweed skeins. Soggy green wigs of algae festooned the walls. Pandora, who seemed to be wearing an invisible tiara, had shuddered. Shelly could only surmise that the woman was so distraught she was just putting on a front—a front thicker than a frogman's wet suit, but a front nonetheless.

"Can you imagine what that poor bloody mother is going through?" Gaby had asked Shelly in the cyclone shelter.

And Shelly *could* imagine, that was the trouble. She had often thought over the last few days, of how her own mother would have broken if her father had spirited her away as a child. Shelly could empathize all too well with the traumatized, agonized state Pandora must be in. Kit might love his daughter, but only a mother's heart could know the intense rapture instinctive in giving life; her own life expanding like an accordion to accommodate her child. Matilda's mother would need calming, consoling, comforting, intravenous whisky even—and Shelly would do all in her power to soothe her.

"Like I was saying," Shelly reiterated, "Kit loves Matilda so desperately. And when your marriage went wrong he—"

Pandora's alligator skin valise writhed on her lap like something alive. "Of course, there are always two sides to every marital breakdown. Mine, and that asshole's. Honestly. I don't know what I ever saw in him," she said, her voice petulant with disappointment. "I must have been on drugs! Oh yes, come to think of it, I *was*. And then, there was that enormous cock of his." She smiled, like a canary-filled cat.

Shelly gasped, audibly. Kit's wife seemed to have the sexual compassion of a praying mantis. But she persevered. "Look, I know you're furious that he stole your little daughter, but try to see it from Kit's point of view. Okay," she conceded, "you're going to have to squint quite hard but . . . "

Pandora gave Shelly a sucked-on-a-lemon look. "Does he *honestly* think I would let him get his grubby little mitts on her trust fund?" The gems in the heiress's rings flashed like traffic lights. "That's the only reason he's taken her. And I must get her back before he *completely* ruins her. She's growing so insolent and impetuous. Just like *him*. I *cringe* inside when I hear Matilda say 'toilet' instead of 'lavatory.' Or 'serviette' instead of 'napkin.' Or 'equerry' instead of 'e-querry.' " (She rhymed it with cherry.)

Or pro-*noun*-ciation, instead of pro-*nun*-ciation, Shelly thought, flummoxed. Was it possible Matilda's mother had flown all this way and forked out all this money to save her child from poor vocabulary? She was tempted to call over the waiter for a second opinion. "She's really a *Thunderbirds* puppet, isn't she?" But the waiter was trying to appease Pandora's hostage negotiators for the absence of bathing beauties. The only topless thing about this pool bar *now* was the fact that the roof had been blown off.

Pandora gave a chilly smile. "But boarding school will sort her out." She was nuclear winter in the tropics. "After all, look what it did for me!"

Quite, thought Shelly. Kit had told her that Pandora's approach to coparenting was that it should be divvied up equally—*between the boarding school and the nanny*. But she hadn't believed that any woman could be so meticulous and loveless. Kit had joked that Pandora's interest in children would be best reflected in a car bumper sticker which read, "I Don't Care Who's on Board." At least she'd *thought* he was joking at the time . . .

"I never really saw myself as a baby person." Pandora fiddled with the foam of white pearls which frothed around her Botoxed neck. "Oh, I thought I might have a child *one* day . . ." She paused, and Shelly nodded encouragingly, "you know . . . just in case I ever needed an organ donation."

Shelly was aghast that a mother's heart could be set at such waxworks museum temperatures.

"But I had no idea how time-consuming motherhood would be." Pandora sanctioned her profligacy with a long-suffering sigh.

"Ugh. All those questions she's always asking!" Pandora winced with maternal martyrdom, before steeling herself. "But children aren't like dogs. One can't just have them put down. So it is up to *me* to train her to an acceptable level of behavior. Children need to be house-trained."

Or mansion-trained, Shelly thought with growing irritation as Pandora's serrated voice cut into her.

As if approaching a slumbering baby, Shelly now began to tiptoe towards the notion that Kit had been telling the truth about his wife. She also peeked over the edge of his accusation of her jealousy towards Matty. Had a subconscious craving for a devoted dad of her own colored her feelings? Not a father like Kit, of course. No—a dad who wandered around waving barbecue tongs, whistling Elvis, and loved her tender, loved her true.

The sole overworked waiter proffered a plate of nuts and potato chips, but Pandora shook her head. She was sucking the liquid center from a sweet with a wet, slurping sound when she addressed him. "So, what are *you*? A Hutu or a Tutu?"

"Um, I think you'll find that a tutu is a ballet dress," Shelly whispered, in an agony of embarrassment. "It's Tutsi. And they live in eastern Africa," she explained, as Pandora proved that it takes more than a manicure to give a woman polish.

"I'm not hungry." Pandora waved the waiter away with operatic grandeur, slicing her long and perfectly lasered legs open and closed like a pair of scissors as she recrossed them.

"Probably something to do with your nose," Shelly said curtly, scrutinizing the telltale ring of white powder she'd just noticed around Pandora's left nostril. "I doubt that inhaling half of Bolivia is actually on your twelve-step program, is it?" So Kit hadn't lied about his wife making Kurt Cobain look teetotal either.

Pandora's eyes flashed. "Anything Kitson Kinkade, or Rupert Rochester, which is his chosen *nom de spin*, has told you about me is a tissue of falsehoods," she declared, fumbling for said article in her handbag to remove the narcotic evidence. "Kidnapping a child is the most grave misconduct. And he will pay!" Her small mouth was taut with disgust. "We flew here via Paris where I got an emergency court order binding in Réunion, giving me custody of Matilda. I have instructed my hostage negotiators to offer the rebels half a million to release Matilda. However, I will also offer them extra money to *keep* Kinkade. A stroke of brilliance on my part. That'll be one way to ensure that shit never *ever* sees my daughter again!"

Shelly felt a jolt of misery surge through her as she realized she'd been laboring under a delusion. *Another* delusion. Hell, the woman needed to join the Laboring Under a Delusion Union. Everything Kit had said was true. Shelly could have wept with horror. She made the sort of noise you make before your car collides with a stationary object. That was what her life had become—one of those terrible automobile smashes that people slow down to gawp at, then, having seen the true horror of it all, choose to leave at speed.

But one person was guaranteed to hang around to watch the carnage. Shelly glimpsed half-hidden behind the fallen debris on La Caravelle's stage, a pair of stout, hairy legs in short trunks patterned in yellow deck chairs and dusky hula dancers, and a spasm of revulsion went through her. "How long have you been filming us, Towtruck?"

"Filming?" Pandora brayed. "Stop imijately!" She snapped her fingers and her Executive Outcome personnel tossed aside the jumble of overturned tables and chairs, to loom over Towtruck with menace.

Towtruck's shifty eyes jumped left to right. "It wasn't my idea." He squeaked like a lost puppy. "It was the Singlet. I told ya she was a two-faced bitch." Away from the jurisdiction of his director, the cameraman became vitriolic about her. "I wouldn't be surprised if she didn't organize the bloody cyclone and the military coup just for better fucking footage!" he squawked.

Shelly knew that Towtruck had little usage, except in methane production. ("A botty breeze" the cameraman called his melodious farts.) But the reality TV director was the *tricoteuse* at the guillotine: getting close-ups of emotional executions.

"Where is she?" Shelly demanded, as Pandora, bookended by her bodyguards, flounced off to check into what was left of the hotel. Towtruck, still terrified, pointed into the shubbery. Shelly angrily parted the fallen palm fronds.

The upper lips of the guilty don't often perspire, except in movies. The guilty usually remain cool and calm. "So, are you ready for your close-up?" Gaby asked with equanimity, filming with her steady cam.

Shelly narrowed her eyes. "Gaby *Con*ran. How aptly you are named. Have you lost all your self-respect?"

Gaby shrugged and glanced around. "I guess it's around here somewhere . . . probably under something."

"Why did you really squeal on Kit? And let the rebels know about Matilda's value as a hostage? Not to mention luring Pandora out here?"

"To make things more pathetic and desperate, of course," Gaby said, with a glazed expression of smug self-righteousness. "There is only so much interest audiences have in watching young, beautiful people with all their chances laid out in front of them—especially when they're not taking them. It's when their chances are all *behind* them that things get really riveting. When it's Shrimp Cocktails for Two at the Last Chance Saloon," she concluded, with calm and calculated cruelty. "TV is a piranha tank, Green, and I say that with the greatest affection. Oh, by the way, here's your next installment. £25,000." She took the thick wad of money out of her shoulder bag. "Just a little incentive to keep you camera-friendly," she said, moving towards Shelly for that close-up.

"Put that camera down! . . . Unless you're heavily insured and have a death wish! Thanks to you, Kit and Matty are now chained to some radiator somewhere eating rats and trying to gnaw their own feet off!" Shelly snatched the proffered money. "I'm looking on this as early release from my contract—time off for good behavior."

Gaby seized her shoulder. "Unless you cooperate with me, I will have no choice but to use the footage taken of you in the limo. On that first day. With hidden cameras. It makes for very . . . juicy viewing."

While Shelly absorbed this appalling revelation, it was Silent Mike who became indignant. So indignant that he stepped out from behind the cameraman, removed his headphones, opened his mouth and actually uttered words for the first time, and in a lovely, lilting Irish accent. "But . . . but what about your woman's contract? No filmin' on the bog or when havin' sex, you said."

"Well, they weren't having sex exactly. Kit was just dining at the Y, darling."

No-longer-silent Mike downed his boom and unplugged the battery. "I went along with Towtruck plantin' the dead dog at the dive site in the hope of lurin' a reef shark . . . And you spikin' Shelly's meal with chili so she'd throw up . . . And us stealin' Kinkade's clothes on the island . . . And you pretendin' to save Shelly from Towtruck trying to get off with her so she'd trust you. And all those other wee pranks . . . " They all looked on in amazement as the unprepossessing little guy stuttered his confession. "But I never, ever agreed to makin' no porn movie. What would me mammy think? You know what? Coups, cyclones, no feckin' beer in the bar . . . you can stick your job right up yer hole."

"I think I preferred it when you didn't speak, you poisoned dwarf." Gaby then pointed at her cameraman. "Come on, shit-for-brains. You can operate that boom thingy, can't you?" she ordered, revealing the extent of her technical expertise.

Towtruck shook his head with relish. "No can do. Union rules. I'm afraid the Show Must Go *Off!* Think I'll go whack one off and get a catnap," Towtruck announced with a yawn, before shadowing his newly loquacious soundman down the beach.

Shelly, who'd finally relocated her vocal cords, now emitted one long, startled, hollow howl. "You filmed us secretly? In the limousine? Oh God. Towtruck's right. This isn't a documentary. This is porn."

"Yes. And that's what makes good television," Gaby announced, with grim enjoyment, as she kept right on filming.

"No. *This* makes good television." And so saying, in a surge of anger, Shelly scrambled on to the stage and dashed Towtruck's camera to the ground.

Dead bodies, devastated villages, distraught fathers—while none of these had moved Gaby Conran, her mouth now twisted into an agonized howl. "No!!"

Dominic had chosen this selfsame moment to make his grand entrance in the part of New and Improved Boyfriend. He was showered and shaved, his Calvin Klein aftershave set to Stun, his tight trousers—"French grape-smugglers" Kit called them—leaving nothing to the imagination. This was a man definitely ready for his close-up . . . Open-mouthed with shock at seeing Shelly smash the camera, the entertainment officer's interest in her deflated faster than a poolside lilo at the end of summer vacation. "You broke ze camera?" he thundered. The man seemed to have undergone a precipitous mood plunge. "Ziz is my big moment! You sink I want to teach zese fat, ugly hags, zese *vieilles peaux* in ze pool forever?" He jabbed a finger like a bayonet in Shelly's face. "Ziz is my chance to get noticed, internationally!"

What Shelly had never noticed was the man's dental-drill voice—as relentless as it was painful. And it suddenly irked her. She found herself missing Kit's honeyed twang. "So this whole time you've just been seducing me to get your face on T.V.?" she asked, confounded.

"Mon dieu! I don't *seduce* women! I am French. Women, zey just fall at my feet."

"What? Drunk, are they?"

French charm, Shelly realized, is like mayonnaise: you definitely need something else to go with it. So Kit had been right about Dominic after all. Actually, he'd been right about a whole lot of things.

"Oh, go and drink your bidet water, noodle boy."

"You are *not* going to turn Dominic down," Gaby growled. "You will not wreck my *dénoue*-fucking-*ment*. I've handpicked him! He's the end to my story!" She took off her grimy spectacles and squinted at Shelly while she frantically cleaned the lenses on her shirttail. "Dominic is that rarest of creatures—a man with no faults!" Shelly watched Dominic's face glow with pleasure. He tossed his head in a glory of self-congratulation.

"Um, but I think that's a fault right there; thinking you don't have any," Shelly retorted. At least Kit knew he was profoundly flawed, which made him pretty much perfect in her eyes. "You know what a woman really wants? A man who's perfect enough to understand why *she* isn't."

"I need a happy fucking ending, goddamn it!" Gaby's cold eyes made neat, surgical incisions into her subject. She catapulted onto the stage. "And *you* are going to give it to me!" She almost wrenched Shelly's arm out of its socket. "Dominic is the French antidote to that arrogant Yank bastard, Kinkade. Dominic represents the civilized European culture. Kinkade epitomizes all Americans—with his head so firmly planted in the ground!"

Kit might have his head in the ground, Shelly realized with a surge of pain, but she worshipped the ground his head was in. She felt sick to her stomach. She looked at herself in the mirror behind the bar. She had that jaundiced, ill look that meant she had either just eaten a bad oyster, was coming down with the flu, or was truly, madly, deeply in love. "What happened to the sisterhood, Gaby? What happened to us girls sticking together? The pathetic thing about you is that you've turned into the very type of ruthless, arrogant Alpha male you hate."

As Gaby frantically tried to resurrect her camera, Shelly bolted towards her bungalow to pack. The ground seemed to billow beneath her feet like a waterbed, the shapes of buildings slipping and sliding. Despite the relief of sunlight and oxygen after that day in the sweltering bunker, Shelly, sprinting past the pool, felt as bleak as Wuthering Heights, colder than Mrs. Danvers.

What Shelly had thought was the roar of the surf turned into the sound of armored trucks and police vehicles barrelling up the beach road. The resort, usually a favored beauty spot with its fishing port and sandy coves, was becoming incongruously crowded with mortars, howitzers and rocket-propelled grenade launchers. In the once fragrant grove there now skulked two camouflaged lorries with radar equipment. Shelly was so distracted that she bumped smack bang into Pandora's hostage negotiators, returning from their resort reconnoiter.

"Hostage negotiators?" Shelly faked a warm smile. "Wow! How exciting!"

Their suspicious eyes darted around her like buzzing flies. "Although my first thought is—poor old kidnappers! Have you met Pandora's daughter? Well, believe me, that kid'll question them into submission in no time by the sound of it. Who will live the longest? God, the Easter Bunny or Santa Claus? . . . Does the Statue of Liberty wear panties? . . . Those rebels will be staggerin' down the mountain in a few hours begging you to take the hostages back. Bloody hell, *they'll* pay *you*! They'll probably even throw in a few complimentary rum punches. 'Quick! Before the kid asks me one more time where roads end!'"

The two men didn't smile exactly, but they stood at ease. One of them even went so far as to remove his suit jacket, revealing a swastika tattoo.

"And that awful hubby of hers," Shelly persisted. "No wonder Pandora instructed you to offer the rebels $500,000 to hand over the little girl, and more to keep Kit."

"Keep, ja, or even better, kill," said the heftier of the two, in an Afrikaner accent that smacked of buffalo hunting and biltong. "Cheaper than divorce." He winked at her, but it was a humorless wink, full of warning.

"Ja, till bladdy death them do part," jeered the other, a half-chewed cigar lopsiding his face.

Leaving Pandora wasn't grounds for divorce—apparently, it was grounds for murder.

Reality splashed like cold water. Amidst the sinister

speculations swimming in her head, Shelly was only sure of one thing. She had to get to Kit before they did. But how? Once more that classical music degree was proving itself so damn useful. And even if she did make it to the rebel headquarters ahead of the hostage negotiators, what then? Pandora's money couldn't buy her love, but it would certainly put her in a better bargaining position. . . .

The Differences
Between the Sexes:
Humor

Men maintain women can't tell jokes.

Women maintain this is possibly because we marry them.

19 Mobilization

Vacationing these days mourns more early deaths than stunt-doubling, bullfighting and space travel. Yes! Do come and vacation in the French Colonies! Give morticians more employment!

This is what went through Shelly's mind as she entered her room and locked the door, only to discover, as she turned, that something was moving in the shadows. A primitive dread electrified her nerves, her skin prickling and crawling as though invisible creatures were creeping over her flesh. As her eyes adjusted to the gloom, the sensation that she was being watched intensified. Shelly fumbled quickly through her undies drawer for Coco's gun. Violence was out of character for Shelly, but necessity and urgency had mutated her anger into pure purpose. Suppressing thoughts that this was the way serial killers got started, she cocked and aimed the gun. Not only did Shelly not have a licence to kill, she didn't even have a learner's permit, but the gun proved persuasive enough for her assailant to come out of hiding.

"*Merde!* I wondered what 'appened to zat gun." Shelly snapped open the blinds to reveal Coco getting up from her crouching position beside the bed. She extended her hand. "I will take zat."

"Um, actually, what you're going to *take* is me, to the rebel stronghold."

Coco laughed. "I don't sink so. I am going, but alone. Zere are roadblocks and gendarmes everywhere. I come 'ere to borrow your clothes." Shelly noticed that the terrorist had discarded her military fatigues and was wearing one of Shelly's sun outfits—a dress as full of flowers as a field, a dress which—Shelly's heart realized resentfully—looked much better on Coco.

"An' now I must go," Coco said.

"And I'm going with you. Kit's there and he's in real danger."

"Not unless you give me my gun."

Shelly handed it over and Coco secreted it in her voluminous backpack with her combat boots. "*Au revoir, chérie.*"

"You promised to take me with you to Kit."

"You will never make it," Coco scoffed, adding sunglasses and sunhat to her casual resort wear disguise. She made a tentative sortie outside the cabin door, then, reassured, sauntered barefoot towards the beach.

Shelly stuffed a few possessions into her knapsack and raced after her.

A day ago there'd been a rebellion and a hostage crisis but already the glass-bottom boats, jet skis and waterskiers were jostling for position as usual in the tourist-infested seas. Vacationers had reverted to normal with surreal alacrity.

One thing was for sure. Shelly would definitely need the holiday from her holiday that Kit had promised her. What had happened to the languid days lazing in hammocks, gazing out at golden sand she'd hoped for on Réunion? So far she'd enjoyed cyclones, corrupt cops, revolutions, kidnapping, aiding and abetting terrorists, being held at gunpoint and was now on her way to incarceration in a cramped Third World prison where, emaciated and dysentery-riddled, she would no doubt spend her days having confessions beaten out of her by psychotic dyke prison wardresses handy with a Coke bottle.

On the positive side, Shelly was so frightened of her future imprisonment that she'd forgotten her terror of Mother Nature. On this part of the island, curvy beaches stretched from the coral-tipped hotel cove to the extinct volcano. To avoid the gendarmes, this was the way Coco was heading, away from town and towards the jungle.

"Stop following me!" Coco hissed at her stalker, fifteen minutes later.

"I'm not following you. I'm just going for a nature walk."

"Oh yes?" Coco pointed to the dark forbidding stretch of river before them as it spewed into the sea. "'Ow do you feel about salt water crocodiles, Ms. nature-lover? Ze resort hires out goggles and snorkels but"—she chortled—"*zere is not such a good return rate.*"

"I'm not intending to swim, Coco." Shelly marched over to a rocky ledge where one of the resort's aluminium boats had washed up during the storm and dragged it to the river's edge. "You see how useful I am?"

Coco gave her one of those "about as useful as a solar-powered vibrator on a rainy day" looks, but climbed aboard. The engine, after a preparatory convulsion, jerked into life and Coco took the helm. The boat puttered along the coast for a while until they saw a behemoth lumbering up the beach behind them, which came into focus as an armored tank. Coco automatically headed out beyond the reef into the roiling foam. The little boat was groaning in the swell. Though Shelly tried to hide her seasickness, the green and yellow blotches on her forehead, her red-rimmed eyes and damp hair gave her the look of a woman in a Picasso painting.

Aware of Shelly's weakness, Coco did everything she could to terrify the English tourist out of her mission. First she informed her that if they capsized, she should stay with the boat. A waterlogged boat was safer than trying to swim for shore in these treacherous waters. *Coco* would swim to shore, of course, but only because *she* was an excellent swimmer. If the boat was lost at sea, she lectured Shelly, it might be days before she was rescued. Therefore Coco advised her to eat the seaweed that would be growing on the hull of the boat. "Fish, zey will shelter in it too. You catch zem because, by zen, you will be desperate for water, so you squeeze liquid from zeir raw flesh and suck zeir eyeballs."

Needless to say, for the rest of the journey Shelly continued vomiting over the prow and onto the giant sci-fi jellyfish washed in by the storm and just waiting to sting her to death if she fell overboard. Daylight waned and the shadows of Piton des Neiges volcano were stretching ominously across the water when they pulled into the rocky shore. Coco strapped on her walking boots while Shelly, a natural outdoorswoman, managed to slip on the algae and get an ass full of sea urchin spines.

"Zat's enough," Coco sighed. "Go back now. It will be night soon an' I do not 'ave time to 'elp you."

But Shelly would not give up. As she toiled her way up the mountain's slopes, panting to keep pace with Coco, La Tigresse was forced to continue her terror campaign. Her first piece of advice was that if Coco should fall to her death into one of the sheer walled canyons, leaving Shelly lost out there, all alone: "You must stay on ze ridges not in ze valleys because zen you will be easy to spot by rescuers." She told her that a triangle of chocolate wrapper tinfoil laid out on the rocks was a universal sign of distress. "Only, shame, we 'ave no chocolate. Which means you will be very 'ungry. But you must not waste energy running around trapping animals for food."

Trapping animals for food? Shelly had only been on one camping trip in her life, with the Girl Guides. It was *catered*. And even *then* she'd had trouble feeding herself!

"You can go several days wizout food," Coco went on, "but naturally not in ze cold and, you know, it gets really cold on the Cirque Ma Fate. If you 'ave no food, zen roll in mud and leaves to keep warm, find shelter and just pray zat you do not get 'ypothermia. Zat is where bits of your body freeze, zen snap off from frostbite. You die, slowly and painfully." Coco told her to collect water by tying rags to her feet and walking through the dewy foliage in the mornings. "Or if you are too cold to walk, drink your own piss," she added, cheerily.

"We must be nearly there!" Shelly wheezed, fear and exhaustion flooding through her body. "I mean, we must have been through three time zones already!"

"So, you go back now?" Coco asked mischievously.

Shelly risked a glance back at where they'd come from. The milky sea looked curdled beneath the moon. Then she looked up ahead at the obdurate landscape. In the darkness, the trees and ridges took on a terrifying malevolence. But anxiety and guilt propelled her on. She clambered over rocks, following Coco until the moon went down and it became too dark to walk any farther.

Coco made a bed of leaves and Shelly copied her. After Shelly had lain down, Coco said helpfully, "Zere is only one spider you must be careful of. It sprays deadly acid from its backquarters. *Bonne nuit.*" And with that she curled over on her compost cot and went to sleep.

As Shelly's eyes scrutinized the secretive shadows, she became all too aware of the presence of millions of multi-eyed creatures in the bushes, waiting to devour her. A startled bird made the noise of a murder victim. Even the backbone of the mountain ridge seemed like that of a beast poised to pounce. What could be making all those weird rustling noises? The rabid Afrikaner bounty hunters? Or a herd of lethal acid-squirting spiders taking aim with their hindquarters? As her eyes strained to see in the darkness, a snake slithered out from the undergrowth. Oh, how much nicer it would look on the belt of a catwalk model, Shelly thought, as she vaulted up the trunk of a tree and decided that actually she wasn't so tired, after all.

Eyes pink and sore from lack of sleep, throat parched, her butt porcupined with sea urchin spikes, she sat, shivering, hunched against a branch, and wondered how the hell she was ever going to make it. And even if she did, what kind of welcome could she expect? These rebels were the sort of people who would kill for a Nobel Peace Prize. And anyway, at this very minute Kit was probably doing something rash and stupid that would get him shot—thus rendering pointless her whole hazardous journey. It might be unlucky to see the groom just before the wedding—but bloody hell, it could certainly be worse luck to see him after!

But the thought of Kit was like an embrace in the dark. Shelly fingered her mental rosary beads, praying for him and Matty to be safe.

The biggest inconvenience for brides was supposed to be a husband who couldn't get it up. Hence the peek-a-boo lingerie in the trousseau and the battery of marital aids. If she ever got out of here alive, she'd have an enlightening contribution to make to *Bride* magazine. What the modern woman needs to pack for her tropical honeymoon is something much more useful—say, an *undercover SWAT team.*

The Differences
Between The Sexes:
Partners

Men often complain: "Well, what are women looking for?"

And women attempt to answer them.
"Oh, nothing special. As long as he has pectorals, a Ph.D.,
a nice bum, a nonsexist attitude, a top tan, a well read
penis; can cook soufflés, arm-wrestle crocodiles; wants a
loving relationship and can provide bone marrow—melting
sex . . . now, is that too much to ask of a billionaire?"

20 Retreat

Live long enough and you'll eventually be wrong about everything. That was the lesson Shelly learned when Coco finally led her safely to the rebel camp.

Rebel headquarters turned out to be a half-collapsed shack, which looked as though it had been sat on by Pavarotti. Actually, at first sight, Shelly had mistaken the tattered, ramshackle clutch of thatched huts as the nests of large ants. At second glance, the camp of the mighty resistance force, hidden in the cleft of a hill, resembled the home of the Clampetts before they left Tennessee. The sentry, slouching half asleep in the sun, was wearing a T-shirt which read, "Jesus is Coming. Look Busy."

Teenagers in sneakers milled around, kicking footballs and occasionally scratching their ears with the muzzles of their rusty Russian rifles, circa 1802.

What a military force! It looked as though the Liberation Front would have trouble holding its own against a woman with PMS. The only danger Shelly felt herself to be in was the forced purchase of trinkets she didn't want—such as ashtrays made from coconut shells, seashell bras and hideous woven things carried by the kids who swarmed to greet her.

Until she saw the rebel leader, that is. She knew he must be the man in question because Coco threw herself into his muscular arms and locked her lips feverishly on to his. And who wouldn't? thought Shelly. He was the total romantic revolutionary cliché. Smoldering eyes, sensuous lips, black hair tendrilling around his tanned face, combat boots, jungle fatigues and that bottomless indignation endemic to ideologues set off the Che Guevara image nicely. Coco whispered in his ear, and then Gaston Fock palmed his beard in thought, put down his AK-47 and addressed Shelly in perfect English.

"This Cirque is where my ancestors fled from colonial authority after the slave revolts. Then they organized themselves into villages run by democratically elected chiefs and fought to preserve their independence. And we are still fighting."

Shelly got the impression that small talk was not the order of the day and opted for an encouraging nod.

"Even now we do not want to use force," Gaston said, in a gentle, soothing voice. "I was a teacher. But the French are ruthless. They will not negotiate. It was the Treaty of Versailles in 1919 which imposed such savage conditions on the defeated Germans that made Hitler inevitable. Of course, when Hitler appeared, France simply capitulated. Or should I say 'collaborated.' And the word 'Vichy' entered the English language—a byword for treachery. After British and American troops liberated France, how did De Gaulle show his gratitude? By using his veto to prevent you British joining the Common Market, keeping Americans at arm's length when Nato was established and now not supporting them in the UN."

Shelly nodded enthusiastically once more, while glancing around anxiously for Kit. Coco, however, was hanging on to Gaston's every word. As Monsieur Fock sermonized, Shelly started to feel like a bobble-head dog on a car dashboard. His pontification was just a long-winded way of saying that revolution was nothing more than a chain reaction to chains. The upshot was that Réunion would soon undergo a complete renovation and reopen under new management. Shelly, who now had whiplash from nodding her head for so long, was nearly ready for a neckbrace when he ceased his diatribe and finally offered her a drink of reviving "fire water."

"Better known as 'Kill Me Quick,'" Coco decoded.

One sip of the local brew was enough to convince Shelly that Cava was not going to replace Champagne as the favorite aperitif of the free world in the foreseeable future. This was followed by offers of food—a spinachy vegetable called *brédes* and some spicy tomato chutney known as *rougail*. Shelly declined the fish stew, having severe qualms about the wisdom of ordering seafood this far inland with no refrigeration. Salmonella soup, mmm. When she asked for the ladies' room, Coco let out a howl of derision.

"Oh, we 'ave five-star mobile toilets," she said. "Ladies to ze left of the camp and men to ze right."

After squatting nervously behind a shrub in what turned out to be a patch of stinging nettles and getting a leech on her labia, Shelly felt her patience fraying a little at the edges and, returning to camp, hinted to Coco that perhaps it was time she got to see her own knight in shining "amour." Coco laughed again, no less derisively than before. Watching her confer with Gaston, Shelly realized that in the mountains GMT did not stand for Greenwich Mean Time, but Guerrilla Maybe Time.

"You have the ransom?" the rebel leader abruptly asked Shelly.

"Well, some of it. I was hoping for a bit of a discount, being British and having been screwed over by De Gaulle and all," she busked. "Remember Dunkirk . . . " His face remained impassive so she tentatively handed over her double installment of prize money, a measly £50,000.

As he counted out the money, the militant leader's face took on a cloudy cast. "This partial ransom will ensure the return of one or two of his teeth, perhaps. There is a French arms dealer meeting me today." He turned his hard, anthracite eyes upon her. "What can I buy with this? A slingshot? This is not David and Goliath. I need arms. Where is the rest of the money? You have only one chance to supply me with an acceptable answer."

Shelly watched his hand move towards the machete resting across his knees. Realizing that this was the kind of place where you could talk your head off, *literally*, Shelly was thrown into a kind of stupor. "Ah . . . the rest of the money," she stuttered. She was saved from giving the wrong answer by Coco, who removed something from her backpack with a theatrical flourish: Pandora's small alligator skin valise.

Gaston got busy elegantly hacking open the case locks with his machete. Coco explained, "I was 'iding in Pandora's room. When I saw that bourgeoise bimbo counting 'er money, money earned by ze sweat of other people's brows—serfs to her aristocratic family, I thought, hmmm. Better to be *nouveau* than never to be *riche* at all, no? So, I 'it her over ze 'ead."

Shelly laughed with approval. "She's so rich, she'll never even miss it. When that woman writes a check, the bank bounces."

Coco laughed too. "I will come for you lovebirds soon and take you down ze mountain. I am such a, 'ow you say in English? 'Sucker for love.'"

She nudged Gaston, who gave the nod to a couple of kids with pistols, and Shelly was led through the jungle to the prison hut. She took a deep breath and muscled open the rickety door.

"What in God's name are you doin' here, woman?" Kit said angrily, as Shelly ducked her head under a beam and entered the dank hideaway. He was lying on a threadbare mattress with little Matty asleep beside him. He looked like something the sea had pitched back onto the beach, exhausted and bedraggled. But Shelly's heart began beating out quarter notes, now eighth notes, now a sixteenth-note polka called Cardiac Arrest in Adoration Major. "Christ. Just tell me you didn't bring the damn cops. What the hell's goin' on?"

"Actually," Shelly replied, "I think this is the part where you peel me grapes and fan me with lotus leaves."

"I told you I never wanted to see you again."

Shelly felt a squeeze in her heart. She'd expected a cold response but this welcome was positively Siberian.

"So, why the hell *are* you here, Shelly?"

"Rescuing you and Matty, actually. With some help from Coco. I'm sure I'll feel a pang of regret about stealing the ransom money from Pandora one day for maybe, oh, *two seconds*."

Kit took a beat to drink in this change in his fortunes. "You're a special type of stupid, do you know that?" His voice, which had been edgy and tense, softened with relief. A wide wound of a smile slashed his war-weary face as he pushed up from the camp bed and stood before Shelly, amazed.

"Coco's coming to take us down the mountain. So now will you grant me your forgiveness?" Shelly requested, formally.

Kit twinkled. "Wouldja like fries with that?"

"So"—she smiled for the first time in days—"what do we do now?"

301

"Well, it's probably not a good time to start whistlin' the *Marseillaise*," Kit advised, smiling back at her.

"Shelly!" Their commotion had woken Matty who launched herself at Shelly like a cruise missile. Shelly was awash with joy to hold the little girl again with her warm tangle of limbs and sleep-encrusted eyes. "A snake came into our hut! Daddy killed it. I thought it was a worm."

"No, it was definitely a snake," Kit said, gathering up his things.

"Snakes and worms are related, you know. But only by marriage," Matty said, innocently.

"Ah," sighed Kit, "from the mouths of babes. Matty, pack up your things, okay, sweet pea? So, Pandora's here?" he asked warily once Matilda was out of earshot.

"She flew in yesterday. My God. The deepest thing about that woman is her tan. Pandora may be beautiful, but Christ"——Shelly lowered her voice——"she's so ugly on the inside. Callous, unyielding, hardhearted. I mean, God, I was stupid to judge you before I'd met her, Kit. It was knee-jerk and narrow-minded. It was also idiotic to tell Gaby. You were right about her too——a total piranha through and through. I can't believe I was so moronic."

Kit gazed at her mischievously. "Stop callin' yourself stupid. You're gonna wreck it for everyone else." He smiled. "I tell you what else you've wrecked for me. I can no longer go around thinkin' all women are bitches. You did a very brave thing, Shelly."

Shelly's face was burning. "Yeah, well, I don't know about brave. Right now, I'm more interested in getting these sea urchin spines out of my butt.'" Matty giggled.

"Please," Kit volunteered, taking a slight bow. "Allow me."

Shelly dropped her jeans and bent over the wooden chair.

"Christ! How the hell ja get these little bastards?"

"Ouch! Pretending to be Jane Bond. Anyway, you've wrecked

it for me too. I can no longer go around saying that all men are bastards. Because, you know, ouch! Having met Pandora, I'd be talking out of my ass."

"But hey. With an ass as cute as this, *chat away*," Kit grinned.

Shelly tugged up her jeans, and smiled, coquettishly, relieved that from now on they would banter, not bicker; relieved that they had finally called that truce in their sex war. A *real* truce. No. There was nothing Chamberlain-esque—"peace-in-our-time" about *this* pact, she decided. . . . Was there?

"Anyway, I'm glad you don't hate all women anymore. I was sure your obstinacy must eventually wear off."

"Obstinacy! Hey, I was just waitin' for you to dismount your high horse."

"High horse!" Shelly felt her smile tighten. "*Hello?* You did lie to me from day one. That's why I got up into the saddle in the first place."

"How 'bout I meet you halfway," Kit teased. "I'll admit I'm wrong if you admit I'm right."

"Imagine that," Shelly replied, thin-lipped. "There I was thinking I'd married Mr. Right—without realizing that his first name is Always." Shelly had a terrible feeling that Hitler was about to invade Czechoslovakia.

"Come on," Kit objected, a slight irritation creeping into his voice. "You just refused to believe that a *man* could be done over by a *woman* 'cause it's not in accordance with the Prophecy of Mom."

Shelly's attraction to Kit extinguished itself like a snuffed candle. "God, you're arrogant! You should have just asked for your *own* hand in marriage! I can't believe I risked my life to save you when—"

"Life? What life? Music teacher to teenage Noiseniks? The highlight of your life before you met me was a free box of chocolates from a gas station."

Shelly narrowed her eyes at Kit. She'd been wrong. It wasn't love she'd felt. It was obviously the flu, or food poisoning.

"Yes, I wanted to live a little . . . but living with *you* is dangerous to a girl's health!" (Oh, paging Doctor Freud to Reception. Shelly now concluded that her initial reactions had been right after all. The man was just a carbon copy of her father—selfish, reckless, feckless. A right royal pain in the ass. His misdemeanors chalked themselves up in her mind like a shopping list. A list of things She Did Not Want. One thing was for sure, she thought, the secret to a happy marriage sure was a well-kept bloody secret.)

Matilda tugged violently at her father's hand. Both adults peered down at her somber, dirt-smeared little face.

"What, baby?" Kit said.

Matty pointed to the door of the hut. La Tigresse was leaning there, watching them through suspiciously slit eyes, gun slung over one arm.

Shelly thought that as Coco was such a "sucker for love" perhaps it would be stupid, not to mention downright dangerous, to break up *just* yet. Peering down the barrel of a Kalashnikov would prove a bonding moment for any couple. When arguing with Kit she wanted to have the last word, yes, but just not on her *epitaph*.

"Coco," Matty said curiously, hands on tiny hips, squaring up to the revolutionary. "Crime fighters fight crime. Firefighters fight fires. Well, what do freedom fighters fight? It can't be freedom 'cause you're gonna let Daddy and me and Shelly go now, right?"

Oh God. Like father, like daughter. Shelly despaired. She and Kit both glanced at Coco with trepidation.

But La Tigresse just laughed out loud. "Coming up ze mountain, I could 'ave killed you, Shelly, at any time."

"Oh, right," said Shelly, as casually as an imminent cardiac arrest would allow.

"But, Matty . . . " Coco shrugged. "Like me, Shelly is *romantique*. At ziz moment in 'istory everyone is so cynical about idealism. But I say what ze world needs is crazy dreaming . . . And an AK-47." She slung her gun over her shoulder. "I told Gaston 'ow you 'elp me, bailing me out of prison and zen 'iding me from the Super Flic. We 'ave Pandora's ransom. 'E eez 'appy to give you back your prize money." Shelly took the brown paper envelope gratefully. "Eet eez not over yet, your little 'oneymoon adventure. You must go to Madagascar before Super Flic smells your trail. Zere is a little fishing village near 'ere. You can charter a boat. But if Kit, 'e eez acting like a *grand salaud*, zen maybe you should kick 'im in ze balls and leave alone?" she suggested, slyly.

"Come on." Kit laughed, edgily. "Hey, Shelly and I have our minor differences, sure, but our union is solid because we have so much in common . . . "

"Yeah, mutual contempt and utter abhorrence." Shelly opened the envelope containing the £50,000 and handed Kit a cut of the winnings. "Once we get off this island, we can just go our separate ways." After all, she sighed inwardly, she was a very busy woman . . . She had a vibrator to take in for its 1,000-mile service.

Coco tossed a set of car keys skywards then snatched them out of the air with expert ease. "You are coming, Kit?"

"Well . . . " Kit placed a finger to his chin in thought. "Gee, I don't know. There is my Erotic Feng Shui class to consider—Of course I'm comin', woman!"

What would probably be classified as a traffic hazard anywhere else in the civilized world, Coco saw as an actual road. The French revolutionary's battered old Saab careened and catapulted and nose-dived its way down mountain dirt tracks until they finally hit the coast. It was a car journey that threatened to shake the fillings out of Shelly's molars. In village after village, the damage of the cyclone was evident. Flimsy houses had folded like origami into each other and doors hung drunkenly by their hinges. Concrete stumps, from which fibro houses had been wrenched, lined the road like teeth.

When women get hormonal, large amounts of chocolate are consumed, usually accompanied by a little light shoe-shopping. But Mother Nature's mood swings are less easily mollified. And it soon became clear that, despite her stormy outburst, she had still not vented all her fury.

Matilda was the one to notice the gray snow. She clapped her hands with excitement and begged to stop to make snowmen. At first Shelly presumed it was ash from a forest fire, but the closer they got towards the capital, Saint Denis, the more gray soot was dandruffing down on to them. The sky darkened, although it was only midafternoon. The wind shift brought a strong smell of sulphur.

"Oh *merde*!" Coco gasped. "It eez old Smokey."

"What?"

For a minute Shelly saw Coco mentally grope for the least alarmist words. "I am sorry, people, but zere really is no good way to say zat you are about to be burned to death by a sea of lava."

An earthquake tremor rocked the car, explaining the situation more succinctly than Coco could.

"Holy Mary, Mother of God," Kit, the lapsed Catholic exclaimed, as a massive cloud of incandescent gases came hurling earthwards. "Don't tell me. The volcano. It's eruptin'."

"The *volcano* is *erupting*?" Shelly swiveled around to the back-seat, repeating the words to Kit in an effort to understand the baroque absurdity of it all. A cyclone and now a volcano? The weather here was more melodramatic than a soap opera star.

"Do not panic. I am only joking. Le Piton de la Fournaise erupts once a year. Eet is ze most active volcano in ze world," Coco reassured them.

A seismic tremor rattled up from middle earth and the car corkscrewed to a halt. While Coco bickered with the ignition, Shelly's eyes detected movement through the ashy haze on the road ahead. Like a biblical plague, snakes, mongooses and giant millipedes were twisting and writhing and scrabbling down the mountain's flanks and right across their path.

Kit, his teeth clenched, wanted to know why the vulcanologists hadn't predicted that the mountain was getting ready to rumble.

"Zere was an observatory, the Institut Physique de Globe, but ze cyclone? It destroyed it," Coco explained, casually. "Le Piton de la Fournaise is to the southeast of ze island. Zis volcanic mountain zat we are on now, eet is extinct. Zere is no-zing to worry about."

But as their car lurched around the mountain track, it became clear this was blatantly untrue. It wasn't Le Piton de la Fournaise that had blown its top. It was the mountain they were on, Piton des Neiges, which was having a geographic ejaculation. God, was Shelly the *only* one not enjoying any action? Even the mountain was getting its rocks off: Coitus Eruptus. But as they careered around the next bend, Shelly realized there was nothing to joke about. The summit had heaved and split and red-hot rocks and molten lava had spewed towards the sea, the magma flow swallowing up all houses and cars in its path. The hot, searing porridge was oozing down the mountain before them at a hundred miles per hour, with pumice and ash raining down. All around them vegetation was bursting into fire.

Fear licked like flames around Shelly, too. "I thought you said this volcano was extinct?" she squeaked. Until her honeymoon, she had occasionally worried about life after death. These days she only seemed to worry about life *before* death, i.e., *was she going to have any?* Shelly would regret marrying Kit Kincade to her dying day—if she ever lived that long. It was a case of Sudden Adult Death Syndrome. Yep. As a way of shortening one's life expectancy, Shelly could heartily recommend marriage.

"Jesus H. Christ. We're in real danger, right?" Kit enquired, urgently.

"Right," Coco grimly concurred.

For once, even Matilda had no questions.

The Differences Between the Sexes: Health

Women get colds, headaches, the blues.

Men with exactly the same symptoms, get the flu, a migraine and midlife crisis . . .

"Hypochondria" is a euphemism for "man." If a man denies this, then hypochondria is the only disease he doesn't have.

21 Kamikaze

There are many reasons for sudden religious conversion. A particularly good one would be finding oneself stranded in the path of an active volcano in a car holding both a fugitive and a wanted terrorist while being stalked by an exwife's bounty hunters and a psychopathic police chief.

Shelly was praying as they gunned the engine and raced the lava down the mountainside to the sea. As tarmac gave way to disillusioned dirt, Coco swerved the car left towards the fishing village. At first Shelly felt a tidal wave of relief wash over her. But as they approached the hamlet, she saw it was a ghost town, gift-wrapped in volcanic ash.

"Where is everybody?" Shelly asked desperately, frantically searching for movement in the gray ash.

"I think we have to conclude," Kit said evenly, "that any locals who seem a little remote and unfriendly . . . Well, actually, they're *dead*."

"You will 'ave to try your luck at ze airport," Coco decided.

But a few miles on, it became clear that they were not alone in their determination to get airborne. The entire remaining population of the island of Réunion seemed headed in the same direction.

The sun was now obscured by cloud, the sky a dark yellow-gray. The ground was rumbling like a giant's belly. It felt as though the world was on the move. An unnaturally hot wind gusted down the slopes, as though fleeing the mountaintop. It was like being blasted by hell's hair dryer. Smoke rolled in waves, hissing like breakwater through the pine trees. Shelly thought she had ash in her lungs from the rotten-egg air. Or that maybe a small pile of grit had settled in her stomach. The rational world seemed to have spun completely out of its orbit. There was another low, loud grumbling, followed by a boom as magma burst into the air in a Roman candle effect and more lava sluiced down the shuddering mountainside.

Shelly looked at Kit. His body was so rigid he looked like he'd been shot.

"Have you noticed there are never any members of the travel industry around when you need them?" he said airily for Matty's benefit, as she turned frightened eyes upon him.

Shelly's stomach heaved as if storm-tossed on a big sea. Life had suddenly gone cold turkey on her. "Do you think about dying much?" she whispered to Kit, mournfully.

"Christ no," Kit replied. "It's the *last* thing I want to do."

"How can you joke at a time like this?"

"How can you *not*?"

Ash was now pelting them like black rain. Cars turned on headlights to make progress—not that much progress could be made along the jam-packed roads. Eleven miles to the airport would take hours in the gridlocked traffic but took Coco only ten minutes along the backstreet alleys she knew uncannily well. Headlights snapped off, she deviated through a shantytown of one-way streets and decrepit fishing co-ops.

"Where are we going, Daddy?" Matty asked in a tiny voice.

"It doesn't matter," sobbed Shelly, her head in her hands. "All roads lead to hell!"

"Oh, can we go someplace else? I'm married. I've already been *there*," Kit quipped, strain tightening his speech. He hugged Matty closer as the car screeched around a corner on two wheels. "The volcano looks so beautiful from here, look." He made an effort to distract his daughter, pointing out the mountain's hot orange lips pouting up at the sky. But it had the opposite effect. Matty gasped as a new wave of red maggots seethed from the earth's open wound.

Shelly patted Matty's hand. "The only good view of Réunion Island will be from the window of the airplane as we're getting the hell out of here," she said firmly.

Coco pushed them out of the car at the end of the runway. She pointed to a hole in the fence. "Zat way you bypass Customs. It will be chaos in ze departure lounge, which is good. Good cover. Look after your chakras, you crazy dreamers!" The fake hippy and not-so-fatale *femme* winked at the three bewildered tourists. "When I look into my crystal ball, you know what I see? . . . Goldfish. And now I must go and run over some dogmas with my karma." She cackled, as her bomb of a car rattled away down the deserted road.

The dart across the tarmac into the airport proved uneventful, but still, once inside, their feelings were as hushed as their footsteps on the scuzzy acrylic carpeting. The fluorescent tubes of garish, pitiless light seemed to cross-examine Shelly with every step. But Coco was right. If you are going to sneak into an airport, a volcanic eruption is just about the best camouflage you can have. Nobody was interested in people getting *in*, just in getting *out*. Pandemonium ruled. There was one Air Mauritius 747 leaving with 350 seats—and about five thousand people were trying to get on to it. Air France, with the finest of racist sensibilities, was taking only white expatriates, together with their dogs and other household pets, leaving behind their Creole servants. While Shelly watched over Matty, Kit went to try to scalp tickets.

Moments after he left, an announcement was made first in French and then in English that the airport, so recently reopened after the cyclone, was closed again until further notice, due to volcanic dust in the atmosphere and debris raining down onto the runway. This obstacle to takeoff seemed minor compared to the tidal wave of angry people surging towards the information desks, yelling incomprehensibly. Like two kids knocked over in the big surf, Matty and Shelly went under. Matty was sucked into the maw of the crowd. Shelly panicked, flailing out to find her. She finally seized her hot little hand from amongst the dervish tangle of arms and legs and pulled her close.

"Watch where you're going!" Shelly was yelling at blank faces when Kit found them. "Oy! Don't you understand plain English?"

"Um, Shelly," Kit said, amused, "they're *French*."

But at least he'd returned with positive news. CNN had chartered a seaplane from Mauritius to collect Gaby and her precious footage. He led them to the secluded end of the departure lounge and pointed through the window at the old, bulbous-nosed seaplane moored to a pontoon in the bay. It looked as though it had drunk too much fuel. It was W. C. Fields, with wings. Shelly sighed with relief, but if they'd been in a movie, sinister music would have welled up to indicate the arrival of the baddie . . .

"Can't chat." The voice was Gaby's. "Got a plane to catch," she said, pushing past them.

Behind her, laden down with lights, recording and camera

equipment, plus boxes and boxes of videotape, trundled Towtruck. His face was splotched floridly with drink, and desperation was oozing from him like rancid sweat. It was clear the cameraman's nickname of "Towtruck" was now obsolete. The man was no longer headed for a breakdown, Shelly thought. He'd arrived. Big Time.

"See you on board," Shelly volunteered recklessly.

"Or *not!*" Gaby responded with malice. "Good-bye, Kit. What a dramatic end to my documentary—groom lost in mysterious volcanic tragedy. I feel a Bafta coming on," she announced with chilling triumphalism. "You can come, Green. There's only one more spare seat so you can bring the kid. We can reunite her on camera with her mum. Punters love that tearjerker shit. Pandora left by private helicopter for Port Louis an hour ago. Urgent leg wax appointment apparently."

"Gaby," Kit begged. "If you would only leave behind some of your heavy TV equipment, we could all get on to that seaplane."

"Yeah," muttered Towtruck. "All we really need are the tapes."

"I wasn't born a bitch, you know. Men like Kinkade made me this way!" She kicked Kit between his legs. "That's for fucking up my doco." Then Gaby and her Bafta award–winning CNN footage disappeared into the small departure lounge designated for the lucky seaplane passengers.

"I think she's warming to me," Kit said to Shelly, through clenched teeth.

"Really?"

"Yeah. She's only kneed me in the nuts once today."

"What did Gaby mean about there only being two seats?" Shelly demanded.

Kit reluctantly told her that since the French pornographer and the rock star and his It girlfriend had already bribed their way on board, the Mauritian pilot had told him the plane could only accommodate one more adult and one small child. The CNN-sponsored plane was close to exceeding its maximum takeoff weight.

"Shelly, you will leave with Matilda. I'll charter another fishin' boat. With a good wind, and no mood swings at the port authority, it's only a day by boat to Mauritius."

"Include me out!" Matilda, who'd been quiet as a mouse, suddenly cried. "I am *not* leaving without my daddy. No! No! No!"

"Daddy knows best, sweetheart. Shelly will take care of you."

"No, she won't. I'm not going on that plane," Shelly insisted. "*You* are."

"Just shut up, Shelly. It's already decided."

"Hello? Do you see a typewriter in my hand? I am not your *secretary*, so stop *dictating* to me!"

"Oh look. Ze 'appily married couple. Zere is no need to fight. Ze point is, neither of you are going. *We* are."

Breaking their state of Holy Deadlock was Gaspard and his mistress—the waitress from the hotel bar. Shelly felt a spidery crawl of horror up her spine. But while she thought an appreciative silence might be the best policy to adopt at this point, Kit groaned audibly.

"Christ! Not *you* again! You're like some friggin' creature from a horror movie that just won't die!"

"My life, eet eez in danger. The two seats on ze seaplane? You will give zem to me."

But all Kit gave him was the finger. Shelly just hoped and prayed the French police commandant would think it was the Vulcan sign for Live Long and Prosper.

But the police chief's attention was focused on the window, through which they could see the procession of passengers—

Gaby, Towtruck, the rock star and the pornographer, picking their way across the tarmac towards the storm-battered pontoon. Gaspard lunged urgently towards the lounge door, mistress in hand.

"You can't possibly take the last seat from a child!" Shelly chastised Gaspard's anorexic mistress who, come to think of it, was about the same size. Shelly turned her attention to Gaspard. "Don't you have an uprising to quell? Although, why should it surprise me that you're so cowardly? The French name for police is *le poulet*, isn't it? Chicken. Obviously, brave men run in your family."

Gaspard stopped in his tracks, returning to slap Shelly sharply across the face. Once, twice. It would have been thrice, except that Kit seized his hand mid-strike.

"That's what I like about you French," said Kit. "You're so suave, so discernin', so discriminatin'—discriminatin' against women, blacks and us Yanks, that is."

Shelly's anger with Kit immediately ebbed. Okay, her husband might be the only man she'd ever met who burned his bridges *before* he got to them, but she had to admit that Kit Kinkade didn't just have balls of steel, he had balls of titanium. And, by the look on Gaspard's face, he was bloody well going to need them.

The interesting thing about looking at a knife aimed at your husband's groin is how small the tip of the blade is, and yet what a huge hole it would make in your future reproductive plans. Shelly pulled Matty out of the way and held her breath.

Hatred flared across the Super Flic's features, red-hot anger. "I should just kill you for zat," Gaspard seethed, jabbing the knife at Kit.

"If I had a corpse for every time you've said that"—Kit jeered, darting expertly away from each thrust—"I could open a funeral home." He was backing towards the baggage carousel, drawing Gaspard and his knife as far as possible from Matty and Shelly.

"But why aren't you stayin' to put down your little rebellion? Oh, but of course. Retreat is a maneuver you Frogs have been perfectin' since 1870. *Vive les wimps!* The French army only has practice in the finer points of military surrender, right? Still, to wave the white flag while remainin' pompous requires real skill. Which unit are you from again, Gaspard? The Régiment de Collaborateur Français, wasn't it?" With one deft lunge he kicked the knife out of the commandant's hand.

The most important rule of air travel is that the passenger with the weapons has the right of way, something Kit was slow to learn until Gaspard began beating him in the face with the butt of the pistol he brandished from his coat pocket. The cop was furious, frothing, beet-faced, oblivious to the wail that tore at Shelly's throat and Matilda kicking and screaming at the top of her lungs, her face distorted into a mask of horror. Oblivious until the loud curses of his mistress provoked a shift of attention to the imminent departure of the seaplane.

An abandoned suitcase had broken open during Gaspard's psychotic attack and disgorged its gamey underwear on to the carousel. Kit collapsed back among the soiled laundry. Shelly was too preoccupied picturing her husband with a tag on his toe to see the police commandant leave, but she heard the heavy click of the departure-lounge door locking, as final as a submarine hatch closing.

Matty climbed onto Kit's lap, sobbing, great bubbles of snot pouring from her nose. Shelly gently laid Kit's head on her shoulder. The blood on his face was dripping onto her leg. It looked fake, as though from a B movie.

Through the huge glass windows they watched as Gaspard and

his lover crossed the runway to the wind-worn pontoon then clambered aboard. They watched with increasing despondency as the plane taxied across the water, then took off straight into the wind to safety, intercepting the declining sun. They sat in unnatural silence, breathing in the pungent effluvium of jet fuel and cordite.

"Don't worry," Matty piped up. "Daddy will save us. He's like that American movie star. Arnold Snort-snigger."

It was too much for Kit. "I've failed you both," he said, and his voice was juddering, broken. "I am so, so sorry."

"Sorry for what? For loving your daughter? I know you've done some crazy, no, make that downright stupid things, Kit, but you have only ever acted out of love. Which is what makes you so . . . " She looked at him. Kit *was* like her father in that he was a pain in the ass when he was around, but he was *unlike* her dad in that he was also a pain in the heart when he wasn't. And, most important of all, he was also always around for his little girl.

"Makes Daddy so *what*?" Matty was tugging on Shelly's sleeve.

"Attractive," Shelly whispered, embarrassed.

"*Attractive*? D'ya think you'll still find me attractive after twenty years in prison?" Kit asked, dispiritedly. "Which is where Pandora is gonna put me."

"Which is why I've kind of . . . " Shelly pushed on. Well, it was now or never. "Fallen in love with you, goddamn it." She bit her tongue, punishment for what it had uttered. An endearment to a *man*? Was she mad? "Although it could just be the flu."

But Kit seemed unaware of the momentous emotional ground Shelly had just given him. "You didn't *fall* in love, you *stepped* in—and now it's time to wipe me off your shoe," he said, barely able to lift his eyelids. "Pandora is right. I can't even look after myself. Let alone my daughter. Failure is the only thing I've ever been a success at. I'm always screwin' things up."

"You know what?" Shelly said, robustly. "You're right. You've screwed things up for me too. I mean, there I was feeling all justified in my absolute hatred of men and you have to go and start being Brave and Heroic and Self-sacrificing and Nice to me. How selfish you are! You heartless bastard." She gave Kit a playful punch in the arm, which prompted a wan smile from him.

"D'ya know what? I must've been on this baggage carousel for too long 'cause I'm startin' to find *you* attractive again, too. And not nearly as bossy as I'd remembered."

"Either getting knocked around the head has made you more mature and intelligent," Shelly replied, "a thesis for which there is little public support, or, for once in your life, you really do mean what you're saying—"

But Shelly didn't get her answer because just then Coco, panting and disheveled, burst around the corner and ran towards them, her black hair streaming out behind her, a bandanna over her nose and mouth.

"Dieu!" she gasped. "I am so 'appy zat you are still 'ere," she puffed.

"Why?" Kit and Shelly said simultaneously.

"Tourist dollars. Zat eez what supports ze regime, no? Gaston just gave ze order zat planes carrying tourists 'ave become legitimate military targets. Sank God you did not get on zat plane."

"So what are you sayin', exactly?" Kit demanded.

Coco paused, glancing with foreboding out of the window up into the night sky. "Zere eez a bomb."

"So," Shelly's brain was befuddled, but she was trying to achieve a kind of clarity, "what you're trying to tell us is that seaplane protocol allows terrorists to preboard?"

Coco nodded. And then Shelly took the only option possible after such a day—and passed out.

The Differences Between The Sexes: Sex Drive

Men think "sex drive" means doing it in the car—probably because of that little sign on the rearview mirror which reads, "Objects in this mirror may appear larger than they are."

22 Terms of Surrender

"What do you want to be when you grow up?" Shelly asked Matty as they stood on the secluded shore, drenched in a wash of syrupy sunlight. The sky was as pale as milk, with curlicues of creamy clouds.

"A doctor, a nurse, a barrister, a solicitor, a judge, an actor, a garden-lady and a wok-star. Also a giant, a wizard and a wizard's servant."

"Do you mean a sorcerer's apprentice?" Shelly smiled. The big, easygoing sea, a deep, still, sleepy blue, slurped at the sand as it washed in over their feet.

"Yes. And a knight. And the Queen of America. What do you wanna be when *you* grow up?"

The question stumped Shelly.

"That's easy." Kit, who had just joined them, supplied the answer, "A concert classical guitarist."

"Daddy, shhhh! Let Shelly answer," Matty said in her best headmistressy voice. "Shelly," she persisted, "tell me and Daddy. What are you going to be when you grow up?"

"Um, taller?" Shelly grinned mischievously at Kit.

Kit gave her an appraising look. "Still a Bach Suite driver, huh?"

"Ha, ha." Shelly grimaced at his appalling pun.

"Daddy! The baby submarine!" Matilda pointed to the overblown tadpole which was just breaking the surface of their secluded cove. "Oh, isn't she cute? Where are her mummy and daddy?"

"You know what? I don't think she needs a mum or a dad. I think she's swimmin' just fine on her own, don't you, kiddo?"

Kit bundled Matty into his arms where she beamed contentedly. Shelly tried to imagine what it must feel like to be protected, cozy, safe in the deep folds of her father's loving embrace. And she experienced a twinge of longing which pained her.

"Coco said the sub will drop us in a fishin' village to the south of the island. Then we can hitch a ride to Madagascar on a trawler."

"Are you sure it's safe?" Shelly asked, surveying the giant windup bath toy bobbing on the water before them. "I mean, just once it would be nice to have a get-together where one of us doesn't leave in a police car or an ambulance."

"I can sincerely promise you that I won't do anythin' to get you on to the evenin' news ever again," Kit said, hand on heart.

"But Madagascar? How will I get back to England?"

"Whyja wanna go back to that shit-hole? You can't really wanna keep teachin' cover versions of 'Dead Girls Don't Say No' to bands called Red Hot Sticky Helmets and Big Dick and the Swingin' Willys."

There was truth in it. A couple of months ago the piano teacher had been carted out of the music department in a strait-jacket, sobbing, "It's a fucking quaver, you cunt!"

"You can't leave us, Shelly!" Matty piped up. "Because, you know—don't listen, Dad!" She put her hands over her father's ears, and whispered to Shelly, "I found out that my dad is the tooth fairy."

"He is?"

"Yes. Shhhh. Don't tell him that I know. But how can you let him go out every night to do his job as the tooth fairy and leave me at home all alone?" Her green-flecked eyes, so like her father's, were large and moist with pleading.

Shelly felt her heart contract. "But what's the alternative?" She looked at commitment-phobic Kitson Kinkade. The man who liked being footloose and fiancée-free. The American Love God who believed in life, liberty and the happiness of pursuit.

"Well, um . . . " For once Kit's voice groped. He couldn't choose the right sentiments to give shape to his feelings. "I thought you might, you know, um, hang out with us."

Kit's words hovered in the air, verbal parachutes, little hopeful silken things. His eyes glinted, like sun caught on the sea. The world glimmered and fractured as the sky thickened into a band of gold. The warm wind was like an embrace.

"Can I get that in writing?" Shelly replied finally. "This is not like a wedding vow, Kit. I mean, *this actually counts.*"

Kit gave her a speculative, salacious smile, a smile full of promise, possibility and pleasure—and an involuntary shiver shimmied up her thighs.

The stolen mini sub, the Blue Safari 800, could accommodate six passengers and the Creole pilot, whom Coco assured them had trained at the French Naval Academy. The sub comprised two transparent glass bubbles interlocked by a door. The view from each cabin was panoramic, allowing them to peer with wonderment into the Neptunean world. Although the mini sub was descending, Matty, Kit and Shelly were buoyed up by their escape, not just from the island of Réunion, but from the Grim Reaper himself. Cyclones, volcanoes, armed insurrections, terrorist bombs—his intentions had been a dead giveaway.

The spotlight beam illuminated the silent fish symphony, as clown, lion, parrot, puffer, butterfly and surgeon fish darted in their colorful choreography in and out of the coral massifs. At 25 to 30 meters undersea, a skittish and slightly peeved gray nurse shark stooged by, but Shelly was in too much of a quandary to notice.

As they bubbled along the sandy-ribbed bottom of the sea, Kit left Matty with Coco and the captain and joined Shelly who was brooding quietly in the back cabin. "Hey, haven't I married you some place before?" he asked, playfully.

"It won't work, you know, Kit." Shelly looked out at the shadow-latticed, corrugated sand of the ocean bed. "We're so opposite."

"Yep. I'm a human, and you're some kind of Klingon girl. But, hey, the French are right about one thing. *Vive la différence*." He closed the interconnecting door. "Opposites attract."

"But we have absolutely nothing in common—except a marriage license."

"Ah, but true love conquers all." A sly light stole in from the underwater world as he pulled her to him.

"No, it doesn't, Kit." The air seemed wavery, filled with the aqueous opalescence that rippled into the cabin. "It doesn't conquer the fact, for example, that you are used to glamorous women like Pandora. I am so *unglamorous*. I mean, look at my hair! It's gone all Christian."

"It has?" he asked, bemused.

"Yes. All flat and oily and straight." She tucked her straggly strands behind her ears. The last few days had been so stressful, she'd started to look like her passport photo. She flinched in the spotlight of his scrutiny. "Don't look at me."

"Christian, eh? I hope that doesn't mean you're gonna be good?" He fondled her breasts, rolling the nipples between his fingers with firm intent. "An' what about your other hair? How is Farrah Fawcett-Major?" He slipped his hand down her jeans and into all that musky heat.

Her body rocked against his, disobeying her every order. "I did warn you that you might find the legendary lost temple of the Xingothuan tribespeople down there, didn't I?"

Kit laughed, huskily. "Strangely, I ain't found no *Big Brother* contestant who hasn't realized the series is over yet, either."

Shelly stopped moaning to hit him. "'*Ain't found*,'" she cringed. "Really! Nor will love conquer the fact that you think elocution is how they kill inmates on death row in Texas."

He moved his fingers over her body slowly, as though conducting the legato movement of some carnal concerto. His languorous touch soaked into her skin like sunshine. "D'ja know what? You're right, Shelly. It would never, ever work. I'm a free agent. Impulsive. Reckless. Whereas you are used to the spontaneity of those snotty English society hostesses who book you three years in advance and post you the seating plan, then sit around discussin' Clitean geometry. Who wants to discuss Clitean geometry when you're *Hard*?"

Who indeed?

"Clitean? You mean Euclidean geometry," Shelly corrected, trying to quell the ache of excitement in her bones. "Nor will love overcome the fact that you're so uneducated. You think Dante is how Italians cook spaghetti."

"What? It *ain't*?" He nibbled her ear. "Yep. You're right on.

327

We're a perfect mis-match." The heat of their bodies mingled as they writhed against each other. "You're highbrow, I'm low," he breathed into her neck. "You're an uptight Brit—you do hospital corners on your beach towel, for Christ's sake—and I'm a laid-back Yank. I'm the type to get back to nature, while you like to get back *at* it. Honestly, Shelly, by the time you've sunblock-sprayed and insect-repelled, there'll be no ozone layer left in the entire goddamn Indian Ocean."

As he slid her jeans down over her thighs, Shelly felt as sparkly as a sequin. As light as a wish. "And then there's the fact that you're suspicious of all women."

"And then there's the fact that *you* hate all men."

"Yup." Shelly ripped at his jeans and he kicked them off. They landed, legs flung wide at a quarter to one. Although nearly naked, they were spinning a cocoon of breath and sighs around each other with each caress.

"If only there were a third sex available to us," Shelly panted.

"If only." Kit ran his hands over her waist and hips, where her body curved like a guitar. Shelly felt faint with bliss as he strummed her. She panicked momentarily, that she was getting in too deep. It was narcosis, that's what it was. The pressure forces nitrogen into the bloodstream, which makes you crazy, so light-headed that you don't even realize your oxygen has run out. It's called "the rapture of the deep."

To anchor herself, Shelly reached between his legs. A convulsive start shook his frame. Kit, too, seemed to be suffering from the emotional "bends." "The worst thing about this honeymoon is that you've made me stop seein' women as the weaker sex. And I can never forgive you for that."

"*Weaker* sex—isn't that the type of sex you have after you're worn out from having children?" She knelt before him.

"Are you ever gonna find out for yourself?" he murmured with pleasure into her hair. "I could definitely do with another kid. I mean, it's only a couple of years before Matty goes to her room and I don't see her again until she gets her driver's license."

Shelly pulled him down on to the floor. "Well, I can never forgive *you* for making me fall in love with Matilda. Because now, against my better judgment, I do so want to have a darling little daughter."

"All that time people spend worryin' about whether they're happy or fulfilled. The best thing about havin' a kid is that you're too damn busy to keep askin' yourself that question."

But, with his hands on the bare skin of her belly she was already happy, so happy she couldn't believe she didn't have her own cloud. "I also can't forgive you, Kit, for making me redefine my thoughts on men. I have now had to change my allegiance from the All Men Are Bastards school of thought to the *Most* Men Are Bastards school. And it hurts!"

Kit laughed, that late-night, frayed, sexy laugh she hadn't heard for so long. "Ya know, bein' opposite ain't all bad. We can complement each other, enrich each other. Maybe we could call that truce in the sex war, after all . . . "

She removed her gold ring and slipped it on to his little finger, then kissed him, drinking in his hot moan.

"Only if you're now ready to negotiate your terms of surrender, Kinkade."

"*Your* terms of surrender, you mean." His was an octopus embrace, all hands everywhere. Kit held her arms above her head and pressed his body into hers so hard that she couldn't breathe or move or think. "I've taken you prisoner."

"I won't cooperate. Not even under torture."

"Oh yeah? What if I said I was goin' to make you go on a honeymoon in Réunion Island again?"

"Okay, okay. Anything but that! I'll do anything you want."

"Anythin'?"

"What did you have in mind?"

"Occupation." He parted her legs with his knee.

"And what if I give resistance?" She sunk her nails into the flesh of his back, hard enough to draw blood. "I might be booby-trapped."

"In that case, I'll just have to give you a full strip search." Pinning her arms now with one hand he used his other to shuck off her half-mast jeans and tear open her shirt.

"I think you're going off half-cocked, Kinkade." Shelly bit his neck. His head jerked back from the unexpected bestiality of it. She bucked him off her body and, slippery as a fish in his hands, rolled on top of him. "You're underestimating my independence movement."

"So, you won't grant me safe conduct?"

"I think I could give you refuge and sanctuary but only once we've worked out a balance of power." She pivoted on her knees and lowered herself onto him with perfect equilibrium.

They needed to have peace talks, to arbitrate, mediate, negotiate, they really did, except the trouble with the language of love is that orgasms tend to do all the talking. There was nothing to say but "oh" and "yes" and "take me now" and "mmmmmmm" as they finally surrendered, blissfully, to each other.

And so, in the end, they could have made the evening news after all—the first heterosexuals to be admitted to the Mile Under Club.

Matty, meanwhile, sat with Coco and her pilot at the submarine's controls, pootling through sun-sequinned seas that were wild with fish.

"Eet looks as though you 'ave got yourself a new mama," Coco winked at her.

"About time," Matty said. "Grown-ups are soooo dumb. They're always backing talkwards, you know?"

"Ees that so?" Coco queried, amused.

"Well, Shelly told me that men and women will never get along 'cause men are from Mars. And Daddy told me that men and women can never get along 'cause women are from Venus. But men and women are from the same planet," she said, matter-of-factly. "The planet Earth. So"—she gave a philosophical, and rather French, shrug—"deal with it."

The Differences Between the Sexes: Needs

Men: marriage suits men much more than it suits women. Married men live longer than single men, have less heart disease and fewer mental problems.

Women: well, basically, if our vibrators could kill spiders in the bathtub, light the barbeque grill, kiss our upper eyelids and tell us we don't look fat in stretch Lycra, would we need men at all?

23 Casualty List

It's a week later—seven P.M. and cheery people of all ages, colors and sizes are being decanted from a free bar to a large TV studio in South London. The studio, set up for a dating program, is all curvy pop art with groovy music. But music and set have been subdued for the somber tone of this transmission.

The British viewing public watch transfixed as the presenter, with his heavy metal rock star hairdo gelled into submission to suit the sobriety of the occasion, recalls the tragic events of the extraordinary reality TV *Desperate and Dateless* experience, which the tabloids are reporting as "the most bizarre honeymoon in human history." There is no documentary footage, no bride, no groom and no director. When cataloguing the couple's experiences on the island—the cyclone, the hostage situation, the volcanic eruption, the tragic plane disappearance in which all are presumed dead—the earnest presenter wonders if the fated couple ever did manage to call their truce in the sex war? If they ever were able to discover a reconciliation of opposites?

The presenter goes on to say that there is one poignant reminder of the bride. A tape arrived the day before of her playing guitar. The show then cuts to a scratchy video of Shelly, playing, with eloquence and panache, Bach's Fourth Lute Suite, all the way through to the end.

Across town in Mayfair, Pandora Vain Temple is watching the show on television when an officer from the Inland Revenue serves her with a summons for tax evasion.

Needless to say, shares in Pandora's panty-liner company immediately plummet, despite having wings.

On an uninhabited island in the Indian Ocean, Gaby is washed up from the plane wreckage onto a deserted beach. The reality TV guru begins to think that this is enough reality already! She hopes, for a pathetic moment, that perhaps she is really just a secret participant in *Survivor*, where people are sent off to a deadly, snake-infested desert island, with nothing to eat bar beetle larvae, except with secret medics, backup emergency supplies and nice friendly film crew around to sneak you treats when you need them.

For a whole day she searches the island for film crews, only to discover that it is, indeed, deserted. She finds nothing. Zilch. Nada. Except for something even worse than all the poisonous snakes and vile, creepy-crawly things she's encountered. It's her cameraman, naked, bar a penis gourd he's fashioned for himself.

"Thank Christ!" he shouts. "I thought I was doomed to do meat-saber practice with Captain Solo forever more. But now you're here to scratch Yoda behind his ears!"

"Ugh. I wouldn't lay you if you were a floor tile," she replied.

"So, what are you gonna do, Gaby? *Fire me*? So come on. Let's take the pigskin bus to tuna town!"

Gaby could only think one thing. I'm A Nonentity, But Still, Please, I'm Begging You, *Get Me the Fuck Out of Here!!!*

In the rebel camp, a great shout of joy goes up when Gaspard is reported missing, presumed dead. He is also denounced *in absentia* by the international press for his overzealous handling of the uprising and abandonment of his post.

Coco, a closet Catholic, is more circumspect. "The man, he was a prick, yes," she said in French, "but he just got blown to smithereens by a bomb. If you can't say anything good about the dead, then you should say nothing at all."

"He's dead. Good," said the rebel leader.

Dominic, in an effort to sweep an aged heiress off her feet, was showing off with some hang-gliding stunts when he was caught in an updraft, possibly caused by his own hot air. He was last seen by a startled B.A. crew, headed for the Mir Space Station. Rescuers are looking for an overly tanned man with gold chains and a generous appendage.

On television talk shows and radio stations and in newspaper editorials all over the world, pundits discuss the sex war. No woman is an island. But if we were, would we want to be colonized? Told what to do? Have our affairs run for us?

"Love *can* be democratic," pronounced one commentator. "Equality within, solidarity without."

"Then why do men and women spend all their time itemizing each other's failings with such monstrous efficiency?" demanded another.

"The point is," castigated a female panelist, "how can we ever end the sex war when we keep fraternizing with the goddamned enemy?"

"Because fraternizing is such fun, goddamn it!"

"But men and women! We want different things," she retaliated.

"Yes, men want women, and women want men!'

Whether Gaspard joined the Mile High Club with the rock star's It girlfriend, and whether the French pornographer documented their stunt, will only be known once they recover the black box from the bottom of the Indian Ocean.

In a beach bar in Madagascar, Matty is reading *Aesop's Fables*, which, she assures her dad, is written by some Greek guy called Aesophagus—and decides she will write her own fables called *Kids Are from Pluto, Parents are from Some Other Galaxy Entirely*.

Kit Kinkade and Shelly Green are declared Missing—Presumed Happy . . .

A story to be continued, Shelly and Kit hope, for the rest of their lives . . . as long as *she* stops making him eat pongy cheese and faces up to the fact that all-you-can-eat-nights at the local hotel are what constitutes "fine dining" for most men. As long as *he* admits that Americans do have such overinflated egos that sitting behind them in a theater should be classed as restricted view seating, and *she* admits that the English really are a society of Lilliputian divisions. As long as *he* not only makes the bed but remembers to put on the decorative pillows, and *she* stops thinking that, just because there are subtitles, the crap film about the one-legged Polish lesbian who takes an interminable bus ride through Romania to discover her inner existentialism must be Art. As long as *he* stops yawning whenever she wants to discuss their Relationship and *she* stops yawning whenever he wants to discuss miles to the gallon. As long as *he* refrains from saying, every time she asks for "a little respect," "To eat here or to take away?" and *she* refrains from informing him a week in advance that she can't go to the baseball match because she's "not in the mood." And as long as *he* learns that fluffing the blanket after farting is not an effective odor-eater, and *she* learns that men will never overcome their dependency on the remote control. As long as he learns that he, too, can be the Designated Driver goddamn it, and *she* learns that it's possible to quietly enjoy a car ride from the passenger's seat in silence for Christ's sake. As long as *he* also realizes that staying awake after sex is not an Olympian feat, fuck it, and *she* realizes that men are genetically incapable of noticing when a woman has had her hair cut. As long as *he* understands that women are also genetically incapable of walking past a shoe shop sale without buying something irrational and strappy and *she* understands that men are psychologically incapable of doing their Christmas shopping before Christmas Eve. And as long as *he* comes to terms with the fact that women are forbidden by the female code of ethics to have a phone conversation which lasts less than thirty minutes, and *she* realizes that when men are being quiet, they're not holding back on you, they are in fact thinking about nothing and . . .

Acknowledgments

The material gathered for this book on the sex war was taken directly from the species in the wild, at serious personal risk to the courageous author! But thanks must also go to Geoffrey Robertson, as ever; my editor Suzanne Baboneau, who puts up with the whining of people who think they can write (a delusion most prevalent amongst published authors!) with such grace and good humor; Alison Summers, a dear friend and lethal red pen-wielder; "Doc" for the diving tips; Antoine Laurent for teaching me that there are more words in French than *lingerie, liaison* and *rendez-vous*; John Talamini for checking my American colloquialisms (plus great cawfee); my Mauritian friend Guy Ollivry for Creole pronunciation; Jane Belson for legal advice; Denise Fisher, the Australian Consul General to Noumea; my agent Ed Victor, the Ed-ocet missile; Melissa Weatherill and Tabitha Peebles for practical help; Robert McCrum for the title, which is dead sexy; Patrick Cook for always making me laugh; and of course, to my bonsai darlings, Julius and Georgina who've put up with my long working hours without writing the sequel to *Mommy Dearest*. Thank you.